Daimon

DAIMON
ABEL POSSE

Translated from the Spanish by
SARAH ARVIO

ATHENEUM
New York 1992

Maxwell Macmillan Canada
Toronto

Maxwell Macmillan International
New York Oxford Singapore Sydney

•

Copyright © 1978 by Abel Posse
English translation copyright © 1992 by Macmillan Publishing Company, a division of Macmillan, Inc.

Atheneum
Macmillan Publishing Company
866 Third Avenue
New York, NY 10022

Maxwell Macmillan Canada, Inc.
1200 Eglinton Avenue East, Suite 200
Don Mills, Ontario M3C 3N1

Macmillan Publishing Company is part of the Maxwell Communication Group of Companies.

The three lines quoted on page 106 are taken from Willis Barnstone's translation of "Spiritual Canticle," by San Juan de la Cruz, from *The Poems of St. John of the Cross,* copyright © 1972 by Willis Barnstone, and are reprinted by permission of New Directions Publishing Corp.

Library of Congress Cataloging-in-Publication Data
Posse, Abel.
  [Daimón. English]
  Daimon / by Abel Posse; translated from the Spanish by Sarah Arvio.
    p. cm.
  Translation of: Daimón.
  ISBN 0-689-12123-7
  I. Title.
PQ7798.26.078D313 1992   91-33837
863—dc20

10 9 8 7 6 5 4 3 2 1

Printed in the United States of America

DESIGN BY DIANE STEVENSON/SNAP-HAUS GRAPHICS

For Alicia Posse de Parentini

Lope de Aguirre
(1513? – 1561)

Self-styled the Tyrant, the Traitor, the Wanderer. Anti-imperialist. From the Amazon jungle, surrounded by monkeys, he declared war on Philip II, founding thereby "the first free territory of America." Demonist. Timid but tenacious erotomaniac. Rebel. His cruelty is proverbial. Amoral as a tiger, as a dove. It seems that he believed solely in the will to power, the revels of war, the heat of delirium (lethally disdaining those who disagreed, or were lukewarm).

He eliminated his superiors and almost all members of the Expedition, some seventy in all, including ecclesiastics and women. With two liberal jabs of the dagger, he killed his fifteen-year-old daughter, to relieve her of life (he concurred with his betrayed King Philip II that this is a vale of tears).

His ambitions were grand despite his modest circumstances: consolidate the Marañón Empire, seize Peru (swelling his ranks with an army of one thousand blacks), conquer Spain, and take over the world.

He perdured in the Eternal Return of the Same, which is a spatiotemporal spiral.

I

Epic of the Warrior

CIVILIZATION

When I arrived here they sent me two girls, exotically garbed: the oldest could have been no more than eleven, the other seven; both were as shameless as whores.
—Christopher Columbus, Letter VII to the Kings, Jamaica 1503

SAVAGERY

Oh, may I never die! May I never perish!
There, where there is no death,
there, where we dwell in triumph, there I go.
May I never die! May I never perish!
Only to sleep have we come, only to dream:
No, oh no! Not to live on earth do we come,
but to turn to grass in the spring meadow.
May my song stir the souls of my dead friends!
—The Poet-King Nezahualcóyotl, 1-Rabbit 1402–6-Flint 1492

1

A Major Arcanum:
Le Jugement des morts,
the Judgment of the Dead

Those who have returned ring Lope de Aguirre. The Expedition is mounted. "From essence into form." Variations on nondeath. The horrific war of the dead. Native beasts and men discover Europe (October 12, 1492). Aguirre and the Fiend. The Sermon of the Deep. Yearning for unconsummated loves.

AMERICA. ALL is desire, juice, blood, sap, panting, systole and diastole, food and dung, in the relentless cycle of cosmic laws that seem new to the world.

Sacrifices and slaughters are followed by the rhythmic panting of copulations. Births, assassinations, eradications, cataclysms. In the night the serene dew-drenched flowers open to give birth to the seed of the giant araucaria. Jaguars bound toward their cubs at dawn bearing the dead stag that drips hot blood. Roused by the rubbing of the high wind-ruffled branches, the jacarandas burst into fecund clouds of yellow dust (the heliotropes, bold messengers of love, bear the burning pollen to the calyces of lusting females).

Within three days, fallen coins, if not minted in gold or silver, crumble like the second-rate lumps of beet sugar manufactured by the Dutch in wartime. (This they knew from experience: the profile of Charles V cropped out on a wild jasmine petal just where Anémona Salduendo had buried her savings, out of reach of the cook, Gianni Delano, pederast and rogue.) A sword left plunged in the earth by Antón Llamoso, to mark the rainfall, dawned as a dagger: beheaded by the juices of this fierce earth. It was fact that lost bullets sprouted blossoms the following spring (flowers easy to spot because hummingbirds shied away). Spring came suddenly amid torrents of wintry rain. In this world there was as yet no fixed progression of seasons. The smoking volcanoes seemed newly erupted.

Returning to camp in the first light of dawn from his nightly war with the dead, old Lope de Aguirre came upon the humped sleeping bodies of his troops in the dense, drenched air of the jungle, where wild creatures wander. They sweated, swaddled in blankets and hides to thwart the slakeless plumbing of mosquitoes and above all the sleek vampire bats (partridge-size) with the art of sucking through dainty wounds welcomed in troubled sleep like the caresses of mothers. Some, opting for imaginary breezes, slumbered in high branches, from which they sometimes fell into the bed of mud below like giant ripe chirimoyas.

In the growing light, he sat down in the clearing and watched them rise, one by one. Diego Tirado; Roberto de Coca; Nuflo Hernández, the Standard-Bearer; López de

DAIMON

Ayala; Blas Gutiérrez, the Chronicler and Scribe; Alonso de Henao, the Priest; Geronimo de Spinola, the shrewd Genoese; Rodríguez Viso; Sánchez Bilbao; and Diego de Torres, the falconer with his sights on sainthood. Solemnly they passed before him and perched on the rocks along the riverbank. Only Nicéforo Méndez, the negro with mulatto ambitions, the servant to whom he confided his goblet and his furors (who had died in Cumaná, a barber relating tales of the Omagua and El Dorado Expedition to his idle customers and hoping against hope for a job on the police force), ventured an unctuous smile.

Shy, still burdened by the grave. As though born again, and just as awestruck. They listened to Aguirre's yammer: "Marañones! Marañones! Looks like none of you strayed far from my rotting carcass! Look here, Custodio Hernández, I see you coming! Look at my hand! Look at it here in the air! You, who they dispatched to Mérida with my right hand, to serve as warning! And you, *mulatto,* who constructed a cage to transport my head as though it had feet or wings! Look at me good! Where are those eyelids stuck shut with dried blood, those burst eyeballs?"

A long silence ensued. The Old Man looked around with a touch of regal pride: the half-hearted avenger secretly flattered by the unconfessed loyalty of his people. *Doña* Elvira, his fifteen-year-old daughter, keeping her distance from the officers, demurely approached in a sort of see-through shift, as though just rising from sleep. As sexy and silly as ever. Aguirre confirmed what he had always thought and felt: her breasts were not pigeon chicks, but two small Seville oranges; her thighs two dorado fishes on the brink of entangling in battle. Behind her came the splendid *doña*

7

Inés de Atienza (who had not relinquished her nobility laid out cold and flat). In silent reproach, she bled her wounds and they gleamed in the moonlight. He had inflicted them, but with love.

They barely saw each other. They were passing from essence into form, expounded the Priest in a whisper; he had not yet renounced his rudimentary Thomism. Although words were superfluous, Aguirre extemporized (without too much vigor, for he sensed that no persuasion was needed). "What is the grave? Cool languor. At first the bliss of dying, the pleasure of liberation from the body, a sack of potatoes dragged from Oñate to Vitoria. The bliss of leaping free, of bounding to treetops, of sleepwalking on rooftops . . . But how long does that last? Nothing, maybe only two intense seconds, as long as a dream and then what? Nothing, nothing . . . " Now he seemed to be recollecting: "And the fury for what was never had and what was never done, for loves and vengeances, for all that was good and bad! Gold, women, El Dorado! I say nothing is discovered! Nothing is finished!"

Planting his feet—a bullfighter braving the bull—he drew his sword, more rust than blade, and like Pizarro, etched a stripe in the sand. "Those on this side are coming! Everyone else, to the grave!" But the hunger for life was great in these men who had lived and died with the fear of death and had wasted their best years fearful and trembling. All of them jostled and crowded into the space the Old Man had poorly reckoned between the stripe and the river. A grand success. It was clear that in spite of everything, both killers and victims had reveled. They preferred the perils of adventure to limbo. It was certain.

"You, Diego Tirado, with your grimy beard, shall be

Captain of Cavalry! You, Roberto de Coca—murderer!—
shall be Captain of the Guard!" Insults, fond military salutes
that did not mask Lope's joy.

After the requisite sentimentality, a whoop of glee rose
from the supernumeraries who had hung back meekly
among the trees observing the melodramatics of the leading
players. Nation of conquerors: soldiers, harquebusiers, reg-
imental whores, cooks, workers, mulatto porters, zambo
pimps, the two lepers, the Jew Lipzia, and the natives—
wronged but no less swept up in the thrill of resurrection.
(Let us not forget Carrión, the executioner, whose dinner,
like that of the lepers, was stewed in a separate pot.)

"You, Serrano de Cáceres! Muster the people! Expedition! Grand expedition! We're off! Prepare the palanquins
for *doña* Inés and *niña* Elvira! You, Padre, wipe those scru-
ples off your face! Celebrate the mass!"

The women set to washing clothes and their peasant
song rose from the still pool of the river. The cooks scrubbed
their pots and pans with wet sand. When the Old Man
stretched out in his palm hut and shut his eyes, he heard
the happy cacophony of a regiment on the move. Shouts,
bickering, whistling, songs and muttered threats. Gunsmiths
greasing harquebuses. The acrid smoke of swords tempered
in manatee or mule oil. A line of gossipers waited at the
cobbler's with their worn-out shoes. Someone was slitting
the great paiches strung from the branch of a ceibo and
tossing the bloody entrails to the stream. Babbling, mulattas
mended fine garments with needles strung with gut of young
monkey. Native women prepared tamales wrapped in banana leaves.

The Priest hunted for a good sun-warmed stone and

patiently began to deworm his missal. He filled his cruet with manatee oil twice refined over the flame, and then, off by himself, mixed it with sweet-potato flour and piously laid out more than one hundred wafers to dry on the back of his cassock. He muttered: "Let us celebrate the mass, indeed we shall celebrate the mass! This time the Lord will win, cursed Fiend!"

Night. The Old Man waded ankle-deep into the river, reaching his left hand into Space. He tried to control the trembling of his arm to take a more precise measurement (after the wars he was left with three fingers, which he employed as a natural astrolabe). Tipping back his rusty helmet, he gazed hard into the sprinkling of stars. The Magellanic Cloud. Orion. The Serpent. The Centaur. Venus. Beyond, grazing the treetops, the guiding lights of the Southern Cross. It was easy to sight, having just risen. Luckily no comet threatened the precarious harmony (Lope feared the fickleness of comets).

He stretched out on the sandy shore and gazed upward, vaguely distressed by an old fear: that the Supreme Order would transform into pure Chaos. That all would revert to the first page of the Bible. Heavenly bodies, planets, stars in a scramble, a wild whirlwind, as forecast by some bitter, alarmist Florentine astrologists. The colliding of spheres. Waters of the seas mixing with the winds of space. The horrifying mingling of the dead with the living. This was his fear of God. His simple fear of God: like the fear of a huge, not so tame bear or of some hotheaded Galician losing a game of *tute*.

DAIMON

By the hut he found Nicéforo sleeping packed in a
layer of mud (to shield himself from mosquitoes and chiggers). The silence was utter. By and by he heard someone
lurking near the watering hole. He thought of Spinola, the
Genoese, who often corrupted the deer that came to drink.
Then the silence closed in again and the only sound was the
faint sighing of a newborn orchid.

Then he saw, firmer now in the soft light, the shadow
of the Priest. "Is that you? Is it?" On his cassock, bloody
red stains began to show, and the gruesome garrote strap.
No answer came. The Priest must be good and dead, floating
in idiotic eternity, he thought. Then he heard a groan, of
weariness or disgust. "Is that you? Speak! Come on! You're
still speechless with rage because I garroted you? You once
told me your idol was Saint Sebastian . . ." The Priest's torn
mouth was an appalling bloody grimace. During his execution, Lope had commanded that the garrote collar be fitted
between his teeth, to increase the suffering. It was difficult
to understand why he had come. The Priest had never cared
for life (never even aspired to be a bishop!). He must surely
have told himself he had a priestly obligation to his flock.
The Priest was fully aware that to live was to risk Hell, as
life is the only seat of temptation and sin; and in fact, he
feared the annoyance of insects, the bishop's prayers, the
obligatory torments of Holy Week, the *peno porque no muero,*
the quinquennial examinations in Latin, and above all, his
inability to believe in God. It was considerable. But here
he was, passing "into form." Perhaps he was bound to
Aguirre by some dark vow, some ineffable fascination, some
love-hate that might reveal its meaning with the decades.

Restitution of the circle of power, the perambulant Palace. Blas Gutiérrez, the Chronicler, languidly approaching: pale, tormented, the eternal debtor. Then Lipzia, the Jew, always crusading for the latest craze in culture: he begged permission to enter from a distance of some fifteen feet, the estimated length of Aguirre's imaginary drawing room. "Come in, come in . . . See anything in the cards, Jew?" "Yes, I felt clear today so I threw them. Turned up the *Jugement des morts*." And Aguirre: "More dead? Haven't we had enough yet?" "No. It's the card of rebirth, of the cycle completed, of jubilee. Look, sir, this figure standing in the grave could be Lazarus. It's rebirth, with a lust for life that can arise only from the grave . . ."

The Old Man chose to change the subject, fearing witchcraft. "And you, Blas Gutiérrez, color of parchment, what's this you put in the Chronicle about me? I know you had it printed in Seville. Tell me, don't be afraid . . ." Lope laughed. Blas Gutiérrez, quaking like an accountant caught in an error, read out meekly: "The Tyrant Lope de Aguirre was a man of near fifty, very slight of body and spare of person, and ugly, with a small, pinched face and piercing eyes that glowered beneath his helmet, especially when he was wroth. He had a shrewd, quick wit for an unlettered man . . ." "That's fine, at least one in favor. Proceed." "He was said to be Biscayan, born in Oñate. He was hardy and could bear much fatigue . . . in all the years of his tyranny he was rarely seen to sleep . . . though now and again he napped in the daytime, he was always up through the night . . ." "Fine! Fine! Don't be afraid, Pastyface. I see that you've tried to capture a personality. What else?" Again the tremulous voice of Gutiérrez, who feared for life and limb: "He renounced his King and his God, and often professed his allegiance to Satan. He founded a rebel principality under the name of the weak-willed Fernando de Guzmán, after the execution of Orsúa, the Frenchman, legitimate leader of the Expedition to the land of El Dorado. He killed Guzmán and crowned himself Prince aboard some rafts adrift on an unknown river. He planned to liberate the blacks of Peru, a good thousand, and mount a regiment named Liberator. During the years of his tyranny, he slew with his own hand upwards of seventy men, women, soldiers, ecclesiastics, and even his own daughter, a beautiful fourteen-year-old half-breed . . ." When he said "beautiful," the voice of the Scribe seemed to leap a ditch. "That will do," said Aguirre, glaring. For a moment all expected the worst. But evidently Aguirre attached little importance—as of yet—to the written word.

"Hey, Lipzia, getting back to that card, the joojemon dee morr . . . , is it the dead who judge God, or God who judges the dead, because . . ." He guffawed dangerously. Then he lapsed into a meditative silence and stretched out on the brush mat. "And this thing about my nondeath—what do folks say?" Lipzia took the floor: "They say that when you were hit twice by the harquebus you crawled away in the darkness, and that the two negroes assigned to cut you up mistakenly worked over old Antinori. Remember him? The Milanese watchmaker who suffered from piles. He was just returning, the night of October 27th, from the land of the Pisaguas, where he had taken a magic cure for his malady." "So then what?" "They say that at dawn you were still not dead. That you saw, plunging through the forest, a great bird the size of a royal eagle but with the plumage of a quetzal bird and a golden ruff. Probably the Phoenix, descending to light his fire with branches of the cinnamon tree, so as to be reborn for another 540 years of resplendent life. They say you were ravenous—wounds always made you hungry—and that you ate it half-cooked. That would explain everything . . ."

"Not at all. The negroes simply found you and quartered you. That's fact, Aguirre," said Blas Gutiérrez, with the usual priggishness of historians. "Or how did Antinori turn up twenty years later with a luxury clockmaker's shop in the Piazza San Marco? How could your body parts have been sent around the viceroyalty as a lesson? Tell me if I'm wrong. Reportedly those dumb negroes washed off your severed head by dunking it in that laguna of eternal youth your pal Ponce de León was searching for . . ." The Old Man was wistful: "Ponce! Poncito! What a life! And what of Hernando de Soto, who squandered his youth tramping around searching for the fountain of youth? Is Antinori the one who mended the watch Almagro gave me?" "The very same, sir." "What a pity, now I remember. He was a nice old fellow. I remember his fit of madness when the clocks started running counterclockwise in the Sierra de Parima . . ." Aguirre glanced at Padre Alonso, who was listening in silence. "Some say it was you who did it, Padre. I've been told you craved vengeance after I garroted you between the teeth. And that on dying you implored God to make me tramp forever through those wretched jungles, finding nothing, no Amazons, no gold, nothing . . . Is that true?" The servant of God turned pale. "Is it true? Was it you?" Lope's laugh, more sane than not, was somewhat reassuring (they had learned from experience to rank his laughter; the worst was a stifled sarcastic bray, which invariably meant death or torture). "Your God's a fake: he claims to listen to martyrs, but he can't stand 'em. He's on the side of victors." The Priest failed to produce a quick, neat retort, for he yielded to the temptation to impress upon the others his intimate rapport with the Creator. He lapsed into silence and luckily Aguirre was distracted by Lipzia's timely remark: "Some say that after the atrocities of Sacsahuamán, you were hexed by the *amautas* of Cuzco. That they doomed you to come back to life as an Indian, so you'd see what it felt like . . ."

They made camp after tramping knee-deep in rotten swamp water for an entire day.

As his horde dried off by the fire, the Old Man lay in his bed contemplating the splendid butterfly *(Morpho cypris)* that Nicéforo, knowing his pleasures, had captured. Lipzia boldly contended that they occurred not only in blue and white, but in pink and ivory too. "Where have *you* seen them, Jew?" Aguirre was in a foul mood, for he had noticed that it was no longer possible, at his age, after so much damaging dampness, to close his fingers on the gossamer wing of a butterfly. Nothing more delicate, not even a Chinese painting. Who needed paintings and painters and Titians? A butterfly's life-span was brief: one day. All for only one day and never knowing if there were witnesses! "They live only one day and die at dusk . . . Are you going to dispute this too, Jew?" No, of course not. "Do they drop dead in flight or stop still to die, like the elephants?" Then Lipzia again boldly asserting that the sun at its zenith was their hour of mating. "You dare say this to me! They mate at their peak, in the fifth hour of the afternoon. Morning's their bloom, noon their prime, afternoon their peak of life. They are not creatures of the night . . ." It was in midafternoon, the Old Man knew, that they secreted the sexy fragrance with which the Queen of the Amazon reportedly anointed herself, twice yearly, for her naked dash through the jungle to entice *caciques*. An erotic rite the thought of which never failed to fluster the Old Man.

Nicéforo, who was scratching his master's ankles, accidentally jiggled the bed; the butterfly flew up and lit on Aguirre's brow. The dainty pat on his skin bethought a snowflake, a Christmas night in his boyhood: amid forgetfulness, a glimpse of those immense, amorphous, time-entombed joys.

He caught the butterfly. Crushed it gently on a strip of white bark and passed it to Nicéforo, saying, "Paste it on nice and tight and take it to *niña* Elvira for her collection . . ."

"Send for the Scribe! Tell him to bring his portfolio! I need him!" Lope's bad temper was plainly growing worse. He was in no mood for Lipzia's highbrow dialectics, or to humor his scientific notions, which he found naive. "Instruct Blas Gutiérrez to come forward." Summonses rippled through camp. Lipzia understood that his audience was over, and judiciously withdrew from the presumed drawing room of the palace, backward. He knew that Aguirre's bad temper could degenerate into one of his vicious personal pogroms. "The Jews are wicked and deserve extermination not for killing Christ but for siring this idiot!" Lope had uttered what in the Spain of his day was the worst possible blasphemy.

Blas Gutiérrez showed up with parchment paper the

color of which had contaminated his face. He carried a baroque inkwell and some prized feathers of the *Coloris* parrot, deemed superior to those of Valladolid geese (he planned on someday procuring the export license).

"Do you have quality lightweight parchment?" The Scribe rummaged in his portfolio. He delayed his reply, as though thereby granting himself some sense of autonomy in the realm of paper. "Here's a good one. Two sheets of trimestral llama fetus. Veinless. Grained with the faintest tiny dry veins . . ." "I did not call you here to listen to your insolence. This is for the King, therefore write in your best hand. Put down: 'To His Most Gracious Majesty, King *don* Philip II, native of Spain'—write it just like that—'son of Charles the Invincible. *Don* Lope de Aguirre sends you this second Declaration, having received no reply to his first, dated eleven years ago today in the Marañón Empire, at the time of his conviction and abominable execution.' Put it down as I say, and don't change a comma or I'll scramble your brains.

"State that I declare war on him again, now as then, Prince against Prince. And put in that sentence about how he should stick with his God and I'll take my Devil. That if we are the way we are after fifteen centuries of so much Christ, I invite him to try the way of the Devil and see what happens! Take down this sentence carefully: 'Most Excellent Sir, I'm preparing to make a long expedition whose end I cannot see. It is the American Expedition. With my executioners and victims I will roam these fabulous lands. Once again I sign this missive with my traitorous title, not easily revoked. For if I am the Rebel'—like so, with a capital R— 'I must betray you.

" 'Your priests and theologians lie to you, Sir, when they tell you that Lazarus sat calmly among his sisters on his return from the grave. They lie, for when a man returns from death or the brink of death, he feels fire and fury, not calm. He knows all he had to do and never did, and he hates the void. So many people to kill and love! He is tormented by the magic of life, source of all pleasure and pain and error. Though it may shock your theologians in their silk shorts, I say Lazarus did not sit quietly among his sisters at Jesus's table, waiting for Monday so that he could go back to work . . . If he indeed rose from the grave, I vow there was an uproar in that house, a real ruckus!'

"And close the letter like that! Same as last time, set down the names of the members of the Expedition according to rank and don't go and hide under the flourish, pen the name Gutiérrez nice and clear—for what it's worth. Under my name, put 'the Wanderer, the Traitor, the Rebel,' all just as I tell you, in caps."

This done, they brought in a falcon trained by Diego de Torres, who had mystical tendencies and was grooming his creatures with the secret hope of someday sending messages to the Creator. They affixed the missive and set the falcon free by the river, in the direction of Cuzco. It would perch in the bell tower of Santo Domingo until the King's men came upon the challenge.

The Old Man felt calmer. He thought of Cortés the day he sank his ships. He lay down on the mat and gazed at the flittering of the giant postmeridian butterflies, as big as medium-size roosters. Through them God was clearly testing his abstractions and transparencies and diffusions of color and form (many Quattrocento theologians went so far as to speculate that the Lord was Italian). God (in a manner of speaking) amazed him less with his astronomical scenery—which alarmed him and unnervingly alienated him from Him—than with his supreme and exquisite skills as a miniaturist: that elegant mosquito with the perfect little suction tubes, standing on stilts like one of Carpaccio's pages; the armies of armor-plated ants with panoramic vision and nocturnal antennae, which man lacks (He who created you also created the jaguar?). Such peerless patience. And so as to all seem necessary!

Aguirre had drifted off to sleep dreaming of the slow flutter of the giant butterflies. He awoke as always, with a presentiment of the panting of the jungle at nightfall.

The jungle, an immense feverish animal. The air grew thicker in its jaws. Suspended by the laws of night, the visible universe ceased. The other code. The birds—flocks of snipes, whistling ducks, herons—prudently returned to the protection of their high nests. The elusive owls hooted evil omens and alit to contemplate the horrors like academic philosophers (whose symbol is aptly the owl). Scorpions, spiders, jaguars, toads, blind crayfish that live in mudholes, vampire bats, green-eyed panthers that seduce and then devour their prey, anacondas that hunt in the parched mud of riverbanks, hyena dogs that eat only rot, homosexual monkeys denied daily life in the tribe, giant bird spiders that first hypnotize and then slowly devour live birds. (These are the horrific *caranguejeiras*, half of whose weight is poison. Terror of the nests, they exert parapsychological power over rats and small birds. And yet they are defenseless before the flies of the underbrush, which immobilize them by biting the dorsal nerve and then inject their eggs: the bed of larvae grows in the living body.) With the first signs of darkness, the players began to stir, enacting in the theater of night another cycle of silent and necessary cruelty, of hushed and necessary love.

And also the dead.

Aguirre shrieked impatiently. "Nicéforo, damn it! You asshole! Where are you hiding?" No one in sight but the guards, along the edge of camp. Nicéforo showed up limping as though dragging a dry eucalyptus bough. He helped him on with his two coats of mail and handed him the helmet and the rusty weapons. Then he followed him through the brush to the place of the dead, lugging the extra weapons, a halberd and a mighty saber the Old Man never really used.

He had learned that to combat the dead with any success it was necessary to league with the darkness. Sometimes he had to lie hidden in a ditch full of stagnant water or behind the fallen trunk of a big *viraró*, enduring the creep of vermin. Sometimes he had to rush out howling and take them by surprise, shocking the night with the clang of his armor.

He waited until the faces began to issue forth, thin, pearly-gray mists. This was the moment for action. Attack, endure thorn scratches, attack. It was not easy: they were maddeningly skittish, maneuvering like guerrillas, incapable of head-on battle. "Don't run, damn it! Yah! Come on! Fight, you bastard! Charge! Come on! Fight! Yah! Yah! I see you, Salduendo! I see you! Turn around and I'll show you, I'll show you!" But they did not get moving, they were as obstinate as bulls. Without hands. With a stare that neither hated nor feared but would exasperate the most even-tem-

pered. "I saw you, Guzmán, I see you! Goddamn fool, don't
climb, no!" Sword thrusts at the air. Panting. Always three
steps ahead, they slipped back and forth through the boundary of death. Nothing could be more elusive than the silence
and subtlety of the dead: they sashayed in the branches, just
beyond reach, and seemed to be laughing with the dots in
their eyes. Sometimes they shamelessly flaunted the blood
dripping, or not dripping, from their wounds. Vanishing with
the nimbleness of deer, they popped out a bit beyond with
blank, bleary gazes. As Aguirre knew well, there is no worse
enemy than he who has known death. He knew that an
invincible enemy, though he does nothing to win, wins in
the end. Being a military man, this drove him to distraction.
He had to cope with people who slipped in and out of "the
divine medium of death" (as Teilhard de Chardin would
much later term it) like fish through water. "But someone
has to put a halt to the antics of these brazen sons of bitches,
damn it!"

The Old Man got even by kicking the negro, who lay
facedown in the mud, terrified that he might see a dead man.
Then Aguirre took his post and waited. Melancholy, mild,
and courteous, the murdered men began to crop out again.
Flemish shopkeepers killed in the age of the *tercios*, big-
bottomed browbeaten burghers fleeing a Rembrandt painting. Those done to death on the island of Margarita. Com-
rades-in-arms with reproach in their eyes. And then a silent
red wave, the army of Indians who had lost their heads at
Cuzco and Cajamarca. It was amazing! Not only did they
possess souls, as established by the controversial Council,
but they were authorized to lead an ultraterrestrial life!

Aguirre listened to the blood gurgling thickly over the

cobbles of Cajamarca. Here the quantity, which under normal circumstances legitimates massacres (and indeed Wars),
was overpowering. The trees were veiled in a mist of faces,
an opalescent gray gleam. Daggers swished as they sliced
the necks of kneeling men, blood gushed. Rending cries of
daughters and widows. Then the melopoeia of the bards,
who had set their verses to funereal music:

> *Death, rape, and plunder!*
> *Our blood spatters the feet*
> *of the foreign conqueror*
> *who deals death with a promise*
> *of pardon and eternal life.*
> *Death, rape, and plunder!*
> *Ravaged cries on dry dust . . .*

Then the plangent howling of the women. The jungle
aflame with horror: a sudden dawn. The Old Man had no
choice but to strike out in fury. He stabbed at the fleeing
shapes. Fell and struggled up again, still more furious. Mud-
splashed, he huffed with the last breath in his lungs but
bloodied not even the tip of his sword. Lunged forward,
slashing spider webs painstakingly woven. Slipped on the
bellies of amazed, meditative toads. Roused whole families
of wrathful monkeys who avenged by splattering him with
excrement. Distressed the birds, which fled upward to their
nests in alarm.

On October 12, 1492, the animals and men of the
kingdoms of the jungle discovered Europe and the Euro-

peans. Thereafter they progressed from disillusion to desolation at the passage of these pale creatures more powerful by dint of guile than of true superiority. They regarded them as a tormented but treacherous congregation of outcasts from Paradise, from the Primordial Oneness no man or animal should have reason to renounce.

Those who came ashore were robbers, hustlers, skinflints. They organized their delirious visions of time under the name of History (a kind of metaphysical racetrack).

They comported themselves with the utter brashness of those impelled by bone-deep fear. Their triumphs perforce brought unhappiness: they exhibited a radical incapacity for comprehending balance and the natural order of things. Picking pineapples, for instance, they clung to rigid harvest schedules, and also cut the green baby fruit, causing mass colitis. Fishing, they could not spot the female dorados and paiches in spawning season. Hunting, they spared neither the father nor the pregnant mother monkey. Admiring a Rainbow parrot gaily cheeping, they raised their crossbows and shot it down, so as to study it sprawled dead and spoiled amid boots and mud. One scientific fellow made sketches of the corpse.

Their god and sacred symbol was those two crossed sticks for nailing up bodies: an instrument of torture.

The white-faces deemed it best to perpetrate a mass, preventive death. All was threat: from a Caribbean hurricane to the song of a native child wandering on a sylvan path. Only via death (of others) could they achieve the stasis they required to launch their "Civilization."

The men and animals of the jungle (and naturally the plants too) soon learned that the white-faces had a temperamental propensity for rapacity and plunder, and a passion for murderous death (not the inborn biological death of normal species).

Soon the jaguars and the confederations of monkeys scorned them. These first, then almost all else. On sight the gentle manatees dunked, because the white-faces hunted not the understandable one or two for lunch but thirty or forty: someone had mentioned that selling the oil wholesale in Cuzco brought a good profit. The habits of these people became so excessive that the birds stopped singing. At the first whiff of the Iberian horde, which smelled of widowed skunk, the colorful flocks fled, denying them the pleasures of the eye.

Only the eternal traitors colluded: vultures and other consumers of carrion, some runaway dogs hankering for a home life, and the immoral foxes. (One befriended Lope and often brought him gifts, a fat snipe or a few herons, which the cook prepared for him *à la française*. The fox evidently foresaw a not so distant imperial triumph on the part of the white-faces.)

They were unfit for peace or tolerance. Why? Someone, at some time or other, in those lands of productivity and misery, had told them that *being* called for *doing*: that we were born not to be but to bring ourselves into being. This barbarity, or philosophy, the grim details of which the Indian chiefs could not yet comprehend, bespoke itself in each of the acts of the invader.

With fantastic tenacity they instituted what they themselves—bafflingly—called the "vale of tears."

*   *   *

Cool of the coming dawn. Breeze sailing over treetops. Aguirre sat down on a smooth rock on the riverbank and felt a strange urge to meditate, a sort of expansion of his interior silence. This, he knew, was the required prelude if the Voice of the Fiend was to reach his ear. (Not really a voice, but various vague intimations in his inner fog.)

The other god.

The horrific hour that precedes the dawn, when the night begins to putrefy like the wings of a rotting bat. An acrid taste in the mouth (all men have tasted it): anguish, all fears of life and death, the sense of lost time, pining for the past, guilt. Hour of evil. (Midday and siesta also have demons: which lure the satyr to the nymph, which quaver in the skin and pulse in the groin, which set fire to the games of cousins.)

Aguirre was sure his demon had crept in during venereal contact: a Syrian slut in Istanbul (too late he saw the tiny breast between her legs). Or perhaps the blind men of Bruges had poisoned his wine the time he cheated them at dice, in the age of the *tercios*. When he first heard the Sermon of the Deep, he was captivated: *Blessed are the powerful for they shall possess the Earth! Damned are the weak and sick for they shall inherit solely the yoke of slavery! They shall eat shit, and love one another!*

All good had come from the Devil (this he had pondered at length in the grave): the creation of the Marañón Empire, first free territory of America, in defiance of Philip II and his solemn god and his murderous priests. (Let the chroniclers, scribes, and clerks say what they will! At least he was someone. Yes! The Devil creates.)

He might have been a humble Catholic. Might have

married the dairymaid next door (Dolores Iturrylarigoyaz-conbeytía). Might have stayed home in Oñate, his biggest gamble two reals on the seven of *oros* in the Saturday night game. But the temptation had been great. Devil of defiance. Or perhaps, luxury of rebellion. The Devil had shown him that this was the only way to lower Heaven to Earth. The body! The body and now! Postpone the soul forever like that meddlesome aunt busy with embroidery and the stingy virtue of the old and sick.

He who would follow me, let him follow. This too was written in the Sermon of the Deep.

Asking for life! Asking to do it all again: all crimes and all torments, pardoning nobody and begging nobody's pardon! Again the Marañón Empire! What a fiesta! The whirlwind of war!

Aguirre felt a surge of life. But the Voice of the Evil One still eluded him. "Come forth! Right! Do it!" He threatened him: "I'll cast you out! I'll exorcise you! I'll douse you with holy water! You'll writhe like a worm drenched in brine!"

The Hidden One's designs were hard to understand. The Expedition would set out again, but would not be understood. Aguirre suspected that the Devil needed him. He was so vain as to suppose that who gave whom the helping hand was debatable.

Dawn was breaking and the Evil One's suggested meditations were trailing off. While Nicéforo tidied the mat, Aguirre went to the river to piss. He felt content: the Expedition was launched. He had released his men from the perversions of peace, and remitted them to adventure. The inanity of peace, which mutates men into boozers and cows and fishes.

Pissing took a good while; he had once been kicked by a horse. For the same reason, his ejaculations were superlatively long, his sperms spurted out in delicious Indian file, so to speak. Herein he had no cause to envy women, or the panda bears of the East.

He had formerly weighed matters of State when he pissed: with the passing decades, he was apt to wax sentimental.

The Moorish girl with firm, sunbrowned breasts. Eyes like embers, of a nun in heat. First seen in the Córdoba cathouse, near the Judería. At the end of that street of his youth, seafarers with exotic aromas and new words: jute, coffee, clove, tobacco, feathers of fantastical birds, aphrodisiacs, amulets, America.

The Moorish girl, luscious and piqued in her room under the roof: "If you don't buy me that yellow-and-violet feather I'll never see you again!"

And also Sister Angela. He was only twelve when his uncle, the pork butcher, barked: "Get ready! Tomorrow we're off to the Convent of Guadalupe." The fulfillment of a fervid vow to the Virgin, for he had palmed off the leprous pigs. This was so, but he would also try to sell his nephew to a band of subverbal mule skinners.

Cold rainy morning. Bleak wind whistling through the rose window in the Cathedral façade. Handbells tinkled by the altar boy at the instant of the consecration, when the miraculous gust of chill wind descended from above and for one moment held aloft, in its invisible hand, the coif of Sor

Angela, the Girl-Nun kneeling one row ahead. An instant that would last forever. Exceedingly white skin of her unforgettable nape, exquisite as the skin of rich babies or newborn kittens. Tender, fragile region on which he vowed the sun had never risen (intimate reverse of the Spanish Empire, where the sun never set). Above, a mane of chestnut hair coiled and waiting, at the start of time, to break into a wild, undulating dash. Oh! Nuns were not bald, as he had always believed. Guadalupe, October 17, 1525.

Thereafter he had often met the Girl-Nun in the seclusion of an imaginary convent whose flying buttresses were the trees of the jungle. She waited for him sweetly as he wallowed in the mortifications of Guilt.

In his delirious, fever-racked despair, the Moorish girl had often reached out her hand to him in the darkness.

With time the two became one: lived side by side, silent and separate, in the house of desire. Performers in the bawdy dreams of lonely men. Tenderness and lust. "Sor Angela, you! Oh, Sor Angela! I am so alone!" The Old Man pleaded. But he at once regretted revealing to his men, who were presumably spying, that he was in love. "Damn!" And he pretended to have slipped in the damp sand.

2

Tarot XV:
The Devil

Ordeals of the march. Love of Tertiary monsters. Aguirre's love for the murdered woman (doña Inés de Atienza). Rebellion against the Devil: ritual exorcism. Local men and animals offer their own indignant version. The Tyrant and his fifteen-year-old daughter. What's a man without his demon?

MONTHS AND months of hardship. The first years. They pushed south, but the route was not linear: it was a circuitous tour through the labyrinth. Their purpose was to strike the (presumably) golden heart of the Continent, or an infinite silver sierra.

Almost weekly Aguirre sent Custodio Hernández or Rodríguez Viso, his seamen most skilled in astronomy, up into the tallest trees to check the position of the Southern Cross. "See it or not? See it? Yes? Answer me!" "Yes! I said yes! It's there! It's there!" A great relief: they had not strayed into Chaos, for reference points still linked them to universal order. "Can you see it clearly?" And Rodríguez Viso: "The four stars shining bright, the southern tip nice and sharp!"*

"So get moving! Let's go, move! Out of this swamp!" Lope's fury flicked through the laggard column like the lash of a whip: discipline is not easily rewon after the lethargy of death. The men were still mild and sluggish. They had not yet retrieved fear and ambition, those sure signs of European life-force. The Old Man was forced to have Martín de Flores tortured; racked by fever, by the thirst of the vampire bats, he had expressed his preference for the nonbeing of the grave. "There's no worse threat to a mission than a backward-looking Lazarus! Torture him! Let him serve as a lesson!"

Ordeals of interminable swamps. Mud to the waist and the weight of corroding weapons. Regiments of mosquitoes; bellicose carnivorous plants enraged by the odor of white men; shrewd, stubborn jaguars; jeering parrots that mimicked human cries; sly anacondas that slithered away snorting scornfully after pitching them into the slime (*Serpens gaudius aequatorialis*, according to Linnaeus).

Came August, season when the giant river turtles lay their eggs, they were caught by a downpour that lasted sixty days and sixty nights. They had to search for the air required for survival among rippling sheets of water. Cloth dissolved and hides swelled like drowned dogs. Skin wounds, including old scars, throbbed as though they might burst. The hair

---

*With their sick penchant for torture devices, they had renamed the long, narrow, rhomboidal constellation that the Tupí-Guaraní called Omoy-Coyé (meaning "Heavenly Vulva") the "Southern Cross." (*Diccionario Guaranítico* [Montevideo, Rodrigues & Cohen: 1925])

of many men drowned: upon stroking their heads, they reaped handfuls of smelly wool. At night they slept perched in the forks of trees, wrangling for space with families of irate monkeys.

Horrific damp. On an iron shield from Guernica a little green rust plant sprouted; on the third day the Priest excised it in disgust, alleging witchcraft. Apparently iron putrefied in America, emitting a smell like stunted nuts.

When they saw that tiny fingers had budded on the stumps of the two lepers, there was talk of miracles.

After some weeks thus, several men sank into the false solace of madness. One morning Diego Tirado, Captain of Cavalry, and Carrión, the sullen executioner, climbed into the treetops, laughing and singing. The Old Man halted the column. "Nothing worse than madness, nothing! It spells the end of all productivity and discipline. But wait and see . . . " They swung from branch to branch, humming all the while. Leaped from the jacaranda to the silk-cotton tree with more the bravura of drunkards than the skill of acrobats. Gaped up there as though gulping not rain but dry air.

The first to fall was Carrión, and he thudded like a ripe banana on a tranquil night. They laid him in the fork of a tree. He resembled an eaglet with a broken wing, still gazing enrapt into the vast beyond. "Onward! Onward! Tell that fool to shoulder his weapons and follow along!"

Entering America was a struggle. From surprise to surprise, like touring the origin of the World.

They found jaguar bones four meters long to which the magnificent pelts still clung; tails of horrid dinosaurs extinct since the retreat of the glaciers. Sometimes they stumbled on wandering hulks of ice from the melting insides of which sprang armor-plated saurians and alarming specimens of an animal cycle that predated *Homo sapiens.*

One moonlit night after the flood, hiking through some dry red lands—located, claimed the Priest, near the first circle of Hell—they heard a roar that shook the earth and swayed the trunks of the rigid quebracho trees like reeds bent by the wind.

In a clearing on the red savannah, they came across a pair of creatures from another age, two giant armadillos, or caudate glyptodonts, more than twenty paces long, with domed carapaces. Fear and panic. Cosmic terror among the men. Guilt feelings for passing fraudulently, and without divine authorization, from the Quaternary to the Tertiary. They flung themselves down and prayed, faces to the ground; the females moaned and wailed.

It struck them that the motions of the monsters followed some cryptic pattern. Savvy and subtle, Lipzia declared that he had seen nuptial dances of this sort conducted by crabs on the Travemünde beach during one of his banishments.

Under the giant footsteps of the dancing lovers, the ground seemed on the verge of collapse; as nerve-jangling as watching an elephant cross the Rialto Bridge. And yet, a remarkably intriguing rhythm, an awesome, angelic grace endowed these massive monsters. The huffing and panting that riffled the leaves as far as fifty feet off was presumably Homeric carnal desire.

The monsters mated with the brevity and simplicity of unperverted desire (a pair of Extremaduran peasants). Swirls of red dust rose up, hiding the—no doubt horrible—details.

Then a roar of thunder, surely from the female. "They too revere virginity . . . " the Old Man murmured.

The two carapaces rested on the earth, over the limp sprawl of utterly spent and sated bodies, while a pungent odor, like bitter almonds crushed in ammonia, choked the air for many leagues around. It would accompany them through the next full week of marching. "Damn! That's fucking!" cried Aguirre, pagan at the core. Avoiding his gaze, the Priest averred: "This is not lust but simply the procreative urge, by God's will . . . " He was trying to offer pastoral guidance to the men, who were making gauche remarks.

America. A land of such living power that she routed vigorous men the way a hearty organism repels germs. She bred a perilous sense of distress, the distress of powerlessness: "I feel like I'm drowning in the sea, but I drink leaves instead of water!" One harquebusier complained to Aguirre that he felt like he was inside the belly of a submersed whale.

Maddening fecundity. Roberto de Coca hacked away some cane and brush so that he could lie down in a spot out of the rain; on waking he found himself two meters in the air, cradled by wobbling young shoots of cane that had sprung up while he slept. Like one of those exotic beds the Comtesse de Nesles commissioned for her amatory exploits.

If someone died, on the second day the coffin was sure to shed its classical funereal geometricality and transform into a gay raftful of flowers and young sprouts, floating downstream through the swamplands toward the mouths of great rivers.

This riotous vitality vexed the Europeans: methodical *doers* driven by a biblical imperative to conquer the Earth, thereby wrecking not Nature alone but all humans and animals that stood in their path. In America all was *being*, and human *doing*—doomed, Adamic, postparadisiacal—ran up against a barrier of free existence that to them seemed subversive and unnatural. They were as irked as the alchemist whose droplets of mercury spill, rebelliously, irretrievably, slipping from his grasp.

Aguirre stayed up nights. Nothing soothed him like suspicion, like watching out for subversion, at all times on the rise (History was proof). He skulked among the sleeping men, spied on the guards, and waited for the emergence of the dead, who were always game for a fight. In his wanderings he met those night stalkers that occur in every human group: men set apart by ambition or secret vice. Sablon, the French adventurer, who merged with the zambo Olindo into a peculiar panting quadruped: a bull writhing against a ceibo. Or Lipzia, the Jew, waiting with a sieve in the river current for the unlikely nuggets that would permit him to open a jewelry shop in the great square of Amsterdam. The eunuch Vergara gorging on ripe bananas. The hushed expeditions of the Priest and the Scribe, led by Spinola, the lecher, to fuck the silken contractile orchids, which released them depleted at dawn. (These lipped orchids are sometimes confused with the quinquennial flowers of the so-called barracuda, a critical error: for on sensing the invader's presence—goldfinch, hummingbird, or spider—the lips of the

corolla weep a sticky fluid and pucker with such power that
not even a medium-size cardinal can wrench free.)

The Old Man glided among them as though he did not
see them. His years in command had taught him that the
vices of men are inalienable and that a modicum of tolerance
averts graver breaches or outbursts.

Near dawn, rebuffed by the dead, Aguirre searched
wearily along the riverbank for the body of *doña* Inés: Inés
de Atienza, the two-time widow of Pedro de Orsúa and
Lorenzo de Salduendo, both killed by his hand in the name
of a love he had never had the courage to confess in words.
(His *billets-doux* were mangled cadavers, but *doña* Inés could
not lower herself to that language of horror, of bloody sig-
nifiers.) Only by way of the wounds inflicted by his henchmen, Carrión and Antón Llamoso, had he cast her to the
ground, and only then had she understood, as she writhed
and died, the savage love, or lust, concealed behind those
deaths, her own included.

Wordless punning. She waits for him, prone beside the
still pool of the river, near the spot where the Priest mixes
his sweet-potato wafers, away from the eyes of sinners. She
bleeds sweetly, sprawled there; splendid thighs stranded on
sand, lustering in moonlight. He had found her in this pose
when he hurried into the hut as it began to burn, after his
henchmen rushed out, choking, with their bloody daggers.
Is hers a look of gentle love or vaguely vengeful scorn? Two
toppled torches. Lope loosens his clothing, gathering that
doña Inés is prepared to accept *in extremis* the devotions of
this shy, awkward suitor (Dumb spik! Childish little boy!
You might have spoken sooner!).

Beside the still pool, teased by flames and the chill of approaching death, he lies upon her again and wages battle for supreme rapture.

Coitus interruptus in aeternas. Barely a glimmer of perfect bliss: for death poured into her body like a flood of frigid water, and by then the flames of the burning hut had begun to grill his coat of mail. How maddening and frustrating to glimpse the peak and not be able to reach it! Comparable only to lying entwined with the Moorish girl in the Córdoba cathouse when the hunchbacked houseboy, that hard-bitten bastard, ran through the upstairs corridor rapping with dreadful precision on every door and shouting "Time's up! Time's up! Time's up!"

At the first glimmer of dawn, he shuffled back along the riverbank. "This interminable war! But someone must keep the dead in line!" And later: "What wouldn't I give for an ordinary love, a dairymaid from Oñate—and why not?—with hands that smell of fresh cow's milk . . ."

With a kick he waked Nicéforo, who had drifted off to sleep in the mud on the path to camp. And while the men were preparing to begin the work of the day, he lay down in his bed for a nap, one eye half-open.

Years of tramping. Prodding the few surviving horses through the mud. "Giddyup! Giddyup! Nasty beast! Giddyup!" Lather ribboning from worn-out whips. These existentially eccentric, man-corrupted creatures straggled along, fearing the roar of the ravenous jaguars and the sting of tarantulas that clamped to their hoofs, sudden and vicious. "Giddyup! Giddyup! Dumb nag!" No trace of the lordly centaur, that hybrid born of the bellicose passions of man. All sign of the gallop had gotten tangled up in lianas. The dignified trot of the Spanish School of Vienna had been reduced to a messy skid in the mud. Once a great warrior in the battles of Mexico and Peru, the horse was now a worthless rackabones, a worm-ridden, four-footed wastrel begging for an imaginary mawful of oats.

The dog—man's other collaborator in his aggressive, repressive misery—was a tired clump of mud and thistles crouching between the horse's legs. Hotbed of worms and chiggers.

They prepared to conduct astronomical and geographical surveys, for the night was cloudless. But when they unrolled the maps, they saw that the ink had run, creating delicate iridescences and butterfly-wing abstractions. The stellar charts of Abraham Zacuto of Salamanca (which Blas Gutiérrez was under orders to convey in a watertight case, along with the books of the Chronicle) were ruined: the Arabic numerals, fruit of three decades of calculations, had seeped into the paper. But setting up the astrolabe was the worst. The tripod, carved from the root of the olive tree, had sprouted roots. The cross-staff had so badly swollen from moisture that Antares sat between the Sun and the Earth, and the Moon had landed beside the Magellanic Cloud like the ball the drunken Basque flings in fury from the far side of the court after the game is lost.

All this added to the doubt and distress. Men racked by disappointment came before Lope: "Sir, I wanted a farm! But no good planting nothin'! You tell 'im, tell our Prince what happened to yer beans!" Then another: "That's right. We planted a sack of seeds. Those other plants were waiting for 'em to sprout. And when they were only tiny little shoots, those greedy plants with yellow arms and black flowers pounced on 'em . . . pounced like beasts and gobbled the baby beans right up." "The Conquest's fine, and the Marañón Empire's great, but a fellow wants a garden and a few pigs, no? A fellow wants an export business, no?"

Aguirre had to mollify these frustrated farmers, these troublesome kulaks who grasped nothing of the missionary meaning of the Conquest and even less of the destiny of the Marañón Empire: "Well, well. Give it time. I'm sure the white beans will do better. You must keep trying and keep your chins up. Mark my word, Giménez, this'll be nothing but gardens and vineyards, olive trees by the millions! But first the military phase—the Conquest!" The men returned, less than reassured, to their entrepreneurial dreams.

America comported herself like a monster, by turns playful and pitiless, who delighted in ridiculing the dynamism, the gleaming purpose of these can-do men. Her means of resistance were myriad. The case of Nuflo Ayala, who came across a sylvan stream of fresh mountain water and felt tempted to strip down and take a dip. In short: he bobbed up half a league downstream in the tow of a raging whirlpool, howling with pain, gelded by the nip of a gigantic anaconda that slithered off cackling into the dense brush.

At other moments it was the lavish beauty that unmanned the men. One morning they were tramping under a vast canopy of giant araucarias whose big fleshy flowers were sopped in dew. Suddenly the breath of the jungle—wet and heavy like the huffing of a feverish mule—lifted. A light breeze riffled the orchids. There, at the foot of a slope, lay a blue lake rimmed by Swiss mountains and fed by a quicksilver waterfall. Gorgeous, bliss-inducing silence. Mist rising from the waterfall produced a perfect rainbow that evanesced above the cool blue water; the plumage of two peacocks waving with spread tails from the bare branch of a *viraró* mirrored its colors. Three pink herons rose into the air and hung there with amazing serenity, near motionless beneath the blue dome of the sky, like the Taoist images of Tieng-Tse (T'ang dynasty).

The Priest knew that every manifestation of beauty was the laboratory of the Devil. On seeing the men trapped and panicking in this (unauthorized) numinous atmosphere, he reacted vigorously: "Mass! Mass! Idiots. The God of Abraham, Isaac, and Jacob! Mass!"

Aguirre had no choice but to authorize a quick open-air mass, which in any case shattered the rapturous spell and rewaked Guilt.

No one learns to accept the discomforts of Evil. On reaching the river, which they baptized in the name of the Holy Apostles (today known as the Roosevelt), Aguirre succumbed to the temptation to shake the powers of the Evil One. In fact, it was one of those old projects that never come to pass. In his deepest self he felt, almost indescribably, that the best things in life had sprung from the Fiend (his relationship with *doña* Inés, his decision to garrote the fanatical Priest who was fundamentally incapable of faith in God, his resolve to wage war against Philip II, for what would have happened if he hadn't?: he wouldn't have his spot in History, he'd be some poor bastard with a gun, some nobody!).

But it was grief and agony and eternal stress. He felt that shirking the Devil would be a joyless relief, like castration.

To be a humble Catholic! Or a meek Jew merchant! To give up the luxury of rebellion! To temper the body like an old wineskin passed down through the family! To live with the obedience and virtue of the eunuch!

With all his soul Aguirre longed to be a common man, a nobody (the hidden temptation of Christianity).

They camped for three months, waiting for the return of Rodríguez Viso, who had gone off in search of fresh provisions (due to scurvy 80 percent of the soldiers' teeth had fallen out).

The Old Man never ceased to speculate, at times positing scandalous demonological theories. No day passed on which he failed to summon the Priest or the Jew or the Scribe. "What would a man like me be without the Devil? Nothing! An inkpisser with a gun! Some men are his angels, like Saint Francis, and some are his demons . . . but at least they *are*!"

But succumbing to the temptations of freedom, he agreed at last to the exorcism urged by the Priest. Said Padre Alonso: "In your case I believe it's Asmodeus, the lecher. I think I can beat him."

On the designated day he set out with Carrión and the Priest, followed by negroes and mulattoes weighed down under pulleys, ropes, braziers, Neapolitan boots, hard thorns for implanting under fingernails, jugs of flammable oil.

They hung the pulley on an urunday tree. The Old Man removed his breastplate, his coats of mail, his leather vest, and the tatters of his shirts and undergarments. His scrawny chest looked indecently pale, like the paunch of an English preacher.

He surprised everyone by handing around cone-shaped hoods in black fabric. "Must do these things properly," he said. They bound his hands and strung him up. "Pull, damn it, pull." Carrión and Nicéforo Méndez struggled.

The Priest at last found the page in his amphibious book and in his best sacerdotal voice began: "You, Satan! You, Devil! Come out! No use hiding! *Ecce crucem Domini, fugite partes adversas, vivit leo de tribu Juda, radix David. Exorciso te! Exorciso te! Creatura ligni, in nomine Dei patris omnipotentis! Exorciso te!*" The negro and Carrión chiming in: *"Exorciso te! Exorciso te!"* And Aguirre: "Come on, pull! Pull, damn it! Nothing's happening here. The pulley's not doing a thing! What about those boots! Don't let that fire go out! Come on! Do I have to be telling you how to do it?"

Carrión strapped on the big funneled iron shoes and began to pour in manatee oil, which boiled heavily. The Old Man let out four or five deep, promising roars of pain. The Priest lunged forward and jabbed at his chest with the bronze cross. "Come out, Devil! *Dicas! Dicas! Exorciso te partes adversas!* Come out, Satan! Burn in this holy water!"

Aguirre's howls turned into moans and then into a growl that rose from the pit of his chest. The Priest approached and listened carefully to the growls. For a moment he thought he was making out a few words in low-class Hungarian (one of the Devil's tricks, saying important things in code). "Speak! Speak! Talk clearly, wretch!" But the brief message was lost. The Devil had apparently shrunken into some even darker corner of Aguirre's soul. The Old Man

half-opened an eyelid and glowered. The Priest hurriedly
commanded: "Come on! Stoke that fire! More oil! Move it,
Carrión! You don't wish to be agents of the Devil, do you?
Come on!"

They sloshed a new load of boiling oil into the Neapolitan boots. Though the pain could not be expected to
reach into every crack and crevice of the Old Man's soul,
as it had the first time, the Priest believed that some hope
lingered. He thought he was hearing a mumbled message
in Lope's growls, each weaker than the last.

Slowly the Fiend arose triumphant; he had hunkered
down and foiled the assault of Good. The torture had merely
made him shift position in his bed of squalor, among kidneys, groin, and belly. The Priest knew that the Evil One
occupied the deepest, darkest places, into which the soul
steals on tiptoe.

But he was not prepared to give up easily; his sense of
priestly duty called for heroic measures. He ordered Carrión
to wrap a gut string (the sort used by the fishermen of
Santander for catching shark) around his testicles; the Old
Man whimpered, woozy with pain. "Make a doghanger's
knot! Come on, quick before he passes out and the Evil
One gets the upper hand." This done, he tied the other end
of the string around Nicéforo's chest. Then he lashed him
with his whip and made him run with all his might. A few
meters out, the negro lurched like a bull caught in a lasso,
and rolled. Aguirre let out a shrill cry. But then nothing:
he had fainted. The Old Man's testicles were like teak seeds
from India or those formidable blue-steel minibullets forged
by Solingen armorers.

Then Aguirre opened his eyes. Angry and upset, but too weak to kick or scream. Nothing had been gained! The Priest did not know how to tell him he had lost the battle. He made excuses with an Andalusian lilt, which crept in when danger made him nervous: "He's a tough Devil! He's gotten tougher! He's frozen down inside! He won't budge! Won't budge! He's more stuck than a Galician's tooth! At first he was moving, but later noth—nothin'!"

They unhitched him from the pulley and laid him in a stretcher. He was a wreck. The skin of his feet was stuck to the inside of the iron boots and unsticking it was a horror. They smeared the flayed soles and toes with fresh oil and wrapped his feet in banana peels, to be changed four times daily. For two weeks he raved on his mat, tended by Nicéforo, who whisked away the flies with a plume (luckily he didn't get wormy).

Coming to his senses one day at dawn, he discovered the ultradelicate spirit of *doña* Ines blowing gently on his burning feet. Again he heard the Voice (barely a hiss in the distance, a signal in the fog of his soul). Deep down he felt no regret at having failed to rout the Devil. "Lope, Lope . . . do you hear me? Son, brother, father . . ."

Meanwhile, the local nations and their leaders watched as the men of the New Continent (called Europe) rampaged across America with the misery and fury of those who fight and cannot slay the enemy.

Day after day they scrutinized them from the deep jungle. They drew the conclusion that the white-faces were fleeing the scene of a Great Crime, surely related to that amazingly weak little god nailed to the bronze cross the Priest wore on his chest.

Not solely the men of the jungle tribes, but the plants and animals too, were soon convinced that the invaders were deeply estranged from the Spirit of the Earth. Enjoyed neither harmony nor peace. Had been born to prowl like hungry wolves. After the days of sacrifice and exertion, their pleasures were few. When at last they seemed to be resting, in fact they were weighing the future, drafting feverish plans that reduced the present to a mere waste of time. It was vital to understand that these were the victims of a capricious god who reveled in punishing them by fulfilling their ambitions.

Though they claimed they had come to propagate the institutions and customs of their Kingdom, in fact they had come to cast them off: molested and murdered and indulged in every vice. Apparently they could not fathom freedom without crime.

> *This "true" god from the sky*
> *will speak solely of sin,*
> *his sole teaching will be sin,*
> *his soldiers will be ruthless,*
> *his dogs fierce and cruel.*
>
> *The Earth will burn.*

It was difficult to outwit them, for they believed they were the bearers of the sole religion of salvation. (At a meeting of chiefs on the river Napo, the *cacique* Supé summed up this strange conduct: "By their standards, they are kind: they kill us to save us, to keep us from living without the benefit of faith . . .")

The white-faces were driven by a reckless passion for property. Apparently the power of their Empire was rooted in the wealth of the individual. They expended great effort surveying and parceling out plots, placing boundary stones and ceremoniously drawing up deeds. All were lords of vast estates; to walk was to gain wealth. Evenings they agonized, cards in hand, losing what may have cost months of sacrifice: a cardboard Horse simply trampled a Knave. Apparently they relished slipping from opulence into poverty. Could not live without the fits and starts of their symbols and fictions.

The greed was so extensive and divisive that the Priest was continually reminding them in his Sunday sermons (as if he had paid a personal call to Paradise only yesterday): "It's easier for a camel to pass through a needle's eye than for a rich man to enter the Kingdom of Heaven." Knowing that these were gratuitous words, guidance for death not life, they taunted him under their breaths. They said, "Each man for himself and the Devil take the hindmost!"

The local chiefs had learned that international amity could not be had. Every gift was a ruse, every embrace hid a dagger. After the banquet they would find that Llamoso or Coca or Salazar had nonchalantly nipped the King's gold amulet or was fondling the buttocks of the Princess. Greed gave them no peace, and as for carnal desire, it was simply a monster after centuries of bondage.

And yet, though these things were comprehensible, the actual events roused great indignation. The *cacique* of Aparia reportedly writhed in fury for three days after receiving this message from Orellana's chaplain: "We come to save you! God is with us! Praised be God!"

Eleven months after his departure Rodríguez Viso came back without fresh provisions. They would have to keep on making do with monkeys, turtles, and herons; for salad, slips of tender bark.

Ever since the exorcism, Aguirre had lain in bed with wounded feet. He was forced to submit to excruciating foot-baths of gunpowder mixed with tannin juice to stem the proliferation of the ravenous caterpillars.

It was during this long delay that Lope reconsidered the remarkable charms of his half-breed daughter, *doña* Elvira, a sunny, sparkling fifteen-year-old. Mornings the Girl sang and gathered choice fruits for her father's table (the only man with whom she consorted, as no other was allowed within eighteen paces). Her body surpassed her years, yet was unspoiled by time. Rather like an odalisque of Tetuan turning twenty-four.

From where he lay languid in his bed, Lope saw that the happy frolics of the Girl sank the men in strangely mournful sorrow.

The two wounds he had dealt her (to protect her from the evils of life) that memorable afternoon of October 27th, 1561, had mended into two little red daubs, two merry beauty spots. It dawned on Lope that her death had been like the pruning of a young poplar: each spring it sent up stronger, sounder shoots. Watching her caper near the cald-rons of the camp kitchen confirmed his old idea that death harmed nobody, not even friends and family. (This was the secret of the great tyrants of History, pruners who somehow always turned their cuttings to secret profit.) What would she otherwise have become? A cranky drudge fussing about the kids, wed to her insufferable suitor, Pedrarias de Almesto (duly purged). Her bloom lost: the sags and shrivels of matrimonial eroticide. No! He had been right to lift his dagger and declare: "I have come to kill you, my daughter. Lest you have nobody to protect you in the event of my death." And having inflicted the two paternal punctures: "Now no rascal can bed you down." A great truth, after all. And she clearly had no ill feelings. When Aguirre inquired if she harbored any filial resentment, she would gaze and smile in that naughty, silly way that had in former times stirred the furtive lust of the soldiers.

At around noon, after plucking the fruit and before retiring into the hut to play with her butterfly collection, *doña* Elvira took her bath in the river.

As she waded into the water, wetting her thin sheath, a silence rose through the regiment solely akin to the silence of nightfall in the virgin jungle. Even the screeking flocks of parrots were inaudible, and if someone had something urgent to say, he had to shout into the person's ears at the top of his lungs, like steering through a Caribbean hurricane. All that could be heard was the wondrous murmur of water pushed aside by the shapely thighs of the Girl. And later, after she had dunked her head, the splash-splash of playful washing and her crystalline voice softly singing a silly song:

Tirulirulí liru lí!
Tirulirulá liru lá!

Tirulirulón liru lón!
Tirá! Lirí Lirón!

The men were so flustered by her innocence that without wish or intention they wound up in a mesmerized row along the beach, the cook clutching a slab of fish, the cobbler with a half-sewn boot, the armorer with an unhoned dagger.

Doña Elvira slunk out with the sheath clinging to her naked body. A sight whose torments the Girl could not have fathomed: she had been reared in an ignorant, repressive, prudishly Catholic environment.

Fascinated along with the rest, Lope craned his neck for a better view from the mat.

It struck him that if the Girl was a half-breed, his paternity was only partial. Or perhaps royal consanguinity was like the relationship between an uncle and a niece. Amid these musings, he summoned Huamán, the Cuzqueño *amauta* and polyglot, for an account of the matrimonial arrangements of Incan kings. "What was that you told me? They wed their sisters, how was that?"

Huamán tried to explain that the blood of the King— the Inca—was sacred. That the heir could not be conceived outside the exclusive (absolutely endogamous) circle of sacred blood. He contended that the bastardy of Atahualpa was proof positive of the disaster that strikes the kingdom when strange blood flows in Incan veins.

They were deep in these disquisitions when *doña* Elvira approached, her hair freshly braided, bearing a platter of plump fruit. Her stiff nipples showed like two iron coins through the wet sheath.

Lope (skilled, like all longtime leaders, at reckoning the

mood of the masses) saw that the tension wrought by the Girl's presence had risen prodigiously during those months of stasis. As *doña* Elvira rolled the coconut soap beneath the sheath with her usual playful, perilous innocence, Aguirre said to her: "Henceforth, and until further notice, my little daughter will bathe only at midnight."

One rosy dawn the Old Man felt something fresh and rough lapping his burning feet. Still dreaming, he imagined it was *doña* Inés pampering him with exquisitely loving care. When he sat up in bed, he met the placid, hypnotic green eyes of the panther. Marvel of beauty, innocent evil, primitive cruelty, elegant harmony. Lope was fascinated, but not afraid. When at last he moved his arm to take up the dagger, the beast retreated with that disconcertingly slow, almost nonchalant swiftness of princes. Vanished into the brush with regal poise, conscious of its perfection and its power.

To avoid talk of witchcraft, Aguirre made no mention of the occurrence. But within the week his wounds began to heal. "On to new afflictions!" remarked Sablon, the skeptic, who had no faith in the fate of the Expedition.

As always at the start of a new phase, the Old Man summoned Lipzia to read his cards. The Jew shuffled them carefully on his tattered cape and turned up the card of choice: the Devil. "What is it? Can you tell me anything?" And Lipzia: "Conjunction of Mars and Venus. That's it . . . Lust. Here you see the hoofs of the goat, no question about it, the female billy goat. See the tits? But you mustn't forget it's Satan. Satan, who's basically a challenge to the order men attribute to the will of God. But isn't order what

Satan requires for the perversion of man? It's an Earth card: war and sex, Mars and Venus . . . " "Is it the most dangerous card? The worst?" the Old Man muttered. Then Lipzia: "No, personally I'm sure it's not, but don't forget, I'm a Jew. The Devil's . . ." Then Lope: "Which is the worst?" "If you ask me, the cards that do nothing, say nothing! The cards about the boredom of life!" Lipzia replied.

But the Old Man was far from content. Demoniacal rebellion can also include the urge to not be even the Devil's agent.

Two days later they resumed the march, after those versed in astronomy inscribed date and bearings in the Chronicle. They reckoned it was May 12, 1637 (counting the week the Scribe made no notations because his hand was infected by snakebite).

Reviewing the column on the move, Aguirre noted to what degree laziness and peace are indeed the root of all corruption. They looked less like a regiment than like a procession of broad-beamed mayors in the fiesta of San Benito. They had grown fat. The captains had helped themselves to the five purebred whores (the mulattas and native girls didn't count) and the soldiers resented it, everyone's turn was late. María Schneider, María Fontan, Rosarito Quesada, Anémona Salduendo and Greta Perticari preened alongside their pimps of official rank. Even the dead, emboldened by Aguirre's languor and sleepiness, were rebelling: came and went at liberty through the camp, reeking of old blood and unslaked vengeance.

They trekked eastward by quick marches. Reveille sounded at three and if necessary they traveled in the dark (dawn was moved one hour back for enhanced efficiency).

Accidents tended to be disastrous in the murk of the jungle. They hiked Indian file, led along by the flickering beams of *cocuyos* (giant fireflies), which each man lashed to his back and heels to light the way for the next.

They crossed the incredible village of the Homopuevas (Blas Gutiérrez made sketches in the margins of the Chronicle). These amphibious men took to wheezing at sunset and had to retreat for the night to the swamp floor. Easy to conquer because they lay still and could be skewered with the halberd against the clayey ground.

Some weeks later the Marañón Empire seized the land of the Jomocohuicas: vegetal humanoids that, lacking digestive organs, fed on the fragrance of plants and flowers. The advance of the Spanish column forced their exodus into the mountains, where they were stricken by severe indigestion.

Two years beyond, these wifeless warriors reached the great desire (and fear) of their deliria: the delicious, dangerous land of the Amazons!

3

Tarot III:
The Empress

Drifting hopefully toward the kingdom of women. Hegel and "the men of the Spirit." The Amazons propose a strange war. Sexual novelties. The desert of guiltless gratification. Return to the perversity and complaints of Queen Cuñan. Failure.

*T*HE RIVER was surely bearing them toward the land of the Amazons. The rafts slid slowly through oily waters that concealed the hectic commotion of giant fishes. Here and there by the still pools, fat Indians fished, humming in high-pitched voices with the unmistakable serenity of eunuchs. These were men who had been captured by the Amazons, used in insemination rites, stripped of their manhood (did they really do it with their teeth?), and then freed.

"But I won't make the same mistake as one-eyed Orellana! Never!" Lope could see that the prospect of making love to those far-famed woman warriors had perked up the spirits of his men. The Chronicle states that on June 24,

1524, Orellana's regiment launched into unruly battle with the Amazons, killing seven. "Stupid victory! They were spoiling for a fight! Am I right, Antón?" "Yes sir, beyond a doubt." Then Lipzia: "Orellana didn't wish to risk it, they're reportedly ferocious . . . " The words of the Jew upset the young captains; luckily the Old Man's mind was elsewhere. "I'm sure love is the only war they seek . . . " A fragrance fleeing along that verge of the mind where forgetfulness begins.

Nights, an unnerving swish-swish rose up in the muggy, motionless air: the prow timbers parting the silken water. Many men lay wide-awake against the barrels and sacks, eyes gleaming like coals. At moments they thought they scented some distant brine spiking the hot sweet breath of the Tropics. Something salty or female . . .

"The trick is to seize their city, grab their goods and skip out on those so-called last rites . . . !" fretted the Scribe. The Priest was afraid that his flock would run wild. The troop hussies prowled the rafts, trying to tempt those fiery-eyed men sprawled out sleepless.

By now the peoples and animals of so-called America knew that the men of the Conquest (whom their Hegel would later call "men of the Spirit") deprived their bodies to horrific extremes on behalf of their own intractable beliefs. That many had defied the abyssal monsters of the Ocean Sea, and Saint Brendan's whale, for the undivulged purpose of viewing a naked woman (and slitting her open like a ripe pear, nibbling her, tasting her).

They now knew. In the world of the white-faces, bodies

were suspected of sin: moonscapes over which demons ca-
pered. Clothing (peacetime armor) concealed the flesh and
the curves of the body. The white-faces coupled in the dark,
with set limits on pleasure. (Their stupid god seemed to
clutch them by the sex organs.) They could contemplate the
flesh, the curves, only of their whores—not bodies but
things, cheapened by sin and social exclusion. Llamoso, for
one, mated with his wife through an eyehole in a sackcloth
gown. The so-called Pope, terrestrial manager of the interests of their god, had ordained that the sexes of Greek and
Roman gods on display in the Vatican be covered with plaster leaves. The wrath of society threatened any female (not
whore) who permitted her body to be seen. The Devil
preened in the brazen female who showed herself after the
onset of puberty.

They now knew. After Mexico, after the tragedy of the
aclla cuna, after the fate of the women of Atahualpa, they
knew. The white-faces had metamorphosed the marvelous
fire of desire into a panting dog chained in the pits of their
souls. This they knew. The white-faces would pounce on
their women and tell them that they were not women. That
they had no souls. Were mere things. Indians—they would
say—things, like their whores. Only a poet like Nezahualcóyotl could have found words to describe the misery of
that monstrous destruction:

> *You write flowers, oh Giver of Life.*
> *You sing colors. You sing down the dark*
> *Upon those who must live on Earth.*
> *Even jaguar knights and eagle knights will fall.*
> *On Earth we will live only in your painted book:*

DAIMON

Your black paint blackens brotherhood, society and honor.
You bring down the dark
Upon those who must live on Earth.
Courage! For all must go to the land of mystery.

At dawn the rafts reached a turn in the river. On the far shore the birds were hushed, a standard sign of ambush. Monkeys bunched on dry branches, jostling for the best seats. "Here they are at last! Thanks for the news! Well now! Captain of the crossbowmen! Starboard! Here they are! Here they are . . ."

A dart whizzed through space and pegged the deck. Then another, of yellow parrot feathers (pitched with playful, not mortal, purpose in a quite parabolic fashion), struck the buttocks of Anémona Salduendo, who was napping on a mat in the stern: it wasn't poisoned, and in her sleep she moaned something about mosquitoes, the scourge of twilight.

"We're here, we're here! Here they are! Don't you see? No matter what, I won't blunder like one-eyed Orellana! What good is combat without conquest?" Lope gave the command to shoot two crossbows toward the guava trees. A guava, pinned by an arrow, fell and rolled on the white sand along the shore. After a long pause, another dart flew in on a parabolic course and spiked the bridge. They looked it over; the Priest remarked on its queer smell: as though it had lain on the ocean floor.

While the Old Man was giving orders to turn the rafts windward, suddenly Antón Llamoso, gripped by a rebellious fury, fell to hectoring the men: "Once they're inseminated, they'll devour us, devour us! Why d'ya think Orellana didn't stop! Let Aguirre give us a raft, and the fellows who'd rather not be gelded and slain will shove off! Let's scram! Or didn't you catch what I said?" He ranted for a spell while the others calmly went about mooring the rafts. Tossing a crossbow on the sand as a sign of peace, they glimpsed, on the ridge over the river, several ravishing woman warriors retreating at some command. "They look like Flemish girls with an Andalusian tan!" Diego Tirado sighed rapturously.

They sprawled on the beach, waiting; but when the afternoon elapsed uneventfully, they decided to dine. Not until morning did a delegation come forward, five runty eunuchs with blackened skin. Though they spoke an obsolete common language, Huamán, the polyglot, managed to gather that they came on the part of the Queen, with orders to subdue them for the fulfillment of their rites; the reprisal would otherwise be brutal. One lifted a blowpipe, a sigh was heard, and at fifty yards off a Chanca porter fell: the dart was a deadly poison bee. *"Curare! Curare!* Poison herbs! We're lost!" And Lipzia: "Not even the Venetian alchemists have achieved a more deadly substance!"

They had no choice but to cross the river and follow along. The head eunuch agreed to let them leave behind a small garrison to look after the rafts and whores. The Priest and Sablon, the Frenchman, would serve as spiritual and military leaders, respectively. Diego de Torres, the crossbowman campaigning for sainthood, cast himself on the sand at Aguirre's feet and cried out that he would rather hang than join in the upcoming lechery. "I grant you this because you stink. Stay, fool!" Ayala (himself a eunuch) did wish to come along. "I like looking and remembering."

Escorted by the eunuchs, who were insufferably

haughty, they waded across the treacherous river and turned inland.

All night they tramped past tidy villages set in high, mostly dry terrain. Morning found them in the Capital, where Queen Cuñan (elsewhere known as Coñorí) greeted them from beneath her baldachin. A splendid woman who treated them magnanimously. So elegant that the nakedness of her gorgeous body could at moments be overlooked.

Lope strode forward and pronounced in a firm, calm voice (unfazed by Huamán's slow translation) that he was seizing her, and the Amazon territory, in the name of the Marañón Empire. The Queen listened with polite condescension. Then she spoke crisply. In matters of state her voice lost none of its femininity: "You have been vanquished. In these lands you will remain for ten moons. Or until the princesses and I are with child . . . " And then she turned away from Huamán, who was struggling to keep pace with Lope's words. Stepping out among the Marañones, she summoned them to tour the city.

Charming stone dwellings, curving streets. They stared, dumbstruck and dreamy-eyed, at the girls standing barebreasted in the windows, sweetly swaying their braided hammocks. Lithe, smiling, but none yet near enough to touch. In the street, only old crones fussily supervising as blacktinted eunuchs swept with palm-frond brooms. Now and then one was brutally whipped for gawking at these strange men from beyond the sea.

A closer look at the windows revealed that the princesses, like the Queen, were togged only in triangular *tangas*.

The eunuchs (they were later to learn) assiduously fashioned these *tangas* from hides of unborn fawns, or from a flexible ceramic fabric, made by secret formula, on which they etched ultraerotic scenes of Pompeian caliber.

At the hub of the city was a great garden, rimmed by a grove of palms and the shore of their sacred lake: Laguna Yacihuara, or the Lake of the Moon. Cosmic heart of the nation.

The Queen cordially allowed Lope to walk at her side, though not beneath the baldachin. As they strolled, she informed him that while the baby boys would be given away or sacrificed, the baby girls would be granted the full rights of citizens.

Came dark, the diligent eunuchs dished up a succulent banquet: rare, sumptuously sweet fruits (papaya, mango, pineapple, and others not yet assimilated into the Castilian tongue), monkey *guiso* in peanut sauce, and the ivory flesh of roasted parrots, served on floating leaves.

And as the moon mounted over the Lake, the Queen rose and danced barefoot on the sand, ringed by nine swaying princesses. In hushed wonder the conquistadors heard for the first time that sweet ritual song they would never forget:

> *Ocarominión . . . !*
> *Emahí . . . ! Emahí . . . !*
> *Ocarominión . . . !*
> *Amorehí . . . ! Amorehí!*

To the rhythm of the tambours, these luscious hostesses calmly peeled off their *tangas* and presented them (with poise and charm, and not a touch of clumsy rivalry) to their chosen consorts. Queen Cuñan danced over to Lope and gave him hers; it appeared to scorch the Old Man's hands like a hot sweet potato. He could not help but listen to the vulgar quips and brutish barbs of the troops (more jittery than joyful, like the night before going to sea). "Damn! This is more like it! This ain't bad!"

But when the conquistadors reached out to touch them, all the girls instantly fled. Waiting proved futile, so they rushed from the garden. But the doors were barred, and in the streets they saw only squads of eunuchs and crones with whips. Carrión, Llamoso, Hernández, and a few other hellions tried to bash in the doors with clubs and crowbars, but it could not be done. When a band of eunuchs showed up with blowpipes, they were forced to scatter. Some returned sulkily to their usual pastimes; some threw punches and even pitched stones at the eunuchs, who were trying to prevent them from smashing the manatee-oil streetlamps.

Next morning the girls ventured forth again and beckoned them, as though nothing could be more natural, to bathe in the Lake. On shore they greeted them with long Turkish-style gowns cut from fresh, colorfully patterned cloth. The conquistadors donned them bashfully: the eunuchs had tossed the breastplates, the patched boots, the tatters of Spanish cloth, the moth-eaten berets, and the helmets like the kitchen pots of gypsies into a great heap. The whole mess stank like a dead mare, and drew flies.

In the radiant morning light, the Queen and the princesses (tall and a bit daft, like Northern girls) again began to gyrate to the nerve-tingling, ever-recurring melody of the erotic season. Only later, shielding the light from their eyes, did the Iberians see that the curious monument around which they danced was a huge stone phallus, representing, oddly enough (they were later to learn), God-woman, the supreme Amazonian divinity.

From that noon on, all was a trail of fabulously luxurious siestas, sleepless nights, languid dawns. The long rite of insemination had begun. Just as in England the household revolves around the hearth, here home was designed around the bed. In the hottest hours they used the braided hammock, at night the soft mat. Huamán explained that there was no word for "bed"; the word they used meant "temple."

Lazy mornings. Eunuchs arrived bearing croquettes made of dried fish; tiny turtle eggs just collected from the cool waters of the river; chirimoyas at their peak of sweetness, after which they rapidly rot; wild strawberries (the berry patch on the far side of a hill reminded the Queen of her girlhood: "sweet summer bird" was their word for "youth," said Huamán); and all the juice of fresh-cut coconuts and all the unconsecrated *chicha* they desired.

They stretched, yawned sloppily, and belched. Copulated as though every night were the last. But slowly, as their senses grew sated, they mastered the subtleties of matinal refinement.

Mornings arrived among gerunds only: time dallied, the present had substance! Each hour lingered on the cinnamon skin of these females internationally fierce but intimately tender and playful. Treachery was unknown to them. Time throbbed like the heart of a sleeping plesiosaur; life shared the slow stroll of the moon on the path of each tropical night. "It's Sunday! Hell! Only Sunday? No man, that's not possible, look, listen! No! It's still Sunday!" And so forth.

DAIMON

These men, who had always ridden the bodies of
women with vengeful, voiceless fury (wishing to be free of
them forever?), now discovered a new corporeal time. No
longer felt constrained to dress and depart. Evenings, they
rambled docilely along the rim of the Lake, gaudy gowns
falling open, each with one arm dangling around the hip of
his princess.

The feasts had fallen silent: no more shouts or curses
or (unconcealably vulgar) innuendos. The conquistadors
supped after dark, sprawled on the warm sand, heads athwart
the strong thighs of their vanquishers. Betwixt tamales and
monkey breasts, they were initiated in the art of kissing.
Learned to link lips and share breath, something they had
always deemed the domain of French queers or craven cathouse dandies.

As the girls regaled them with fellatio, they moaned
rapturously with their necks flung back. Succumbing to this
tempting pleasure, they fought off the infernal fear (ancient
among white men) of castration (mythic anthropophagous
treachery), and of the extravagant sinfulness of the deed.

The princesses orchestrated the tempo and science of
love. Tutored them in the application of ointments for inner
and outer use. Knew how to rouse lust with assorted perfumes. Knew how to moan and bite in a fashion which,
though stylized, was not artificial. All seemingly performed
in the only possible way. From time to time they recurred
again to music, and the song rose to the thrum of the tambours:

Ocarominión . . . !
Emahí . . . ! Emahí . . . !

Ocarominión . . . !
Amorehí . . . ! Amorehí!
Ocarominión . . . ! Ocarominión . . . !
Anahí! Anahí!

Now and then the conquistadors would wander toward
the camp they had left on the shore of the river. They felt
as far from all that as a man-about-town from his bygone
days at seminary. There the symbols sat (though far out-
stripped in each man's inner time): the weapons, the coats
of mail, the gems, the small cache of stolen gold, the precision instruments, the smudgy missives from the Universe,
the five tarts, the Priest with his weather-blighted Bible,
Lope's dead men perching in the branches, high-minded
Torres striving for saintship. If they perked their ears when
the breeze blew away the ceremonial song of the Amazons,
they could hear the wailing and weeping of the jealous
wenches (more rage than sorrow). They pictured the Priest
toiling away at paternosters and confiteors to withstand the
temptation of the whimpering orchids.

But the Priest would not accept defeat: after a lapse of
two weeks, fearing that his flock would slip into unregen-
erate lechery, he began, by way of two eunuchs who had
proved easy converts, to dispatch messages meant to summon back the men from their pagan carouses: "The Lord
sees all. He remembers all." Or: "Don't forget your mother
and sisters!"

Mornings, while most of the men indulged in the in-
creasingly copious breakfasts, and the princesses wearily

slumbered, Queen Cuñan and Aguirre often sauntered along the shores of the Lake of the Moon, after brief devotions to Caranain, the Sun. Huamán followed, murmuring his patchwork translations: an attempt to impart the subtleties of poetic language via the crude nominalism of the white-faces.

The Queen was intrigued and baffled. What passions had lured this lusty, hearty fellow from the harmony and pleasures of Earth? What fire licked his heels, driving him always onward? As a woman, the Queen sensed that he was wildly afraid of his own bliss (clearly a common trait among the warriors from beyond the sea). "I must expand my Empire, my lady. I desire that the sun never set over my Empire . . . I have defied the King of Spain, High Prince of the World . . . I must carry on . . . This path will lead only to triumph or death . . . !" Eyeing him with regal poise, the Queen did not divulge her own concerns. Gold was their topic, and she asked him: "Why do you need so much?" But Lope made no answer. Naturally the Lady had learned of their rapacious and conspicuous greed (most of the men had pilfered dishes out of the girls' homes and buried them, like a dog his bone, between sessions of lovemaking). But what answer had he? What could she have understood? Gold meant a place at Court with a powerful, happy, handsomely remunerated regiment whose velvet-clad captains wore hats decked with Cuban parrot feathers . . . Gold meant striding into the Córdoba brothel, clapping his hands and crying: "Wine all around!" It meant meeting the mocking, admiring eyes of the Moorish girl at the door to her upstairs room. What could the Queen grasp of such things? How could he explain that gold was the means by which civilized men procure those pleasures that primitive men always—with silly innocence—enjoy? There was no answer. She did not seem offended by his silence. She went on: "What we wish is a bit of iron. We've seen that it's good for arrowheads . . . and also for daggers. But our prime interest is the secret of gunpowder." Her tone was uncommonly firm, and the Old Man, taken by surprise, felt deeply flustered. Pretending not to understand, he nudged Huamán; a tactic too clumsy for the subtleties of the Empress. He countered with another question (his diplomatic trump in military matters): "Is it true the kingdom of El Dorado, the Land of Paytiti, lies not far from here?" And she: "No, it's not far . . . Such an unhappy land! Those golden sands breed only scorpions and tarantulas. No manioc, no sweet potatoes, no pineapples! The Lord of Paytiti is so unlucky . . . " Lope's eyes gleamed. He murmured, as though thinking aloud: "Unlucky? Bad luck? Man! If life is a vale of tears, I'd rather be weeping with my butt on a heap of golden sand!" And then he added edgily, "Do you think I'll inseminate you soon, my lady?" The Queen did not answer. There was a coy sparkle in her eye. She smiled, stepped apart, and performed a few pirouettes, heating up the tempo of the tambours drummed by the eunuch band. Then she began to sing the ritual hymn.

On the way to the "temple" she pressed him: "But why? Why do you collect countries when there are so few of you? What for? Why so many weapons and coats of mail? Why not go naked in this heat? Captain, why did you give up your lands on the far side of the Infinite Lake? What are you searching for?" And Aguirre: "I seek only the salvation of my soul." He answered by rote, believing that he spoke the truth (the first thing a believer believes is that he speaks the truth). Queen Cuñan looked mystified.

By the second week, trouble had arisen. At first (still fancying they had stumbled into Paradise) the Iberians were touched by the Amazons' elegant ever-present nakedness; by their stunning and sumptuous naturalism. But in no time the racial penchant for gloom and doom set in: they told themselves that this was simply a boring simulation of true bliss. Bit by bit they abandoned the amorous idylls and reverted to pranking and rampaging through the streets of the city in packs.

Divers incidents exposed curious perversions on the part of the Christians, and puzzled their vanquishers. During one morning stroll, Queen Cuñan related several: with the eunuchs' supply of black pigment, Rodríguez Viso and Bartolomé Flores had dyed two of the spare gowns dispensed to them on the first day. They then forced their princesses to dress up like nuns, and raped them savagely. And Lope: "Man! *Caramba!* What an outrage! That's a good one! They'll catch it!"

Another charge: with Tirado's help, Spinola, the Genoese, was attempting to muster an escape party by deluding the girls with sham and shadowy promises: his real purpose was to peddle them in the brothels of Tetuan. Huamán had distinctly overheard their filthy intentions.

Lipzia, meanwhile, who had been spurned by the women and was living at camp, sent over a full assortment of embroidered linens from Antwerp, tiny mirrors adorned with beveled angels, sample embroidered lingerie, and even two flaskets of *eau de cologne*, which awed and thrilled the younger girls. He thus compiled lengthy lists of requests, promising to import them from Seville, payment up front in items of gold, especially those solid statuettes of Iara, the Great Serpent Goddess, that each princess kept at the foot of her "temple."

But this was not the worst. Apparently these perfect bodies, these necks wreathed with wild dahlias, no longer tempted the Iberians. Only eight impregnations had been verified, by means of magic Amazonian methods (using urine and the eggs of certain Laguna frogs).

Aguirre felt answerable for the virility of his men. Ashamed. There was nothing to be said. "Only eight? Only eight, is it possible? Sounds like a covey of husbands . . . !"

That night he toured the city, loitering beside open windows. Amid the smoke of foul, crudely cured cigarettes, he indeed heard screams and shouts: "Get dressed, bitch, put some clothes on! Keep still! Don't budge! I'm the one who's supposed to climb on you! No! Don't take off what I put on you!" The Old Man understood perfectly. The Queen was right. They were straying into incalculably risky territory. "Imbeciles! Assholes!"

But he too was implicated and held little sway over the Queen: two nights before, she had patted the mat beside her and found, in lieu of Aguirre's loveworn body, only an empty space. Until dawn she waited for him, wounded and worried, not daring to divulge this mortifying news to the guards. With the first light of day he returned, sweaty, ex-ultant . . . He had rendezvoused with his dead in the un-derbrush along the river Trombetas and joined battle. She feigned sleep so that she would not be forced to lower herself from regality to petty domesticities.

This realm boasted only phallic monuments and charming "temples": the Amazons knew nothing of the table, the chair, or the wheel. But the white-faces (promptly finding that they favored the friendship of men over the love of women) strung up a crude reed roof to screen out the sun, and built big tables and benches beneath it. They took to rudely relaxing there from noon to dusk, reveling in elaborate *guisos* and nearly radioactive *pucheros*.

The Amazons, who consumed fruit, fresh fish sprinkled with lime juice, and from time to time a bit of roast fowl or tender young monkey, naturally felt repelled by those grease-oozing racks of venison and manatee, in black vats it was the duty of the eunuchs to tend from the hour of ten. While waiting, the men dipped deep into the ritual *chicha* (whose reserves they had found) amid endless games of *mus* that often led to blows and sometimes to drawn daggers.

To top it all, the eunuch Ayala (whose entrepreneurial spirit had survived intact) ambled over from the camp, smelling a profit, and set up a plank across one end of the lean-to to serve as a bar. A genuine tavern in the open air: Ayala fixing *tapas* with manatee ham and fried river eels. Earthy and merry, raking in the coins. "What'll it be? One with sardines? Here are those two beers you ordered!" (Their word for the ritual *chicha*.) "No credit today, try again tomorrow."

Matters did not look up in days to come. The more the

lovelorn princesses wooed them—slighting their manhood—the crasser and brasher the conquistadors became.
Several girls were assaulted, and Queen Cuñan lodged a
stern complaint. By now the love hymn, sung through the
long afternoons, had no effect.

By order of the Empress, the eunuchs turned up carrying a live jaguar the capture of which had cost the lives
of three infrahumans. The Amazons sacrificed it in the ritual
manner before a great stone idol. The Queen then invited
Lope to eat the roasted testicles in front of the others, who
were dished bits of boiled viscera. Though the conquistadors
swallowed as best they could, the ceremony came to naught:
before the moon rose, most were back in the lean-to, around
the bar, ribbing and taunting like office boys out on a Saturday night. They belched noisily after each cupful of ceremonial *chicha.*

That very night a gang led by Carrión raped two princesses. The worst was that they beat them for giggling, for
refusing to resist.

Relations so gravely deteriorated that by the close of
the third week, the frog eggs had confirmed only ten preg-
nancies. Lope rounded up his captains and shouted: "How
do you like that! You've got it and you don't want it! You
can look and you don't! You can touch so you don't! How
do you like that!" The Scribe looked on ruefully: "Nothing
ousts evil thoughts like the habit of nudity . . ."

The Queen matter-of-factly informed Lope that the
time had come to descend into the Amazonian omphalos
for the ritual of the Moon. On this night of full moon they
would swim to the sunken temple near the perfect center
of Laguna Yacihuara.

DAIMON

The conquistadors were served only a light supper. They then gathered on the shore of the Lake and stripped down. Nonswimmers were carried by raft. All others, Iberians and princesses, swam almost a quarter league and then crowded onto a sandbar, neck-deep in water.

The moon pierced the crystalline, silken, amazingly saline water in a single gleaming lane. Into the opalescence they plunged, on the lithe heels of the princesses, led by Queen Cuñan, who even while swimming retained all her air of authority. There, four or five strokes from the surface, the stone walls of a temple trembled amid moon rays. They swooped down—like a host of angels—to the foot of the steps (geometries skewed by refracting light).

Then, still chasing the scissor-kicking legs of the girls, they swam up for air. So stunning and enchanting! More than one fellow tried to last down there as long as possible, by gripping the friezes.

Now the princesses were *duendes*, weaving around the white stone obelisk in the hush of the depths: their hair undulated in the water.

Once again up swam the girls for air. This time they clasped their dazed lovers by the hand, drew them into the depths, and led them around the obelisk. (The Iberians were shallow, not deep-water swimmers.) Thus surely the ritual had been fulfilled! As they popped to the surface, the girls burst into laughter: unfit for surrender to the Waters, their darlings were dopily rubbing their eyes and noses.

The Queen revealed to Lope that according to legend, the *muirakitán*, that magic essence that each princess kept in an amulet hanging over her breast, spawned at the heart of the Lake. Source and force of life.

In the watery half-light only a few skittish paiches and some silvery clouds of *candiru* (tiny fishes), whose attributes the men would not spot till morning. They invade the body, provoking a rash that lasts over four days. Females too contract a sort of localized fever, a fiery itch.

But that week marked the end of the ritual. The artificial elation of those final days gave way to a mood of outright schism. The indolence turned into spiteful violence and moral standards deviously, maliciously applied. Many girls were whipped, others subjected to the torment of constant clothing. The Queen imposed a round-the-clock guard of geldings toting blowpipes.

Moments after entering Ayala's lean-to, Lope smelled conspiracy in the air. From long experience he knew that fear of an external force prompts rebellion against commanders. Wrongly (but with conviction) the men contended that the Amazons were plotting one of their horrific ritual castrations. They claimed to have seen cropfields on the far shore of the Lake tilled by eunuchs in chains, the seed of past erotic seasons. Roberto de Coca alleged that his princess had beseeched him to flee, so as to escape the worst . . .

The men decided to round up their firearms and helmets that very night; Spinola would sing a *canzonetta* to distract the gelding on guard. Escape was set for dawn.

From a lookout in a ceibo, the Queen (tipped off by her spies) gazed with compassion at the flight of these short-legged malcontents, these *doers* miserably unfit for peace, whom she had grown fond of nonetheless. They taunted each other over trivial matters as they went, grabbing every last gold item within reach and making the sign of the cross to ward off the peril of the blowpipe-toting eunuchs presumably posted at the end of the row of houses.

But a shadow dimmed her benevolent gaze: she sensed that these little men, fierce keepers of their own woes, would by degrees come to master the great rivers, the mountains, the vast jungle. The world would belong to them precisely because they could so nonchalantly shun life. Their god—those little gods on crosses—was surely very shrewd. If only she had managed to steal the secret of gunpowder, at the very least! She could not bring herself to command their deaths.

Only after three days of traipsing through savage swamps (the rafts had rotted) did Lope de Aguirre realize that the lump in the pocket of his leather jacket was Queen Cuñan's jade amulet. He tossed it into a pond. He had learned long before that a Conqueror must carry only gold and gunpowder.

4

Fourth Arcanum: The Emperor

Repression. Hatred of paper and the written word. Personality cult. Emerging on the enemy coast: Cartagena of the Indies. Doña Eufrosia's cathouse. An amazing encounter and new frustrations. Economic might of the Spanish Empire. Aguirre, tramper, emperor of deserts. Plans.

H OW DARE you? How could you dirty my trust with those thoughts? Traitor! Puny paperpusher!" The Old Man moaned with ominous sorrow. Three love sonnets had been found, composed with rapture, darkness, and style by the Scribe, who had then clumsily concealed them among Abraham Zacuto's damaged astronomical charts. "Swine! You've damaged my child's innocence with your worst thoughts! What do you deserve?" "The worst," the Scribe answered meekly. "You've sinned in your inmost self! Indulged in the worst lechery, that of the soul! You've entertained perverted thoughts about my little girl! So what do you deserve?" "The worst," the Scribe Bukharinesquely replied, bracing himself for the horror of torture at the hand of Carrión, who had long coveted him (nothing rankles an executioner like an effete intellectual). "What's one more death, cur? Was it you who left that dried clover leaf in the romance she was reading? Confess!" "It was I . . ."

By now the Old Man's eyes were smoldering. "Fire, damn it! Fire! The Marañones will sizzle your balls! Carrión will whip you till you faint! They'll douse your wounds with vinegar to rouse you, again and again! Smear you with honey and leave you to the crotch ants!" He slavered in his fury, the old veins bulging in his leathery forehead and neck. "You've dishonored my little girl in your paper world! How have you permitted yourself such freedom of action? At once! At once! All pages shall be paginated; let nobody dare use a sheet of paper that has not been numbered and signed by me! All paper shall be accounted for! Anyone with old letters will surrender them to the common pile under pain of death! I'll nip this in the bud! An end to paper! You too, Padre! Number and sign the missal and evangelistaries! I'll nip this in the bud!"

Tortured that very afternoon, the Scribe let out grisly howls of horror. Carrión took extra care with his testicles, since he was certain of their direct implication in the question. He treated him not only to the Neapolitan boots, but also to the Chinese lasso, the so-called seafood paella, and other grim tortures.

After dark, Lope, whose rage had receded (it coursed now, dark and ugly, through subterranean sluices), called for Carrión and unctuously inquired: "How's the poet?" And Carrión, with the vile, canny smile of a pleased hyena: "Quite well, sir . . . " The Old Man laughed alarmingly loud. "You hound! What would we do without you! What a wit!"

During the night, Carrión enthusiastically wrapped a prickly pear in nettles and stuck it up the Scribe's anus. Death did not come, but his cure lasted one long year, during which time the Chronicle passed into the ambitious hands of Lipzia, who had sloppy handwriting but was well schooled.

Came a reign of horror for the Expedition. Informers abounded. All was suspect. La Salduendo was denounced for plotting to make paper and tortured. Carrión and Baltasar Salazar, a shifty crossbowman with the air of a Portuguese, shared the task of security, which, though it sapped military *esprit de corps*, was the mainstay of Lope's new terror.

In homage to its founder and benefactor, the 22nd of May was named a national holiday in the Marañón Empire, commemorating the day Aguirre killed Fernando de Guzmán, in the memorable year of 1561, now so distant and historic. It was celebrated beside a tributary on this side of the cordillera, and the whores costumed themselves in airy garments aspiring to Hellenism. A crown of laurel was fashioned for Lope, and the Priest mustered a motley chorus to provide background music for the recital of the terrible political ode: "Hail, Lope, Your Marañones Salute You!" which the Old Man himself had dictated to Lipzia, fielding a suggestion or two from the spectral *doña* Inés. The devilishly arrhythmic text was read under the staff that bore the black satin flag with its two crossed red swords, the Marañón emblem. From where he lay helpless on his cot, the Scribe could not help but overhear the mumbo-jumbo:

DAIMON

Hail great founder!
Aguirre, lad from Oñate,
Father of the first free
American territory!
Prince of the Marañón Empire!
Governor of Chile,
Terra Firma and Peru,
Hail and Glory to your flag!

Years of dual combat: against the living and the dead (always newly rising to the challenge per the rhythms of their scatological schedules). Nations of living creatures subjugated by the Empire as it tacked its claim to tree stumps and sowed the seeds of faith, which with time would sprout into submission and order. Countless Amazonian peoples! Peoples of Paraguay, Tupí-Guaraní. Nomad nations of the parched lands of Brazil. "All we do is conquer and march! We need to stay a while!" But the Priest placated the Old Man: "They've got the seed of faith, the seed of faith, that's what counts!"

"Can you consolidate an Empire with a roving army that always wins? If we were disgracefully trounced, wouldn't we conquer them better?"

During these ceremonies the Voice of the Fiend—the Other—rose above the soft pink hues of dawn: "All you need is gold. What is Empire without gold? The Philips will scoff at you! Emperor in rags! Give a thing and take a thing to wear the Devil's golden ring. Don't forget: if it doesn't glitter, it isn't gold. A golden key opens all the doors."

"Paytiti! Paytiti! Where are you hiding, Golden Prince? Forward march! Forward march! I'm sick and tired of fruit and paiches! Down with green leaves!" He hunted up Padre Alonso de Henao and harangued him: "The fact that the Lord Our God has sent for the Fiend to tempt your dumb Christ in the desert is proof of the Devil's divine nature! Satan tried to save Christ from his wrongheaded redemptions! He invited him to power, glory, and the revels of the world! To splendor! To joy!"

The Old Man was beside himself, almost foaming at the mouth (as in his worst fits of fury). The Priest sensed that he was emerging from the maelstrom of one of those inner wars into which his incubus dragged him. The Archfiend. No point proposing another exorcism after the fiasco on the River of the Holy Apostles.

Moreover, the Old Man's jealousy of *doña* Elvira had grown worse in recent years. On the march and in camp, the Girl was kept cooped up in a reed hut. Twice or thrice daily Lope (who had lapsed into treating her like a sister-in-law) would stop in for a chat, stirring wild suspicions among the soldiers, who were short on facts. Evenings, he went alone with her to the river pools, serving as companion and caretaker during her ablutions; only after escorting her back to camp would he tackle his eternal war with the dead.

At around that time, in a valley on this side of the cordillera, a patrol party led by Sablon stumbled into a band of mule skinners from Tucumán that had meandered off the trail. Lipzia's clever questions brought out the plight of the Marañón Empire. Apparently the Spanish Crown had planted ports almost clear around the Continent (in Lope's mind still egg-shaped). Militarily, a clash could not be avoided: late or soon, the Terrestrial Empire of the Marañones would be forced to launch a battle-to-the-death

against ports held by the Philips. And that Imperial appa-
ratus was elaborate and efficient. From hilltops they had
watched whip-wielding *encomenderos* driving the Indians into
mines of mercury and lead. Apparently the plantations on
the coast favored the brawny blacks, who balked less at their
new gods, and were too rich in bliss and music to be broken
by injustice.

Apparently the riches were hoarded in the north, and
from there shipped to Spain in the galleons of the Fleet.
Thus a decision was made: they would trek to Cartagena to
reckon the power and deployment of the enemy prior to
the attack, and above all to buy new silk underthings for
the Girl, who in the seclusion of her hut had turned catty,
demanding and capricious, and no longer listened with lucid
rosy respect to the sweet counsel of *doña* Inés, Lope de
Aguirre's melancholy lover.

Marching orders were met with all-around joy. Cartagena was a spree! Here merged all the lust for merriment
of Iberian-Americans and Spanish seafarers after three
months on blue water. During the march, which lasted
through nearly two years of rain, the women patched their
prettiest garments and washed their hair weekly with plant
shampoos.

They crept in timidly, shrouded in the cloistral sickly
reek of the jungle. (Those they passed seemed to shrink
away, leering with laughter or disgust.) The Old Man led
the way, fantastically shriveled. All were out-of-date despite
the repairs of recent weeks; the tatters barely hid lesions
and bleeding wounds. And yet no one tried to stop them!

No one showed pity! No one was angry! They were has-beens! Dogs (who can sniff out poverty and forsaken souls) snarled savagely from stoops and garden walls.

Cartagena of the Indies was amazing. Outrivaling even Seville (of so long ago) when the Fleet was putting to sea and all was the hoopla of drunks hoping for a glut of gold, and whores wangling the last coin from those setting sail, sundering life and fortune.

On a stifling afternoon they reached the coast. Air like the breath of a feverish, woolly dog: tropical lull, tranquil tides. How amazing to land on a linear Andalusian street after the labyrinthine jungle! A messenger heading into the Curia reported: the date was June 15, 1719. The Chronicle calendar had erred by only two years and eight months.

An eternal thrumming of drums ruffled the heavy air. The *son*. Extravagant challenges in raspy voices that melted into *merecumbé* and rumba. Intimacy of tropical streets: windows thrown open. Pampered girls behind the grilles of grand houses. Mulattas in flowered skirts humming and making eyes; the brasher girls sitting legs spread on lapacho doorsteps. Everywhere the smell of seafood sizzling in olive oil.

Many of Lope's people flung themselves down and kissed the hot earth, supposing that by an act of magic they had come to Spain.

Though forbidden to do so, *doña* Elvira drew aside her nanduti curtain and stole a look at the mulatto dancers in their rakishly hung canvas trousers.

They shuffled aside for some swells in litters repairing to the Fort for dinner. Sweaty lackeys in white stockings and billowy britches *à la française*.

DAIMON

Year 1719, 15th of June. Sails of the Fleet had been sighted at dawn, and now the city sizzled. Mulattas greased up with cocoa butter, poked carnations in the kinks of their hair and dashed from their seaside shacks toward the fire of the newborn night. Leaped, sambaed, flaunted white petticoats in the shadows of the long evening. Even slave girls ran off for the sake of revels: lords and overseers were seen clubbing blindly at the hedges into which they had scuttled like insurgent cats.

All the girls flocking toward the sailors just off the ships. Among them an Inquisitor, blackened with burnt cork and costumed in the skirts of a pastry maid.

Apparently America swayed to other rhythms on these shores. The ear caught the devilry of a *bulería*; at once was lured away by the hot pounding of bongos. Apparently the scattering of blacks trafficked by the Portuguese and Dutch had swelled into a multitude and laid claim to all that lay below the waist.

Aristocrats whisked by on horseback, raising a cloud of dust, en route to the plush brothels of Getsemaní.

Festivities of a city! The Old Man sensed that even the deadest members of his horde were rattled by this flurry of life. "Damn! What a wonder! Walk out of the jungle, down a straight street, and wind up in a big Spanish town on holiday!"

Near the port of Boca Chica they came upon a fine grove of palms and banana trees and made camp. Orders to meet in two days' time, caution recommended.

"Shouldn't we know what they think of us? Shouldn't we know what measures the enemy is taking? Could we strike without warning, rouse the blacks, and seize Peru?"

Nicéforo taunted Lope: "Out of the frying pan into the fire! Out of the frying pan into the fire! When Philip gets his hands on you, your ass is grass!" Carrión chased him away, flicking a leather strap. Soon thereafter the regiment scattered. As always, the women were kept in camp under lock and key, in the Priest's custody.

Flanked by Lipzia, Blas Gutiérrez, Sablon, Antón Llamoso and a detachment of guards, the Old Man slipped into a vast establishment: chiefly an eatery, with assorted indoor gardens. Five suckling pigs revolved over the embers of an immense grill. A layer of smoke floated just above the floor. They borrowed a pitcher of wine. "*Rioja*, Gutiérrez, *rioja!*" cried Lope as he tasted this wine of the homeland after two centuries of crude imitations distilled by *ad hoc* Marañón vintners.

The Scribe managed to draw speech from the nearly smoke-blinded Andalusian who tended the grill. Evidently since 1570 the British had been simply and solely infidels (they had guessed as much!), the Pope had excommunicated Queen Elizabeth and Waaterral (Sir Walter Raleigh). "About time! At last!" And Blas Gutiérrez, shrewdly: "In Spain a pirate's a pirate. In England he's the Queen's sweetheart, in the end we're the fellows who lose out . . . " They knocked back another pitcher of wine. Sablon noticed that amid the smoke billowing from the grill, death was not so visible. The Andalusian tossed shovelfuls of fine sand onto the tiny flames shooting up here and there. "And what do folks say about Lope de Aguirre?" "Did you say Lope? Lope?" "De Aguirre, Lope de Aguirre, the Traitor, the Tyrant . . . " And the Andalusian: "Matter of fact, something's going around!

But first names are hard, around here every wench has a kid named Aguirre! But hey, something's going around . . ."

The garden floor was tamped red earth. Beds of Santa Rita vines and jasmine scaled roofward. At long tables, mestizo muleteers who had brought shipments of silver from Quito and Lima. Chewing in silence, tamales, *quesillos*. On the porch between two terraces a colossal Negress from Bahía belted out a melody to Xangó. She was tending a hodgepodge *feijoada* that stewed in a giant vat perched on burning logs. She hacked up oranges and dropped the chunks into the thick, slowly bubbling grease, where now the ear, now the hoof of a hog bobbed up. Against the back wall, stacks of white sacks of sugar, and tables where negroes ate platefuls of *tutu de feijão* and dried fish fried with peanuts. They had come from the mills, bootlegging surplus sugar unbought in Amsterdam.

They stole out and headed down to the harbor. The Fleet: brilliant blaze of light in the distance. Topmast pennants limp in the calm, sultry air. On the wharf, bands of guards in Castilian felt hats with (nowadays American) plumes. They rubbed shoulders with the beggars and used-up whores soused on those sour dregs of beer traditionally doled out at the docks when the ships came in. Above, lavishly torchlit, the proud, impenetrable Fort of San Felipe, outpost of the Escorial.

They perched on the bollards that moored the *Guadalquivir* and the flagship *Conde Duque de Olivares*.

The Old Man commanded them to breathe in deeply. "Salt! Sea salt!" From his chest rose the rumble of ancient, marshy phlegm. "Sea salt dries you inside out! A seafarer's soul must have it!" Suddenly the Old Man plucked up a forgotten image: a boy capering in the Bay of Biscay in the radiant light of a summer morning.

Amid ship hulls and wharf piles, excreta of the city: a dog, hideously beheaded, surely by the *macumba* people; a Jamaican rum crate; a fetus, sent back to its source, serenely smiling. At the sight, Lope felt a deep loathing for death. All sign of sentimentality fled: "To the whorehouse! Someone awaits me!" he cried.

Getsemaní, the Calle Tripita y Media, house of *doña* Eufrosia, top-of-the-line. Palace with Greek pretensions (in eighty years the Central Post Office, and later, the Museum of Independence). In the doorway a black man, dead-still, *banzo*-stricken, his eyes blank, his body empty, his soul far away, floating free by now in the Guianese forests. Four surly deckhands swaggered by, singing, and gave him a shove. Though the negro keeled over, his eyes kept staring, wide and steady, into the beyond. "Pick him up and prop him on the column!" Lope barked. "You're going to die, *negro*, you're already dead. Ditching your body was your big mistake, a man comes here to live *in* his body!"

Fine bordello terrace. Corner counter with racks of European liquors. Palm trees, *bulerías*, frenzy of gypsies dancing the *zapateado*. Flamenco laments tangling with revels of Galician rias. Near the tambours, feet of mulattas stamping out the rhythm. Fine-veined feet of skittish colts. Swish of hips, flash of sweaty thighs glimpsed beneath gaudy skirts. Beyond, the broad wooden staircase rising to the upper rooms, and the corridor leading to the back alley through which aristocrats and ecclesiastics entered, on their appointed days.

Air wreathed with the smoke of Cuban cigars, hawked by little mulattas. Wistfully dim light from draped Chinese lanterns. At the back, a mortified group of Marañones (as though the whole room had turned to stare and the band had ceased to play): Carrión, Nuflo Hernández, Baltasar Salazar, Mamani (foreman for the Indian contingent, which nowadays consorted with conquistadors), la Salduendo, accoutred like an officer. Tirado was mounting the stairs on the heels of an overly professional Galician girl who toted what looked like a coil of rope, for use as a whip, and hummed the pop tune "April Is the Cruellest Month."

They drank rum. The Old Man made fond overtures to the Scribe, wishing perhaps to pardon him for past offenses: "You're an idiot. You're the sort that talks about life instead of living it . . . an egghead! But what would I do without you! You're the only one who understands things! Come on, grab that cigar girl! I could see you liked her!" And he gave him an affectionate nudge. Sensing that Lope wished to be alone, Blas Gutiérrez wandered off after the girl. "Teach a young dog old tricks!" Lope sputtered.

He lifted his head, as though straining to catch a scent above the hubbub and hoopla. The Moorish girl. The Moorish girl, a warmth, a fragrance, an aroma. Someone approached through the shadows: a woman (it had to be) clad in a shimmering, sequined black dress and a hat trimmed with net and black feathers. Like that of a leper, or a devout marquesa masking a voluptuous mouth, her face was veiled in a still deeper mesh of net. Her air of authority told him that this was *doña* Eufrosia. She was flanked by two bare-

chested mulattoes in canvas trousers lewdly slung, one tat-
tooed with a toucan, the other with a dragon off a Pekinese
treasure chest; as surly and unsociable as farm dogs.

"I want the Moorish girl, I know she's here . . ." said
Aguirre. "Oh, *mon cher* . . . I don't know if she can see you.
The Moorish girl? I believe she's *besitzendee*. *Il faut* wait a
moment *mon cher!* The Moorish girl, the Moorish girl . . .
Une mauresque toutes les mauresques du monde!" She stretched
out her velvet-gloved hand, studded in aquamarines and
what may have been diamonds, and took up a glass of Veuve
champagne. "*Santé*," she said. "I know *la mia gente* when I
see them . . . Oh, what memories, what *saudade!* To think
that I sang a duet with Bertani in the Königs Oper of Dres-
den! The scourge of Naples ravaged my face! *Santé!*" And
she withdrew, more feeble than majestic.

Lope knocked back one more glass of rum. Rattled by
his heart, which thumped more and more urgently. At last
he caught sight of her: above, perched on the wooden railing,
displaying her peerless Levantine calves. Gleaming eyes beneath coarse black hair raked across her face. Mane of a
filly. Wench! Wench! Woman. Again that steamy, passionate
gaze, those glints of trepidation that always reminded the
Old Man of a nun in heat.

The Madam slowly nodded, a magic *voilà*.

Again the fire. The urgent burning of unslaked desire.
This most secret, enduring passion. A memory reposing
beneath other women, like a dent in the mattress. He
bounded up the stairs, trying to look casual. Lipzia, who
was emerging from Room 3 with a request for panties from
Paris and fragranced alum from Cologne, saw that, *flash!*,

Lope's face had turned young again. It glistened. A smile frolicked on his lips.

She was sitting on the canopy bed, fussily undoing a garter belt designed purely for show. "Wash!" she said without looking up at him. "The water and lye soap are over there . . ." "Morita!" Aguirre muttered, hearing his voice crack. "Wash!" "You want me to wash? Where?" "Come on, I have no time to waste! Have you got the voucher?" "What voucher?" "The voucher, stupid! You mean to say you didn't pay the Madam?" Lope knew that the time had come to grab the bull by the horns or everything would be spoiled: "Hey, Morita! You never change! What a temper! But I've always desired you anyway! . . . Remember the spats in the brothel at Malta? But tell me: have I ever failed you? Remember the shawl I had Alonso de Contreras bring you? Remember the necklaces? The mirror from Smyrna . . . ?"

Gorgeous, the Moorish girl on her back, her hair flowing over the bed. Gorgeous, kicking at the air and huffing with impatience and bad temper: she puffed out her cheeks and spewed air, refusing to turn her eyes from the moth-eaten canopy above her. "The voucher! Did-you-hear-me!"

Aguirre saw that once again she had lured him to that acrimonious place where the sumptuous but delicate tension of passion disintegrates. Resolutely he thrust his hand between her thighs, which were jiggling in the dimly lit air. Then began the angry shrieks, the pounding of running feet, the tussle. The Old Man had just dealt her two indignant smacks when Seven Squalls (the mulatto with the dragon) entered. "Who is it? There's nobody here! Who, where?"

"Over by the dresser, don't you see him?" "Stop yelling, vixen!" "He didn't have a voucher!"

On the staircase it dawned on Lope that all this commotion had nothing to do with desire: desire was sepulchered in that pique of panting, that fury. Once again she had carried the day. The Moorish girl, who gave herself to all men, even Marías, the hunchbacked Cabildo beadle, had shunned him, her eternal inamorato, her old friend. "In Malta I damn near slew her when I found her with that mangy Sicilian!" But neither Blas Gutiérrez nor Sablon could calm him. "Bitch! Harlot! Slut!"

In the street the air was sultry . . . They went down to the wharves and settled against some bales of cotton to wait for dawn.

Morning came under a burning blue sky. The sea a shimmer of flame out beyond the ships and docks. Tropical light pierced bodies. The work of the wharves was under way. The deep, full holds gave off the breath of America: fragrance of coffee and cocoa bean (*theobroma* or "delight of the gods," according to Linnaeus, great gourmand). Fragrance of fruit heaped in crates: pineapples, green papayas, bananas. Chilean lobsters, with copper legs and antennae, waddling among the crates. Planks of wood that would never rot: *viraró*, lapacho, Brazilian pine, quebracho, American cedar dripping thick, gooey sap. Piquant aroma of tobacco leaves, dried, or in black braids oozing tar (shipped out for processing by the Dunhill-Kent Corporation, founded by two shipwrecked Englishmen who had swum ashore on Margarita Island). Medicinal herbs. Magic plants: *peyotl*, mushrooms from the *brujos* of Mexico, *vilca*, sacks of coca leaves and *ayahuaska*, henceforth to serve not sacred vision but the sad maintenance pharmacopoeia of Europeans.

At the bottom of dark bins, mounds of pure white sugar brought from Peru on the backs of mules: lump or granulated, for use at Court. Bales of cotton swaying slowly into holds on the shoulders of quivering negroes.

Salty hides, still wearing the sickly-sweet odor of rotting meat. Skins of red deer, of Amazonian jaguar, of panther, peccary, otter, and boar, of the delicate equatorial ocelot. Dried-up maps of living creatures. The Old Man spotted his friend the fox—the truncated tail was unmistakable—in a bundle of fine skins that a one-eyed negro was lugging toward the *Espléndido.*

A blind hurdy-gurdy man cavorted about his organ while a monkey on a chain (clearly from one of the New Granada families) begged for blessings from passersby.

Foremen flicked whips at black workmen. Though bands of armed men policed the wharves, in the blinding light the Marañones passed unseen.

Near the head of the wharf, crates of silver and gold were being loaded onto a ship with its name concealed beneath a black velvet sash, for bluffing Caribbean pirates. Gold bullion and gold objects: idols of American peoples, vessels royal and sacred. The Old Man and all his people could pinpoint their places of origin.

Foremen kept tallies with great care; the tongues of all black dockhands had been excised, logical precaution. Tunupa, a hunchbacked idol nearly the height of a man, gazed raptly, immutably at the sea as he waited. Llamoso declared that he hailed from the temple of Vilcas-Huamán.

Up ahead, great wicker baskets heaped with feathers of every color. Mockingbirds, herons, toucans, Orinoco hummingbirds, Guianese thrushes, a golden eagle; long and sumptuous rhea feathers, nowadays prized by diplomats and admirals.

Draped as always in deep net veils, the Madam dismounted from a litter conveyed by four mulattoes in velvet coats and trousers, and began to rummage about in the baskets for plumes to enhance the charms of her girls, à la mode in the choice houses of France and Bahía.

"As you can see, sir, the might of the Crown is commerce, nothing but commerce!" Lipzia remarked to the Old Man, who was plainly depressed by this spectacle of power. "I knew nothing of these things, nothing . . . ! I have been a soldier, a Conqueror!"

That morning alone the ships would sink by a fathom. They would put to sea low in the water, like immense galapagos, all sails spread.

The Old Man spotted a familiar stone idol (confiscated more for humanist curiosity than for commerce). Checking the back, he saw the bullet marks: they had gunned it down and buried it in the heights of Tiahuanaco, on the vigorous recommendation of the Priest, who had declared it "sire of all demons of America."

Near the idols was a sampling of (live) American men, chained together in the sun: a colossal Tehuelche from Patagonia, a *curaca* from Cochabamba, as well as several elegant Otavalá who gazed disdainfully at the squat, sweaty Galician guards spewing pistachio shells. Aguirre paused before a young native, a Chanca captured at the request of the Catholic University of Leiden for mechanist experiments designed to illustrate the new theory: that Indians too felt pain, if to a lesser degree than men.

Amid lances, blowpipes, and war masks, nuptial necklaces and aryballoses en route to collectors, they were shocked to find two stalwart, vanished crossbowmen: Pedro Ramírez and Juan Hernández. Motionless, mummified, shrunken to a height of two feet by the perverse science of the Jívaro.* Now two somber, hairy little children journeying through eternity, solemn as two dwarfs on their first appearance at Court. The Old Man felt choked up; Blas Gutiérrez gathered the courage to reach out his hand and touch the tiny space that had been the cheek of Hernández. "Damn! They just wandered off, dreaming about that bean patch!"

Near the foot of the wharf, the Customhouse teemed with swank gentlemen vying for the latest European crazes.

Fishing line from Philadelphia. The famous Steinway & Sons fishhooks. Pure white sugar crystallized in immaculate cubes, as per the European fashion, for which the inhabitants of the Indies paid gold. Cases exhibiting Dutch medicines (nowadays all American plants had Latin names). Surgical instruments. Versaillesque cosmetics. Champagne. Cognac. Côte-du-Rhône wines already spoiled by equatorial torridity. Milanese velvet. Chinese silk for the undergarments of

---

*These tiny bodies may still be observed, inadequately labeled, in the Museum of the American Indian, New York.

the favorite mulattas of *encomenderos*, *regidores*, and proprietors of sugar mills.

Gold and silver recast by the Jews of Rotterdam into costly rings, into pendants and crucifixes fashioned in contemporary design to dwell between the plump breasts of highborn ladies. Fascinating flaskets of French perfume (Louis Quatorze, the titivating Menton). Several had spilled, and through the warehouse wafted the ambrosial aroma of the boudoir.

And crate upon crate of spangles, baubles, cheap jewels, and glass beads with which to subdue, seduce, or reward Indian maidens.

At the customs booth, a venomous dispute between six French *cocottes*—appareled in velvet skirts slit up the leg and musketeer hats—and the inspectors, who could not decipher the bill of lading, signed by an Italian pimp; the merchandise had been requisitioned by a certain Café de Paris, not yet in business.

Great stacks of hoes, sickles, hammers, scythes. Forged of German and Asturian iron. Durable, resilient, even in the hands of the natives and blacks who would work them on the haciendas from sun to sun for a lifetime, and bequeath them, blades good as new, to their enslaved sons.

But what stunned Aguirre and his officers were the firearms. More than a century and a half had meant great progress in this realm. Muskets, musketoons, and harquebuses were now light and easy to carry, some were even repeaters. Rapid-fire, ballistically infallible (millimetric grooves guided the missile). Damp gunpowder was obsolete. Of the grand old swords it seemed that only the steel core— the essence—was extant, in the form of courtly foils and sabers: more fit for patrician assassinations and conspiracy than for war in the wild. The ultramodern Belgian industry offered some small muskets known as "pistols": packing one of these, a man might even pretend to be weaponless.

The Old Man saw that the power of the European Emperors was formidable: they had learned to combine their ancient evil with science.

Pikes, halberds, and crossbows were exclusively ceremonial, passé. Nowadays functional were those rustproof cannons departing Cartagena on the backs of slaves and mules, bound for all the forts of America.

Toward the rear of the warehouse, several Englishmen, claiming to be independent of their Crown, offered tea biscuits in tempting painted-tin boxes with labels, printed in Venice, depicting courtly and even picaresque scenes. The tea itself, now known as Ceylonese, originated in Paraguay or the missions. They also offered plumed balls for garden games, which sleek little misses were tickled to purchase.

And beyond, by the thousands, ecclesiastical tomes relating the life stories of saints, and an incredible store of crucifixes in every material, size, and painful position. Italian religious trumpery, as gaudy as Turkish wedding cake, selling at a premium to whoever would donate it to the church in fulfillment of vows. Thuribles, unconsecrated ciboriums, chasubles for the priest's birthday, inkpots inscribed with the insignia of the Holy Inquisition, reams of papal benedictions with a blank for the name of the eventual user.

Hundreds of dictionaries, the exact contents decreed by the royal academies, lords and masters of the language. And covertly, behind the back of the bribable Inquisition, books condemning secular Catholic authoritarianism.

French books illustrated with unspeakable smut, to be perused on haciendas by gentlemen at the hour of the siesta amid the frenzied buzz of cicadas. And the no less egregious philosophical pornography: Blas Gutiérrez flipped open a book and one line was enough to trouble him for three days or even longer: "Christianity proscribes killing. One may solely commit murder in a multitude, beneath a flag, to the sound of trumpets." Signed by a certain Voltaire.

All finely crafted, especially the new firearms from Flanders, Prussia, France, and England. Spain, it seemed, had been left to embroider the religious paraphernalia and bind the missals. "We're lost!" cried the Old Man. "Fried! Lost! Finished! Unless we can learn to forge muskets and cannon like those rascals can!"

At the end of the wharf, the slave block. Auctioneer bawling in a Portuguese twang: "Virgin from Benguela, age twelve to fourteen, complete set of teeth, healthy skin free of sores, two fully healed scars in plain view, several small-pox spots showing on the right cheek, all hereby certified by the notary *don* Matías de Abrantes!" The hideous clerk lifted his hand. Then the bidding, which was heated. Next, a lot of three Bantu brothers in chains mounted the platform. As there arose no offers for the lot, the brothers were sold separately. One was bought by a Jamaican sugar grower; the remaining two went to Peruvian *hacendados* who made their acquisitions via commission agents.

Beside the Calle del Fuerte, in a timbered corral, a dozen fighting bulls, bleak from their long confinement in the bilge, and stunned by the light, which outblazed even Cádiz. Motionless they mustered their fury for the *corrida* scheduled for the Day of the Virgin, already advertised: 6

MAGNIFICENT BULLS 6. The *torero*, a trifle misshapen, leaned against the sign, smoking a cigar: Joan Velmont, the ad announced. Nearby, a two-bit variety singer bickered with the show manager.

As agreed, Aguirre's captains met in the Fort of Saint Lazarus Tavern to share news and plot strategy. Fragrance of beef *cocido* floating to the edge of the sea. First-rate *tapas*: sweetbreads roasted with a soupçon of garlic, grilled mushrooms and prawns, genuine red sausage, tripe Córdoba-style, drenched in a fiery lacquer of red pepper and olive oil. Wines from Rioja and Ribero, but also the two varieties of cheap American wine, *carlón* and *priorato*.

The men presented their reports. First Antón Llamoso: "Well, they say Tyrant Aguirre was something of a scourge, they do. They say the King put out a warrant for our arrests, but that was ages ago . . ."

"They say, sir, that numbers of us died by your hand, and that you were dismembered. They tell it straight, sir, but they don't know we still exist . . ."

"They've put your story to paper. Made you live, kill, and die in books . . ." Ayala reporting. "They claim you took up with the Devil . . ."

"In New Granada, on the night of June 16th, the *brujas* invoke you. On Margarita and all through the Caribbean, your name is uttered in *macumbas* . . ."

"But the King—that Fifth!—that French parvenu!— does he fear me?" None spoke: their heads slumped over plates heaped with stew. "You mules! Does he or does he not fear me? What was said at Court about my Declaration?" Silence. Mulish silence. "Well! Spread out that new map! Oh! America's no longer an odd egg! Saint Brendan's whale and the mythical wicked dragons no longer ornament her seas! She's a giant triangle with dented corners! Astronomers have measured every inlet, clerks will market every inch! Well, well!" Clearly the power of Crowns lay in seas and coastlands. The shores nearest cities, and the stretches of beach rimming the vast haciendas. Ports and forts: Cartagena, Portobelo, Guayas, the City of Kings, Valparaíso, Nuestra Señora de Buenos Aires, Río de Janeiro, Bahía.

Then Diego Tirado, Captain of Cavalry (from when he had a horse): "They captured the coasts and seas . . ." Then Lope: "Well said. They have the rims but I've got the heart. They have not yet struck America. But there's more to it. What I want to know is, should we attack? What of my plan to foment a black insurrection?"

The Old Man's question lacked conviction. No, it would be foolish, came the daring reply. Then Roberto de Coca: "By my lights, we could slip into the armory through the back, lift a Belgian cannon, and load it on one of those leper fishing boats . . ." But Blas Gutiérrez broke in and spoke Aguirre's mind: "Idiot! What good is conquering one port or one fort? It would be better to lure them inland and battle them on our turf, cut off from the world." That wrapped up the topic. "But what else do people say?" Lope asked.

"That Dutch Jew, the Prince of Nassau, planted Flemish colonists in Brazil and Guiana . . . America's a whale and sharks nip at her edges. The English are all over the map, claiming to be independent merchants with no ties to their Crown . . ."

Lastly, Padre Alonso boldly but blushingly confessed

that he had been named Delegate Inquisitor by the Holy Office of Cartagena.

For the first time Aguirre noticed his captains looking beaten. Sullen, ashamed. With no will to fight. In the face of commerce and finance, the Terrestrial Empire of the Marañones looked like a ludicrous dream. But he was a realist: "Fine, fine . . . They've got commerce, but the land and peoples are what count! They've got the gleaming rind, but we've got the fruit. They suck the juice of the earth, but the land is ours!"

And in his most peremptory voice: "Hey! Scribe! Ink and parchment! Write: 'Cartagena of the Indies, to His Royal Highness the Frenchman Lord Philip V, Prince of Spain . . .' Put down that I—'as already stated in my first Declaration of War and first Insurrection against Philip II— Lope de Aguirre, the Traitor, the Wanderer, the Rebel'— get this all down carefully—'wage my Rebel Campaign, spearhead of the Marañón Empire, first free territory of America.' Write: 'As of this day, my Empire is two hundred times the size of your Spains. Here in Cartagena, which you still wrongfully claim, ringed by your merchants, slaves, inquisitors, and *alcaldes*, I set before you new proof of my rebellion, the eternal rebellion of America.

" 'Sir, hear this: you hold these Indies, this America, this vast, impenetrable, indomitable giantess by the skin, and soon she'll topple over on your royal feet. Hear this: no one can or will conquer this land. Her soul pulses in the swamps, hides in the peaks, flees into forests unfathomably deep. Seeking her, your men will be transformed. Never will they revere you again. Mark my word: in these lands

your Empire is illusion, only words writ in water. Your coun-
cillors of the Holy Office err: it is right and good that these
lands belong more to the Devil than to God; for if these
peoples bore the lash of your whip in God's name, naturally
they would want to try the side of Satan. Though momen-
tarily conquered, though stripped of life and pleasure,
though imperiled by your piety and progress, these peoples
have not been crushed. Sir, hear this: their gods live, and
they do so in the deepest sense: in the hearts of the people.
Thus, building all those churches merely masks the fact . . .'
Get all this down in your finest script. Carrión, you will
hand-deliver the sealed missive to the office of the Al-
calde."

The Cartagena experience had been trying. The Old
Man spent the afternoon pondering the fate of empires and
the vanity of earthly conquest. The secret laws of tribes
wielded more power than the wills of tyrants, despite their
good intentions (as in his own case). After this whiff of
the monetary and mercantile prepotency of modern im-
perialists, he felt like an emperor in rags. Not angry so much
as discouraged and flustered, like a provincial nobody at a
ball.

After decreeing a rendezvous at dawn, he passed the
evening alone. Brooding at a table in a dark corner of the
tavern. For the first time in his long lives, he felt American.
Or in any event he felt American resentment, that rustic,
scenic pride later to be misread as mere folklorism.

For the first time he welcomed the company of Huamán, the Incan polyglot he had once beheaded, and bid him
sit at his side and tell him tales of his childhood in the Valley
of Kings, province of Abancay.

DAIMON

*　　*　　*

After dark that last day, as he strolled alone on the wharves and by the corral where the eyes of the sleepless bulls glittered red, Lope again heard the Voice. Barely a murmur, a hazy hint of a voice.

"The Moorish girl, her burning body. Urge, stress of momentous decision. A traitor must betray all, even his cohorts, his rituals, his dead." Life, a string of betrayals each freeing us from the effects of the last, therein the intrigue, the mystery, the slither of a snake in the shadows. "Ditch 'em all! Orphan 'em! They won't know who to hate! I can just see them! The Scribe, the Priest (Now who will he save? Who will he exorcise? Who will ease his boredom?). I can just see them! Orphans! No father to hate, no father to try to kill! Llamoso, Roberto de Coca, the Jew, Spinola, Carrión, my daughter. All, all. And I with the Moorish girl in a new life. Barefoot in the enchanted Galápagos: glint of flying fish, juicy guavas, palm trees by the sea, her naked hips. Yes!"

At this early hour the persiennes were shut. He knocked hard, again and again, but his fists seemed powerless to wrest sound from the wood. They at last opened up only because *doña* Eufrosia's chihuahuas, those outsized, repulsive rats, were barking and whimpering and sniffing that odor of death and mold and sunken cathedral seeping beneath the door, so different from the daily whorehouse smell of sweat, astringents, and semen.

The Madam herself nudged open the peephole, showing only the veil that concealed her face. And Aguirre: "I know it's early, but I've come for the Moorish girl! I've

brought the gold and diamonds of all my men! Open up!"
The Madam smiled (or seemed to smile): through the veil,
two glints, nothing more, as from a still pool where even
the ray of light stagnates.

"*Oh vous! Monsieur.* Yes, it's early . . . *Mais je regrette . . . Non c'è, la Mora est disparue!*"

The Old Man managed to slip through the slit in the
door, ferociously besieged by the shrill chihuahuas. The
Madam let out a dry, grim chuckle, betraying faint gleams
of gold. Seven Squalls advanced menacingly amid the tables
stacked with overturned chairs and the stage littered with
bongo drums. The tarts, attired in petticoats, flocked around
the bar, trying on indecent feathers. The Old Man bounded
upstairs to Room 1, but no sooner did he reach the hall
outside than he smelled the distinct and dismal aroma of
the Moorish girl's absence. He felt grief and rage. As always
doomed again, the tryst, the missed tryst, the kiss and farewell, the law of that love doomed ever since the days of
Malta and Granada.

Celeste, the hunchbacked maid who looked after the
Moorish girl's permanganate and alum, sneered at him as
she changed the water. Lope flung himself on the bed, where
a pink petticoat lay (oh, the second one, which she always
peeled off with such unabidable languor, so falsely and per-
versely aloof!), and pressed it against his disconsolate face.
A slip of paper fell on the satin spread: "I knew you would
return. It's too late now. And yet one day we will meet, for
such is your fate. No, this is not a matter of gold . . . "

Celeste Alvaret pointed maliciously to two peccary-skin
suitcases. She had departed without her clothing. This made
him even more jealous: her departure was also a rebirth.

"Oh you! Who knows where you've gone off to!" Aguirre murmured, more bitter than curious, and went sulkily downstairs.

The Madam gazed at him blankly. Fierce was the passion of difficult men for easy women: this she knew well. "*Je vous avez dit*, dearest . . . *gefluchteestee!* She walked out on me too, *sans tendresse!* And do you know with whom? With *un vaut rien!* A gypsy, more crook than singer! An *inutile*, the kind that protects sentimental and—*au fond*—vulnerable women!"

Lope looked at her, baffled. He felt that he could barely drag his feet toward the door. "*Vous savez?* They sailed on the *Intrépido* at sunset. *Votre mauresque travestie* like a gypsy! Tricked out like a pair of waiters! *Il faut dire que c'est excitant, mio caro . . . !*"

5

A Minor Arcanum: The Ace of Golden Pentacles

Frustrated commercial endeavors. El Dorado. Pressures of international imperialism. Nation of eternal dancers. Land of No Evil. H. H. Wildcock confesses. El Dorado! Pleasures of golden dust. Dreams of power. The Fiend and Aguirre. Forsake them all! Away! Betray them!

C A R T A G E N A ! Cartagena! The sight had saddened them all. For two years the soldiers sulked; it was like coming home from a visit to a rich cousin. Citified pleasures, clothes, things . . . ! Empire!

They were camped up the river Vaupés, waiting out the rainy season. The dead gathered around, playing on Lope's despair: "You can snatch all the land you like, but if you don't have a cannon you're screwed . . . ! You're out!"

Several *caciques*, ex-*amautas* and medicine men (clumsily purged by Aguirre and his men) vented their scorn:

"Hey, Lope! What's left of your Christianity? Best not to have come to save us. Hah! Make them give us back our gods, that's the only path to peace, don't kid yourself, pal! Our gods were real. They would never've preached wasting your life on a cross!"

They mocked him in the sly, shifty style of American natives (who know their defeat was foolish and futile, because their gods retaliated by granting the white-faces what they so maniacally wished!): "No, we don't want the life of the soul, no way! It's nonsense, Lope! We want bodies! You burned our bodies and buried the bones! Now we can't be mummies—by our ancient wisdom—can't rest hushed and happy among our dear living ones . . . ! Come on, Lope, don't pretend you can't hear us, you know we're right!"

In Cartagena the Marañones saw that their world had been shunted aside by the march of time. All-around gloom. Officers and soldiers saw that there was no room for their rough, warring ways amid the elegancies, amid the homes draperied à la Louis Quatorze (no trace of the rugged Escorial). Nowadays lieutenants comported themselves like lawyers; *corregidores* knew how to read; killings and tortures were conducted within the sober confines of the law. Thin-soled boots: for treading on carpets, not in the rock-ribbed hills. Decorative swords, more symbol than blade. Honors of war were no longer coveted. Documents, edicts, royal favors. Antechamber tactics, victories of seal and stamp. The Knaves of the Spanish Empire had trounced the Horse and even the King. Lowly, groveling servile knaves. They had triumphed in this elaborate artificial game known as real life.

Nothing of man or Manhood or conquerors. These

were things of the past: with the years all had frenchified. Donjuanesque whiskers, curled and oiled; fine silk; the wrists of scribes. Dandified clerks had won out over warriors. If you insulted one of these milksops, you would find yourself facing not the point of a sword but the slippery hand of a lawyer with a summons for the crime of slander, under the new laws.

One night la Salduendo and la Quesada bravely confronted Lope with bitter complaints. "Strike! Whores on strike! We want feathers! How can we wear these medieval ruffs? Aromatic camphor, Viennese permanganate, *eau de cologne*. Lace! That's what we want! Nowadays even scapulars are trimmed with Venetian panty lace!"

They had to be placated with promises. Lipzia dashed off a purchase order; in Cartagena he had been taken on as sales rep for a brassiere tycoon with a shrewd knack for "marketing" and his sights set on millions of native bosoms.

A mood of discouragement.

The captains called an important meeting. Antón Llamoso, Diego de Coca, Rodríguez Viso, the Priest, Carrión (informing for the Holy Office as agent of the Priest). Llamoso: "Sir, we all agree, Cartagena proved it: gold's the word! Gold and more gold. Accomplish the aims of the Expedition, find El Dorado! Torment the living and the dead, but find gold, the gold of El Dorado!" Then Aguirre: "Fine, fine." Then the others: "That's what we said on the way out of Chachapoyas . . ." Then Rodríguez Viso: "The gold's still there! Nobody found it. Nobody found the hidden gold! Nobody found Huayna Capac's chain, which was tossed into Lake Titicaca!" Then Carrión: "We'll drain Titicaca. We simply have to widen the outlet . . ." Spinola, the

Genoese: "Sir, with gold we can buy Belgian weapons and a fleet, if we like! We can pay admirals! We can merchandise brazilwood in the Hamburg market!"

The Old Man sank into a deep, weary silence. He turned over on his bed, burped, and fell sound asleep. An agreement had been struck: a committee was formed, with Lipzia and Spinola as counsel. Under consideration were stocks, bank paper, bills of exchange, letters of credit and capitalization.

Within two months they were launching their first project. Diego de Coca was appointed to transport a load of sugar to be sold in Europe. They bought it from a cooperative of black runaway slaves and loaded up a rickety vessel. Thus commenced an adventure never chronicled by Dr. Enrique de Gandía.

Weeks of scurvy, lost teeth all around. Equatorial doldrums, obligatory regimen of flying fish rolled in sugar. Storm in the Gulf of Biscay felling masts heretofore felled. When the raft (by now merely that) berthed at Wharf 16 in Amsterdam, Coca and his damp, wayworn survivors asked the way to the Stock Exchange (*de Beurs*). The Provost of Merchants was a ruddy, pudgy fellow, clad in black velvet, with the sour temper of new cuckolds; his big bronze pectoral cross swung heavily above the giant ledger. No sooner did Coca open his mouth than he dealt him a blow that knocked him to the ground. "Brute! All shipping is handled through the Dutch West India Company and the Zucker und Trust Gesellschaft, didn't you know?" Another buffet: "Brute! Lout! You have violated Article 12 of the Harbor Laws of the Hague! Your cargo will be confiscated! But since you're a Christian, your life will be spared!"

Before their eyes the merchandise that had cost such great sacrifice was auctioned off beside the wharf to the Golden Sugar Corporation, that great multinational masterminded by the unforgettable Jurgen van Oost (his likeness second from the right in the group portrait *Burghers Smoking Pipes* by the great Van der Dik).

Chilled, wretched, they enlisted with the Neapolitan flagship *Il Fuggitivo*, high-flying for La Guaira with official contraband: pineapples soaked in rum. Signed on as mess-cooks and head swabbers (he, Diego de Coca, helmsman on the Ocean Sea).

Months later the Marañones rendezvoused as planned at 7° 12'', on the meridian that passes through the Arroyo San Gabriel.

Dejectedly they heard Diego de Coca's tale. It was clear that the science of commerce was complex and that its laws were decreed by the economic empires. "By the sword we built the Marañón Empire, but we don't know how to keep it! We can conquer, but we can't last! We're lost!" Lope could see that some secret covenant controlled the livelihood of men and curbed private initiative. "Nowadays you can't just have stuff and want to sell it!"

Two months later they were granted permission by Queen Cuñan's granddaughter to fell forests of brazilwood and other fine timbers. They built a *jangada* and launched it downriver on the Amazon. This venture was the brainchild of the dilettante oceanographer, Rodríguez Viso, who claimed that a "river in the Sea" flowed past the mouth of the Amazon and upward to just south of Iceland and down again toward the British Isles. "We'll sail this *jangada* to

Southampton! In London we'll sell cedar and lapacho to Buckingham Palace!"

They frittered away months at this. Built cabins on the *jangadas*, sturdy and warm for braving the bitter climes of Iceland. "God willing, by November of next year we'll be in London! Stuffing our pockets!"

But it did not flow by (the current, the supposed river in the Sea). The huge tree trunks swirled like wisps of straw in a storm. Tirado, Rodríguez Viso and Spinola barely survived: were swept away on the current and next seen belly-to-the-sun on the festive beach of Maracá.

In the camp, dissipation conspired with commercial failure. Literary fanaticism had not been plucked out. The French corruption spread: paper was fabricated or stolen, they even wrote on leaves. Blas Gutiérrez, the Scribe, was the source of the blight. He claimed he was a poet. He wrote cunning *octavillas*, which the women learned by heart; his subversive pamphlets passed from hand to hand among the soldiers.

The Scribe now affected a big black frock coat he had acquired by teaching the camp tailor's children to read. He wore a flapping bow tie made of black sateen, cut from the petticoat of the strumpet la Schneider (in his odes he called her *la mia principessa*).

After a quick reading of Voltaire he had become a rebel. He drank too much and posed as the eternal hopeless wooer of *doña* Elvira, Lope's eternally fifteen-year-old daughter (as it were).

Literarily he loathed Gracián and most other Spanish authors (the only Frenchmen he read were those whose books, impounded by the Inquisition, could be pilfered from sacristies). When drunk, the Scribe (or Poet) would nonetheless declare that the greatest poet of all time was San Juan de la Cruz, but that he could not say this aloud "for political reasons." He would quiveringly flail his arms and fire away:

> *Si por ventura vierdes*
> *Aquel que yo más quiero*
> *Decidle que adolezco, peno y muero.*

> If by chance you see
> the one I love most deeply
> tell him I suffer, grieve and die.

Often, within earshot of *doña* Elvira, he substituted "her" for "him." And if Lope found out, all hell would break loose: for the Old Man could not love his little girl without capitulating to the demon of jealousy. Cuckolds tend to rue the past, they're by and large retrospective, but Lope was one of those who rue the future—prospective cuckolds, so to speak. Day and night he watched over *doña* Elvira, detailing whole squads of police and a good number of spies. With time Lope was turning into one of those sorry souls barred by Dante from his second circle of Hell.

Doña Elvira had given birth to her fourth. Two girls and two boys, all equally like their grandfather. For two or three weeks before each birth, and up through the night of screams and boiled rainwater, the guard was doubled outside

DAIMON

her hut. Later *doña* Inés would step out with the baby extravagantly swaddled in nanduti lace and cross the camp to the bed of the Old Man, who would mutter: *"Caramba, caramba!* Another little nephew! We'll name him Hermenegildo or Agueda . . ."* The Scribe, chewing his lips, pained and indignant, had no choice but to record the birth in the Expedition Registry.

Padre Alonso was then summoned and obliged to minister a baptism, for which he personally risked inquisitorial indictment. Heckled by the men: "Call him Saint Joseph, it suits him! Name him the Holy Spirit! Get an eyeful, he takes after his mother!" As the baby yowled, *doña* Inés crooned soothing Castilian lullabies in her highbred voice.

The lucky few on guard at the hut craned their necks, at the risk of their lives, for a glimpse, in veiled silhouette under the light of the moon, of the eternally firm alabaster bosom of the mother-aunt, child-wife. Within the month she would slink out, in sight of them all, as young and voluptuous as ever, humming sillily and waving to the haggard poet with her sempiternal innocent affection.

The Scribe (or Poet) felt bound to the Old Man by inexplicable ties: as though some mysterious blood kinship ruled his actions, and whipped his resentment into fury. In fact, Aguirre was his incestuous non-father-in-law. Gutiérrez spoke of "hypocrisy," an absurd-sounding word that nobody in the camp understood; he had borrowed it from a French text (*Moralité et Liberté*). Animosity marred his writings, reducing the free-spirited art of letters to spite and vindictiveness. He penned a novel, set on the Amalfi coast, in which all the characters were illustrious princes and countesses, but who was who was obvious. Between lines of dialogue he slipped oblique assaults on the Faith and the Monarchy.

Doña Elvira was the same sunny, silly girl as ever. She might be found beside a stream at the hour of the siesta, giggling liltingly and dribbling the tiny mojarra fishes between her breasts to feel them flip-flop as they died.

In an eternal pique, the Scribe worked up a surrogate, purposefully passionate love for la Schneider. He dedicated sonnets to her; he pressed her into sentimental strolls at twilight, the hour at which, beneath the banana trees, restless troops with their trousers down would begin to brutishly grumble and groan.

It was around this time that things began to go badly for Lipzia. He tried to explain to the captains the intricacies of high commerce, the Monte dei Paschi of Siena, for instance, or the relationship between buying price, insurance rate, and shipping cost. But his good intentions were misconstrued. Envy abounded: the captains were miffed because in Cartagena the Englishman Mr. Sternius, wholesale exporter of precious stones, had hired him to act as his sole representative in the Orinoco basin.

The captains took the liberty of rifling through the Jew's trunks, and turned up a sampling of innovative objects earmarked for sale to the natives: special knives for peeling sweet potatoes without getting cut; Solingen minitweezers for extracting chiggers from beneath the skin; an ingenious pair of long-handled pruning shears for harvesting the banana stalk whole without climbing the tree; Swiss watches with the dial adapted to Venusian or lunar time (to which most tribes adhered); minialtars to Saint Anthony for jilted or unwed native girls. Lipzia plainly knew how to turn a profit from the push toward mass consumerism.

The invidious soldiers cried out in rage upon finding, at the bottom of a trunk, a signed contract with the Santería Bonetti of Novara for the sale, on commission, of sacred articles and Bibles in fine bindings. This was the limit!

And then there was philosophy. Nights camped under the open sky, accompanied by the Scribe (or Poet), Sablon, and several of the brighter minds (among them la Quesada), Lipzia would expound on the ideas and discoveries radically changing the conception of the world. This infuriated the captains. One night they heard them discussing Newton: "Have you ever seen an apple fall? Yes? Well, that's Newton: the apple falls from up to down, not down to up . . . Right in front of everybody's nose, but it needed discovering, that's science!" "Damn!" The fighting men exchanged dumb, dazed glances. "Damn!"

Blas Gutiérrez, who was ineluctably turning atheist, made use of Newton's discovery to interpose a thought about Diego de Torres, who after many years of virtuous persistence, often freakishly succeeded in levitating to the height of the treetops.

"And what do you know about Spinoza?" asked Lipzia, looking into the faces around him. No one spoke up. And Lipzia: "His teaching is fundamental, that the whole of the Universe is composed of a single infinite substance . . ."

Blas Gutiérrez, staring electrified and ecstatic into the light of science: "We're on the brink! The brink! Man will master the Universe." "*Homo sapiens,*" Lipzia put in cleverly, borrowing from Linnaeus. "There is no God!" the Poet muttered boldly.

Sablon yearning for Paris after Paris, where all was reason, science, *politesse.* He sighed forlornly: "And us out here . . . and we can't even read d'Alembert! *C'est méchant ça!*"

Men schooled in stupidity and stubbornness, like the ex-sergeant Martin Peréz, the new Campmaster and framer of all lay repression, listened in, compiling data for the Bureau of Security. Carrión, still and always the executioner, was in charge of heresy. Together they prowled, viciously berating the incompetent spies. They sensed—unsure of its meaning—the flow of some mysterious insurrection, as slippery and lunar as spilled mercury.

And then one day the Priest, coached by Carrión and other killjoys (police are born, not made), came before Lope in the name of the Faith. He submitted a formal accusation against Lipzia on the basis of documents found in his trunks and on practices witnessed time and again. The charge was grave and could mean burning at the stake: Alchemy!

"Alchemy! Alchemy!" The word swept through camp. The Greek cook thought they were calling his name and turned up wiping his hands on a dishcloth.

Spinola, traitor *à l'italienne* (in other words, never in favor of lost causes), supplied incriminating quotations and read off the list of confiscated items, criminal evidence: cryptographic documents signed in the Devil's unmistakable hand, the Condesa's ashes mixed with bezoar stone, several cat pelts slit up the belly, five bits of "worked" lead (which Lipzia desperately attempted to pass off as fishline sinkers), a crucible, a black silk yarmulke, two chunks of a meteorite, the Torah.

Aguirre was beside himself. "Alchemucker! Scum! Alchemonster!" He gave him a swat in the face. The Jew felt the horror of all imminent pogroms (like the premonition of an earthquake). The air falls still, all eyes stare blankly. All stare at the Jew, all side with the executioner. The most terrible prospect: if one man moves a muscle, all will pounce on the Jew, impelled by an ancestral urge, and rip him to shreds. In the silence Lipzia discerned an itch of impatience on the napes of the executioners' necks.

"He has flouted the laws of here and there! He has schemed against God, seeking knowledge from the Devil!" The Priest brayed. He taunted him: "Tell us: have you metamorphosed stones into gold?" And Lipzia: "No, not yet . . ." "Yet, you see? He said 'yet.' Here is proof . . ." The Priest read from one of the confiscated documents: "*Visita interiora terrae rectificando invenies occultum lapidem.* The stone! This is conclusive! The monstrous *descensus ad inferos!* Unpardonable!"

Lipzia paled. He ventured a limp defense, as do those who believe that no defense is possible. Carrión hummed beneath a willow tree as he laid out the torture implements (although the traditional devices were kept separate from the regulation inquisitorial ones, Carrión, who served both kingdoms, wielded those of God *and* Caesar).

Lipzia spoke: "The stone, the stone, all men can have it! It's hard to find . . . but all men possess the power to do so. The stone all around us, in the flight of the hummingbird, in fishes, in you, in me, in the air!"

"Enough, dog!" the Priest interrupted. "Get all that

down, don't omit a word!" And he glowered at the Scribe, whose poetic heart could always be counted on to side with the victim, even if he was Jewish. "All is spoken. Let not a word be lost!"

Suddenly Rosarito Quesada rushed among them, wailing and weeping, ringed by children, little mulatta maids, and loyal customers. She pointed a finger at Lipzia, her eyes immense with the false terror of hysteria: "That's him! It's him! The monster! I know him! He and Salomón Resnik abducted and ate my third son on Walpurgis Night, in 1638!" Lipzia saw that there would be no deliverance. The shrieking rose. La Quesada would redeem the death of her dearest son by chasing Lipzia up the tree of Jewish Guilt. "They drank his blood! Boiled him in a caldron! Threw in garlic and a spoonful of sugar! Monsters! Is there no more justice in the world? They replayed the sacrifice of the Saviour on my poor child!"

Before surrendering him to the rigorous inquisitorial fire, Aguirre asked to be left alone with Lipzia (now robed in a mortifying sanbenito and clutching a candle). "Come on, Lipzia! We've always been friends, haven't we? Tell me what's up! What's this about your alchemy? Is it true?" Lipzia raised his eyes, which had plummeted (like lead) to his espadrilles when la Quesada burst in. "It's only a symbol, Lope. A symbol. That's power. Not what those fools believe. A great symbol. I wouldn't lie to you. Lead never really transmutes into gold . . . They really wanted it, that's why they're so bitter. The gold you've got after a long journey is only a figure of speech. There's gold, yes, but it's spiritual. The quest has transformed you. Resurrection, rebirth . . . Then you possess the power to see gold in anything and everything, or in gold see mud, as you like. This is invincible power: not dependent on reality. It is you who has been transmuted, from the shit of life, you see, Lope? Dignity. Wisdom . . ."

Lope stared at him in silence. Then he spoke with the tender bonhomie of an old friend: "I see, I see . . . But there's nothing I can do for you. It wouldn't be fitting or proper. This is your destiny, your task, your mask . . ."

Lipzia had no chance to protest. Carrión was dragging him bound with a rope toward the place of torment. The torturer trilled (with the lilt of a habanera), *"Per me si va nella città dolente . . ."*

Lipzia's first shrieks mingled with the melodies of la Quesada, who in the wake of her outburst had set to washing clothes in the river.

Sablon, a learned man, lost his mind in the face of such unreason. This was not simply the standard Iberian illogic, but the madness of a continent, the mania of Earth itself, of America. He had a terrifying experience: on the coast of Guyana he saw an elm tree sprout pears. The triumph of brash, intrepid savagery. The enduring decades-old love of the pollinous pear tree had at last fertilized the lofty female elm!

Sablon could not expel this shocking occurrence from his mind. An assault on rationality, rewaking within him the dark fear of every homosexual man-at-arms: motherhood.

During those months his anguish deepened. He grew gaunt and sad. Without the lascivious thrill of sodomy, he went sleepless.

Fled were the fiery years of his youth in which he had waked in the tropical night, driven by a reckless urge, and run through the camp in a naked frenzy, shouting, "Don't fuck me! Don't fuck me! *Pitié! Pitié!*" (Often accompanied by the fat Italian cook, Gianni Delano.) Until they were subdued by the soldiers, who would whip them and taunt them. The Galician guards: "Harder! Deeper! A good whack! Yes! Yes!"

Another epoch, another mood. That joy, that vital energy no longer redeemed him. The nights were dimming.

After a month with no wish to rise from bed, Sablon resolved to take his own life. He left a brief missive: "*Non, je ne regrette rien.*" With the flesh of a manatee he baited a shoal of "castanet" piranhas (named for the clack of their teeth) and stuck his legs in the water. He learned that his spiritual flesh was inedible: the fiends swarmed around his calves, nipping furiously, but took no flesh. The boiling of bloodless rage.

A cold shiver of fear ran up the nape of Sablon's neck into the roots of his hair. He sensed that he had lost that secret trump of vengeance: the power to kill himself. (Liberation from life can rank with preservation of life; the decision falls to *la raison*.)

He lay on his back and pulled his legs from the water. He had failed.

More than two hundred years had passed since the indigenous peoples and animals of the jungle first communed with the tragic and pitiful nature of the conquistadors. What had they seen during those ten or twelve katuns?

That the white-faces possessed relentless drive (outrivaling the daredevilry of hunger or madness); that they were prone to pathos not lacking in grandeur if at times showing Aeschylo-Shakespearean propensities; that they suffered as much stupid pain as that which they wreaked all around them. The natives knew, evermore, that the essence of these men from beyond the sea was misery. They could only concede, evermore, that they had been crushed by deplorable creatures who worshiped gods that tutored them in the vehement refusal of life.

Those who had seized their coasts and fertile valleys, their mines and sacred cities, were squanderers of life.

The refusal of pleasure seemed to weaken these wretched *doers*. Consuming (other beings and the very earth), they self-consumed. Efficiency alone dictated their actions, but efficiency conceptualized by morons.

But they possessed an invincible power. The desire for victory, which quashed flowers, languor, love.

Of the ancient sacred nations, nothing but the scatter of detritus.

Cuzco. Cajamarca, Tenochtitlán. Pachacamac. Chichén Itzá. What were they now? The mere stuff of dreams, rhymes for the elegies of decadent poets. Now those hallowed walls were foundation stones for neo-Andalusian structures: balconies for maiden, carnation, lover and guitar; balconies yearning for the recital of "La casada infiel" by the side-whiskered swain.

From time to time chiefs, *amautas* and initiates from various regions would gather to revive past glories and to remember the tragedy. Survivors with eyes lusterless and sad, time without end. For they had seen the line of slaves prodded into the Potosí mines under the lash of the whip; seen the laborers bowed beneath the blazing sun, in quest of the myth of productivity (for the sake of others); seen sisters and even wives dealt around like concubines or maids. The only possible resistance was to refuse to collude with the world of the conquerors. Not cooperate, choose silence, choose to *not do*. Or should they help to bring about the destruction of Earth, thereby hastening the age of the Black Sun? They chose the former. But they pined for the past: in every condor glimmered the avenging spirit that would slay the blundering bull that had stolen their land.

The Space gods perdured in that longed-for past: this the Jesuits and Dominicans knew (bands of devout, zealous crusaders tramping into the farthest reaches of desert and jungle to smash up idols, sacred stones, *huacas*). But the natives had already turned back to the source of the gods: they revered hurricanes, fierce rain, wild rolls of thunder. Their gods arose in the dark vastness of night, in the hushed hills, in the sacred delirium-inducing drugs that sprouted underfoot: grasses grazing the hem of the priest-inquisitor's cassock as he rabidly grilled his victim, crucifix in hand.

Black Sun. Age of misery and sorrow. End of an epoch (oh, the horror of regret!). Inti, Bestower of Life, Inti, Patron of Earth, ineluctably turning into a white dwarf!

> *Here is the face of the Katun,*
> *face of the Katun,* 13 *Ahau:*
> *The Sun's face will shatter*
> *and slivers fall upon these new gods.*

DAIMON

Though they made us Christians
they sell us like beasts:
These predators have offended God.

And what hope—what recourse—had a mere jungle animal? A mere "beast" killing its daily catch (no monopoly, no commerce) for the legitimate purpose of feeding his mate and young? What hope had a jaguar, an anaconda, a fox?

Along the coasts it was already apparent that animal life was doomed to extinction: could not coexist with the predators, the white-faces. Their System tolerated only the dog (contemptibly servile companion and guard) and the horse (dumb and good-natured with a load on its back, or dully pugnacious like a careerist provincial captain). Indeed, the animals would be consigned to zoological slavery or merciless death via commercial ornithology or the fur industry. Or the humiliating limelight of the circus (the Barnum Brothers' soccer-playing alligators, the trained bears of Louis XV, Madame de Montsouris's three jaguars bred in the boudoir and fed on liquor-filled chocolates).

To little purpose, the animals rebelled. Waged wild and unruly wars. Huge wolf dogs rampaged in the southern pampas, spurning their backyard fate (besieging Buenos Aires and the road to Córdoba, they severely disrupted communications in the Río de la Plata Viceroyalty). Jaguars attacked villages, though they were not hungry. Monkeys stormed fruit-growing valleys, armed with their own fetid shit. Having offended the birds, many viceregal capitals along the coast were obliged to forget birdsong. To make do with Góngora and Gregorian chants.

The plants suffered. Many female silk-cotton trees fell barren and their lineage ended because the predators had blindly hewn down the nearby males to build countertops and fences. In fact, the pale men never spared a thought for the lives and powerful hierarchies of the plants. Forests died, dunes rose. Rows of tamed, captive plants bore their fruits for the greed of the market.

At a convention of chiefs and *amautas* in Pajatén, the *cacique* of Aparia said: "They will triumph! So it was ordained, for this is a Black Sun. They are strong, and they honor a strange power that to us seems exclusively destructive. They are relentless, rash, and resourceful. Brothers, we would never think of dancing gaily on the hide of a dead bull! They are not content to simply commune with the things of the world; a strange, demoniacal god consumes them . . . We must try to understand the irrelevance of our enemies: in fact, they're drafting our rebirth." The chief of Acaraí, who hailed from a land devastated by the Bandeirantes, spoke: "We are proud of our sons, who loaf on palace steps and will not serve them. They flog them. But the arms of all floggers get tired when they hear no screams or moans. Our sons will not look them in the face or learn to work. They get angry. They bring black men. In the night the black men sing and thump their drums. The blacks live for escape, for freedom. They have no past. The predators prefer them . . ."

> *The world will dawn*
> *in the next Katun*
> *for those with faith in the world*
> *O Great Father!*

Randomly they drifted—in clumsily lashed rafts—down nameless tributaries. Discipline was scant, for "the Devil finds work for idle hands to do" (due to the rise in despotism, this proverb became "Needs must when the Devil drives": see Cejador). Lope lay about, lazy and desolate, afflicted by the abstract promise of empery. Now and then he rose up in a rage and ranted like a millionaire who knows his properties and assets have been embargoed. "And damn! Why can't I sell these cedars and hides and sugar! Damn!"

Adrift through dangerous lands. Somewhere in the central sierras an assault from shore. The rafts were porcupines with quills pointing inward.

Dwarf cannibals jumped them, and stole a nibble from the foot of Nicanor Olindo, the zambo.

With three (Florentine) mother-of-pearl-inlaid crossbows, they purchased peace from the corrupt, degenerate *cacique* Puvis the Chavante.

They basked in the peace of dim-witted but dovish natives who offered them twelve pineapples and three maidens per head, unaware that their cups and plates would be looted anyway.

On a high plateau on this side of the cordillera, they learned of the existence of a small village peopled by the last of the titanic forefathers. Kind and sad, almost blind and almost deaf, subsisting in a state of infertile homosexuality, a virtual repudiation of the female. Giant melancholy pairs of serene and somber males waiting hand in hand for the inexorable end.

Farther south, in Tiahuanaco, once again they stumbled on the magnificent sacred site of the Kalasasaya, whose two great stone gods Lope (on the advice of the Priest) had ordered gunned down *sur place* so many decades before.* Setting them on their feet, they saw that the eyes still gazed proudly and serenely skyward. The musket marks on their chests looked like the merest little mosquito bites. Lope felt unexpectedly embarrassed, and the Priest slunk away, saying that he would make a sketch of the statues of the Gate of the Sun.

Despite this dreary, unfortunate interval, the captains began to feel confident of their progress toward Paytiti, land of gold.

Deep in the region of the river Beni, they came upon a nation of fifty thousand dancers whose eyes drooped as they spun and twirled, led by mysterious means toward the Land of No Evil.

Feathers of southern birds quivering in the sunlight. Perpetual, repetitive rhythms of drums. The dancers stared past the strange Marañones; seemed not to see what stood before them.

"They seek the land of no pain and no death," Huamán explained. "News of its existence has reached them: they claim that when you start to dance, you're on the verge!"

Dancing, they mated and gave birth. Dancing, they fell sick and died. Dancing, they gathered wild fruit and hunted (in the trance of the dance, the finest marksmanship).

"No point in their going to Heaven!" the Priest exploded. "They will sin and the Lord will banish them. Im-

---

*The statues known as the "Fraile" and "Bennet" monoliths, at present the victims of enlightened archaeological tourism, in La Paz, Bolivia.

beciles!" He stood before the leaders, brandishing his crucifix. Demanded a translation of the song. Huamán replied that though the words were created in the act of singing, they nonetheless possessed meaning. The Priest was incensed.

Ajuné, guajuné!
Harú imbajasi!

Land of No Evil, welcoming only those who surrender to the trance of the dance. *Yuy Mará Ey.* Beyond all seas. Perchance at the crest.

No evil, no death, no pain of loss or death, and yet life, full of life, Earth. Only the children, who are closest to her, fathom the form of her nonlimits.

They spotted one white man in the dancing throng, undoubtedly a descendent of the star-crossed people of Irala. But impossible to speak with him: back came only exquisite and rhythmic sounds, with a hint of an Andalusian lisp. Without authorization, preempting powers of the Holy Office, the Priest commanded that Carrión administer torture: "Come on, Carrión, get going. We've got to save this wretch! Stoke the fire!"

He squirmed on the gridiron. Fire at heat 3 (maximum), he began to sing obliviously. Torres, the contender for sainthood, spoke: "He already belongs to the race of the strong. Those who sing under torture. No point trying to induce fright: he's been giving up the ghost for some time now. Nothing can he lose. Nothing can harm him. He feels only pleasure."

Lope strode up angrily and buffeted the Priest, who

fell over in a womanish dither of flying skirts. "Still not satisfied, bastard! Shall I garrote you again? Make you spit out your guts again? Remand you to your god, and let him keep you?"

Three months later, farther south, they received word of the horrors of the Guaranian war, which had rubbed out several nations slow to surrender to dancing.

The Bandeirantes. Men with splotched, leathery skin, rampaging inland from slaughter to slaughter, seizing for Portugal lands already usurped by Spain and assigned by papal authority. They stormed Mato Grosso and the Amazon. Sporting red beards (mestizos of Jewish descent), they fought their battles with packs of dogs fattened on the flesh of Indians (sacrificing two or three per day, and once in a while even a small negro, if necessary). More pragmatic than Christian.

Though they sacked the Jesuit missions, they banded beneath the flag of the cross in the name of Western civilization, because the local nations had rejected both warring empires. At Caybaté, on February 10, 1756, they crushed an army of 1,700 Guaraní, of whom 1,511 died—almost all wounds fatal!—which demonstrates the excellent marksmanship of the Christians (why think anything else?).

Every month or so they ran across European "travelers." Mostly English: Oxford boys led by curiosity, Romantic wanderlust, and the profit motive. Also Dominicans and Jesuits in quest of "pagan American" temples.

DAIMON

A band of vile Galician priests redolent of garlic informed them that Monsieur de la Condamine had traveled to Quito expressly to establish, from that vantage, the precise and definitive shape of the Earth (1735).

Fastidious Germans, with astonishing attention to detail, rebaptized animals, people, plants, and things by species. Thenceforth everything had a "local or folkloric" name, as well as a civilized one.

Commercial agents abounded, painstaking retailers and impassioned wholesalers. Whole nations cast off old customs and perplexedly parroted new ones. The more virtuous tribes fled to the mountains, the desert, or the deep jungle to fend off the boons of civilization.

They came across a skinny, red-haired English infidel who had been waiting naked for three days while his garments, strung up on branches along the riverbank, dried. This fortuitous find was to crown one of the eternal goals of the Expedition. "Who are you, dog?" "My name is Herbert Humbert Wildcock. I'm a permanent member of the Royal Geographical Society of London, I have resided in Milan, and my sole interest is to tour the world and to propagate science." "Shut up, Waaterral!" screeched Lope. "Are you aware that you have invaded the Marañón Empire?" And the infidel: "Only passing through, don't mean to stay. I've been commissioned to reconstruct Orellana's journey . . ." Searching through the Englishman's baggage, they indeed found a map with a dotted line running along the river, from Manaus to the Atlantic. But also an inventoried sampling of cashmeres and serges. Aguirre gave him a smack. "Orellana as a front for cashmeres! As though we hadn't guessed!" The gringo wanly protested: "There's nothing wrong with commerce!" "Torture! Apply torture!"

"He smells like gold," Rodríguez Viso muttered to Lope. "It's not just import-export, it's something about gold."

They cranked the rack, dislocating his limbs. The infidel was forced to admit that on one occasion, from the top of a palm tree, he had seen palaces shimmering yellow in the sunlight. "You saw it! You saw it! He saw golden dunes!" "He admits it! But where?"

Under Carrión's careful hand, the Englishman, with a short-winded stammer (but not the Oxonian kind), spoke to the point: "South of the Sierra de Parima, south, south, ouch, ouch!" And like a cock jabbing his beak in the sand: "South . . . but heading off a bit to the west."

Paytiti. El Dorado. Reachable by river route.

The lifeless white body of the Englishman lay sprawled upon the shore: golf club forgotten on the green. H. H. Wildcock.

They journeyed for two months, galvanized by the proximity of their goal. Strayed into stinking lakes where everything that sprouted rotted within the day. Were fetched away by rivers that dwindled out in the underbrush. Rowed in the black of night, guided by the menacing cries of caimans.

And then only mud. Sunk to the waist they toiled till they fainted. Were beset by snakes as fierce as the dogs of foot soldiers. Dined on lizards. Crushed and consumed leeches like raw blood-sausages.

At last a grove of tall palms. The Englishman had not

lied! Men who had once commanded crow's nests shinned up. Cried out: "Golden ramparts! Paytiti! Paytiti!" ·

All ran. Even *doña* Elvira, who leaped half-naked from her litter wrapped in nanduti lace. Sablon forgot his anguish. With his dagger, Ayala, the eunuch, pricked whoever ran too close. Quaver of rags. The cripples hobbled forward like lobsters with broken claws. Osberg de Ocampo, the blind Landsknecht, veered off and tumbled into a pond.

The early sun rebounded with rare power. Rays lit cracks and crevices, the reverse sides of rags, the bottoms of empty pockets. A golden warmth gilded the air.

The alleged ramparts were dunes swept smooth by the wind. Smooth and shining dunes. Great golden breasts. Some of the men sank their faces in the warm aurum and the precious dust trickled into their ears. From kissing the dune with sweaty faces, all wore masks of gold. Many, overcome by emotion, fell to their knees in prayer: they felt mostly Guilt. The Priest said an outdoor mass; during the consecration he had to twice adjure silence of those romping and giggling and spraying one other with golden dust.

They rolled down the smooth golden flanks of the dune. Stripped off their clothes to better savor the warmth and goldenness. How lovely to toss fistfuls of golden powder into the air and feel it rain down sweetly on their upturned faces, their eyelids squeezed deliciously shut! Lay on their backs and warmed their pale Catholic tummies with rivulets of fine gold.

Upon seeing this frightful quantity of gold, Lipzia's enthusiasm went flat. Not this the small cache of gold that grows and multiplies by dint of guile and greed. This gold was incalculable and unsacrificial, a surfeit, a windfall.

The natives, vassals of the Lord of Paytiti, were dumb, blond, and nude. Like, say, a Dutch regiment that has unwisely camped near gypsies. El Dorado—the Prince—greeted them aloofly and went on with his rites. Public servant of his own opulence, each morning he punctually anointed himself with peanut oil, dusted himself with fine gold, and dove into the middle of the local lake—Lake Sacred—only to emerge sad and ungilded for breakfast in a land lacking fruit.

For the first week almost nobody got a good night's sleep. Nobody in the world was richer. They sang and laughed as they drowsed. This was gold, supreme gold.

For two or three weeks they went about in a trance, digging their feet into the sweet golden dust, lolling and rolling and wallowing. None spoke. None made plans; all were entranced.

Then began the organized dreams, with details. All was possible: purchasing a hacienda in Granada and drifting off to sleep to the deep bellow of purebred bulls; opening a first-class club in Madrid and strolling in swankly at the hour of ten, when things are just getting lively, to see what's what; fitting out warships, a whole fleet like Pedro de Mendoza's, seizing Naples and Sicily. All, all this could be had with two or three pails of golden dust, or twenty or thirty pails of golden sand. Some of the more cultivated sorts would buy cardinalships and set themselves up like popes. Padre Alonso fancied himself as Cardinal Bessarion the day he gave the Marciana Library to Venice. They pictured themselves in black velvet, with platinum chains and crosses, dining with the Colonnas in the Palazzo Farnese. The wenches (who couldn't cease to envisage themselves with a certain whorish flair) in sequin-and-pearl-studded cloaks, bidding their adieux in French to a golden-haired lord who had just charmed them into giving him a castle in Surrey. The soldiers founded whorehouses, and stocked them with Flemish adolescent virgins; mustered armies; waved to the poor King with the condescension of wealthy men. In their boudoirs the girls hummed as they awaited counts washing up with the mandatory La Maja permanganate.

Within the month they were sick of so much magnificence (possessions get boring, power is depressing, man lives not by bread alone). They began to see themselves in austere Castilian castles with the Greek profiles of their devout and exquisite mistresses, alternating placid and yet passionate sessions of eroticism with exalted theological readings. The women, disillusioned by a sweetheart, or by the pomp of the world, traveled to the Carmelite convent of Seville with their entourages, and were cordially welcomed by the Mother Superior, like *infantas* on retreat.

Next the practical questions. How to move the dunes to Europe, the only place where riches of this magnitude had any meaning! Everybody owned a few: you simply climbed up and stuck in a stalk of cane tagged with your name. They went looking for tributaries that would lead to the sea, and developed elaborate riverine routes. But first and foremost they would need one transport fleet and one sturdy defense fleet that could run the Imperial cordon.

Some spent their days forging gold bullion, but it was all the same.

Gradually they began to stir from their gilded trances. Woke from their dreams of power to play the inevitable game of *dinenti* or dominoes. Reverted to the more reasonable daily recreation of wrangling and bragging and whoring. Again the guitars began to sound.

To top it all, the food was inedible. They got tired of eating boiled lizard tails twice daily, the main source of protein in the auriferous sands (the birds flew far away, blinded by the golden shimmer).

Water was scarce; pure but bitter. Vegetables were virtually unknown. The insipid ersatz-celery salads were made of bark.

Aguirre saw that the men awaited his word, his command. Someone had to coordinate all these desperate dreams. It was preposterous to fritter away his days like this after the discovery of El Dorado! But he lacked the strength to organize or lead. He couldn't shake off the doldrums.

And there was nobody to whom he could delegate a bit of power. Nobody had the makings of a leader. A Leader to turn this bona fide triumph into Fiesta! To go forth into the world bearing all this gold and flaunt it in every seat of power.

Carrión and Sergeant Pérez made some efforts, but they were obviously swine—narrow-spirited commoners. Would rather wallow in the mean pleasures of petty revenge and eat crumbs from the plate of an empty-headed tyrant.

The deterioration spread. *Doña* Inés (departing from her customary sweetness) spoke forcefully: "Look, Lope, they're waiting for the snap of your whip! Don't desert them now! What meaning have all your struggles and brutalities and betrayals, what meaning has the Expedition, if you loll there on your mat the very day you find El Dorado!"

There was no simple solution. A great crisis that had

slowly brewed for several decades was on the brink of eruption.

A new sense of life had metamorphosed his values. Nothing less.

Then one morning the unforeseen occurred. The men had been fashioning iguana-tail pouches for transporting the golden dust. Shielding the shimmering light from their eyes, they witnessed the arrival of a delegation of natty Indians, presumably from Cuzco, costumed and mounted in the Spanish fashion. It was amazing! At the sight of the gold, of the metalliferous mounds, the newcomers did not turn a hair. They rode on by to parley with the Lord of Paytiti, who appeared to know them. Not until the following day did they request to see Lope. They were breezy, affected, and aloof. "Lope de Aguirre, our delegation comes to you from the new Inca, Refounder of the Empire . . ." And they read out the salutation of a Proclamation already sent off to the Viceroy, with news of the uprising of November 4th, 1780 (one year before): "*Don* José Gabriel I, Inca by the Grace of God, King of Peru, Santa Fe, Quito, Buenos Aires and the Continent of the Southern Seas, Duke and Lord of the Amazon and of Great Paytiti . . ." Then the Old Man: "Duke of the Amazon, Lord of Paytiti my ass!" "He's our commander, Lope. We enjoy the aloof but dependable allegiance of the Lord of El Dorado. We're at war, and we know you're an avowed enemy of the King of Spain too. Our mission is clear and our flag flies high. We shall triumph! Just so you know, in Tungusuca we put the nasty *corregidor* Arriaga to death. The die is cast ... We need these dunes you've captured, so the Spaniards don't take them from you and convert them into more weapons to be turned against us ... What do you say?"

The captains banded around Lope, sneering at those remodeled Indians. "Just tell 'em yes, Lope! They'll go away pleased as punch! Those suckers'll be ripped to shreds! Those Indian shit-eaters don't understand modern war!" Padre Alonso mused: "After the Refounding, the gods will dump *us* in the foundry, Christ will never pardon us. Just a thought, Lope ..."

The rebels persisted: "Say the word, Lope. As soon as you reach the coast, they'll grab the gold ... We can't let that happen. Queen *doña* Micaela Bastidas is waiting fifteen leagues from here."

The Old Man was surprised to feel himself wavering. He looked at his captains, and at the hostile, wisecracking soldiers counting on his cunning and postponements and treachery. His standard kill-crazy tactics. Then he felt something rasping in the depths of his soul. It was like a (three-door) sideboard dragged across the bumpy floor of an attic. "Was that him? The Demon? The Fiend? The Unspeakable?"

He was no less astonished than his captains and the Priest at his pert, glib, smooth reply: "I'm on your side, I understand you. Tell the Inca that this gold will stay put and that's final. And that the Province of the Amazons is his, even though I got there first, before even Huayna Capac ..." He turned toward his people, who were listening openmouthed, stunned. "I also place my valiant boys at your service ..."

DAIMON

As the emissaries contentedly took their leave, the Old Man felt something truly phenomenal and grand: he had betrayed them all, even *doña* Inés and his own daughter, his grandkids, and his "boys," as he had called them with a touch of depraved irony. It was a grand sensation, a relief. They had all relied on him and trusted in him, and in a trice he had double-crossed them. Another fine betrayal. The looks on their faces, the curses, the shrieks of the whores, was something to see! Something truly grand and good.

Lope repaired to his hut and listened to the classical muttering of conspiracy, of revolt. A delegation composed of Diego Tirado and López de Ayala was sent in to determine if this was a ruse, a tactic. "Not a chance! I spoke candidly and clearly: we have surrendered El Dorado and you are in effect under the command of its new ruler, the Inca." They withdrew, green with rage. It staggered belief.

The Priest came in unctuously to discuss the dangers of a pagan renascence, but Lope turned toward the wall, ass out, as when he wished to convey that he was napping and not granting audiences.

Toward sunset the whispering grew more fervent; sandpaper scraping rust from swords; clangor of helmets.

Near dawn the commotion inside him grew more violent (the aforementioned sideboard). Aguirre heard the voice of the Evil One distinctly: "Simply follow your instincts, Lope. Why did you want that gold? For what? For more of the same? Bourbons, Vatican gold . . . Bourbonize? Vaticanize? That's over, Lope. Under Vallaro's command, the blacks rebelled. Founded Pamplona and Tudela; righteously skewered the white man, raped his daughters. And now Túpac Amaru, the new Inca, the new Lord. America is burning, Lope! This is the hour of nations, don't you see? And what about you? Are you going to do the same thing over and over? Peripatetic king, second-rate emperor? No. This is your big chance! Leave before morning changes your mind! Just betray that pack of parasitic rascals! Ditch them! Drop them! Do not waver."

Then he glimpsed one of those frogs that allegedly guard the treasure of the Inca in the depths of Lake Titicaca. Two fathoms long. The wicked shape was skulking in the brush.

And the Voice: "Don't you see, Lope? Maybe you wanted to rebel with the blacks and Indians! Maybe you've already joined the other side! Maybe you were right to desert them! This is the hour of nations, Lope." Then Aguirre: "In Cartagena, the Moorish girl . . . if only she hadn't run off . . ."

And the Voice: "Don't fret about her. A coin has two sides. The Moorish girl ran off, but a lonely girl-nun weeps in a convent . . ." "Sor Angela!" cried Lope. "Naturally. Sor Angela." The marvelous nape of the virgin-nun's neck as the puff of wind lifted her coif! He had gone to Guadalupe with his uncle, the pork butcher, Pizarro's on-again-off-again partner. Boorish and clumsy, spitting lupine-seed shells between what teeth he had left. "Be a conquistador, my boy!" Fulfilling his vow, a pilgrimage to the Virgin if he palmed off the leprous pigs. Rainy morning and that gust of air lifting Sor Angela's coif at the instant of the consecration.

The Voice: "Yes, Sor Angela her very self . . . She weeps for you, she waits for you. Moans with love in the Santa Catalina Convent, the cloister of Arequipa. I don't think she knows that she awaits you, nor that you know that you will seek her and abduct her and love her. This is the hour of bodies, Lope. How long will yours lie in chains? What use is the diamond-studded crown of the Empire if you're a melancholy monarch dreaming of a virgin-nun? Dump them! What good is it to be an emperor, or to change outwardly, if inside you're a tomb? A tomb full of filthy unslaked desire . . ."

His decision was made. At the first light of dawn, as the guards of his auricorrupted army drifted unsuspectingly off to sleep, he took up his belongings. Glanced at *doña* Inés and the girl, who were sleeping. Gave a kick to Nicéforo, who shouldered the weapons. Chose the three least moribund mules. Set out toward the altiplano.

They would awake deserted and alone, and search for him. Curse him. Retaliate by raping his women; maybe even cut their throats. Wrangle for power like well-matched dogs. Land in democracy. "That's right, democracy! They'll spend their time strategizing, looking after cripples and half-wits! Squander their days in honorable obscurity! They'll all be equals, to hell with 'em . . . They were counting on me to kill them again, but no. I'm falling in love, oh Sor Angela! How could I have wasted all of these years without you! Oh love, love of the palm and the dove!"

He kept up a steady trot. Morning breeze! Joy! Joy of the man who departs, shutting the door to his past behind him! Holy joy of the self-avowed traitor who turns over a passel of nobodies to the executioner! Joy of the sheer will to live!

He had never felt anything like it.

II

The Personal Life

Fed up with power. Fatigue of continual externality. Man cannot be the eternal keeper of others. Cravings for intimacy. Personal life with a wife.

Wild boars too create hierarchies and military chiefs. The chief lives a profoundly unnatural life, and his propensity for abuse and arrogance engenders serious discord among the females. Though in youth he appears to emulate the tiger, with the decline of his powers he transforms into a rancorous old hog and is torn to shreds by the young boars in a renewal sacrifice.

—J. W. Kilkenny, *Zoological Curiosities*

6

Tarot X:
L'Amoreux, the Lover

Solitude at last. Quest for lost love. Driving back the
duendes *of desire in the desert. Conqueror and Nun. Lovers'*
refuge in the City of the Sun. Nuptials and Homeric eroticism.
Awesome envy of the God-Voyeur.

*O**FF, AWAY*. Gone! Roam the
earth, disencumbered, free. Snap the chain of ever-
the-same. Freed from all the status and onus of the past.
Am I Lope de Aguirre? I? No: there is no proof. Who would
dare make such a claim? Lope who . . . ? (And the Old Man's
chortles—the first in so long!—rang out in the empty im-
mensity, quivering the hirsute ears of the mule.)

Riding. Riding.

Exit the stupid, senseless savagery of the jungle. Now
smooth hills, swept bare by high, thin winds. Clop-clop of
hoofs resounding on dry ground. He was drying out, airing
out. Away: to rebirth.

"All of 'em double-crossed! How could I have waited

so long! The eternal nagging of *doña* Inés! And the Girl: just how girlish was she in bed? Her screaming, sniveling babies! And all the loyal swine lusting to gnaw on the bones of my Empire!"

Deep blue air! High air with no flavor of green! No wet leaves to breathe! Dry! This air dizzied and clarified!

"All of 'em eyeing each other! They know they've been tricked! Swindled! Sold to the new Inca!"

Aguirre had never felt so well. Something grand had begun. At last he was alone with himself! No despotizing! No colonizing! No tyrannizing or terrorizing the soldiers (so that ultimately it was they who ruled him).

After the vapors of the jungle this air was like liquor. Further: it was the exact air of that distant morning on which he fled for Bilbao, ditching Oñate and his corrupt, doting uncle the pork butcher, who had tried to sell him to the Navarrese mule skinners. Air of life, of birth! "Sor Angela, Sor Angela! How can I have tarried so long!"

"Something grand, Lope. Love at last? What have women been for you? Nothing! Nothing yours! Other men's women. Mother, daughter. You've never left the fold. You've had many women in your life, never a wife. It's high time! Think of the Amazons . . . All added up to none. You've mounted them . . . but never mated . . ."

Was it the Fiend? "Who are you! Speak!" Miraculously, Sor Angela of Guadalupe floated up bright and clear in the pure remote air. The nape of her neck! Valley of softness, soft blondish down at the base of her coppery golden hair. Wind lifting her coif, a mere instant. The Girl-Nun! Sor Angela! Love makes a man break his word: melts his knees, softens his chin, dazzles his eyes in the tropical blaze. Splendid erection in the middle of the desert, a spear, a halberd riding fiercely into war. Sor Angela! With his left hand he flicked the reins, driving on the mule, who balked at any thought of a gallop; with his right, he gratefully pumped. The consecration bells were ringing on that morning of pure poetry, in Guadalupe. He was swooning deliciously. Ribbons of sperm streamed in the air like the ravels of a torn standard. "Sor Angela! Sweetheart!"

They skirted Cuzco. Headed down through the naked desert (to them still a novelty). What did she remember of Arequipa? Sad, desolate whiteness. Haven for whip-wielding *corregidores* under the wing of Viceroy Toledo the Murderer. Coats of arms fresh-cut in stone. Faint odor of Indian blood.

Colquipata. Quiquijana. Paruro. Tinta (gaiety of subversion, dancing the *huaino* and the thumping of drums; Inca-ri rummaging for his head amid the putrefying corpses and fallen bells of an abandoned cemetery). Combapata. Caylloma. And then, still descending, Pichecani and a pure, lunar desert rolling lost toward the Sea like a pebble under the sun.

Two months before Aguirre's arrival, the Sister of Bitter Mercies (Mother Superior of the Santa Catalina Convent of Arequipa) wrote to the Bishop:

I again call the attention of Your Excellency to new deeds of La Endemoniada, the Nameless (who claims that this is not her name or her time). In the many years that I have overseen this blessed institution, I have never known such a hussy as this

one. *Day and night she wails without cease. She writhes like
an epileptic in her bed of desire, in the thrall of invisible demons.
These summer nights she often climbs up on the bars of her cell
and grinds against them like a monkey in rut (last week she got
badly stuck and had to be sawed free).*

*When she can procure the necessary materials, she melts
rubber and pours it into deep holes that she digs in the floor of
her cell. In this way she acquires shocking, pliable appendages
which she wickedly affixes to the Cross.*

*We have discovered her at the hour of matins hitched to the
Symbol, panting with pleasure. Some of our dear, devoted Sisters
say that she often levitates, especially on summer nights while
inhaling the fragrance of jasmine flowers. They say they found
her bumping against the roof of her cell. To my mind, she inflates
from dirty desires.*

*We have tried chaining her up outdoors (in the street) but
within hours a throng of sullen men gathers at the door of the
Convent, as though it were a brothel. (Among them we have
spotted Judge Montenegro, Malea the apothecary, Odría the As-
sistant Police Inspector; it is well to make note of these names
here . . .) The commotion was such that we deemed it wise to keep
her within, so as not to disgrace the Church.*

*When I call her to my study to reprimand her, she throws
herself sobbing at my feet and swears to her virginity.*

*I require due guidance from the High Office of Your Ex-
cellency. What shall I do? I kiss your ring.*

> *The Sister of Bitter Mercies*
> *Santa Catalina Convent, Arequipa*

In the distance she scented virility: blood, sweat, and
semen of the Warrior. Thrice on his mule he circled the

convent, and he sensed her anxious breathing. They had made contact. The dark attraction of supreme femininity for the Conqueror, bull of war. From over by the convent laundry came a deep roar, like that of a lioness cruelly widowed: La Endemoniada. Then a heartfelt groan: "Darling! Darling! I'm over here . . .!"

"Sor Angela? Oh you, my Girl-Nun! It's me, it's me!" The nun's moans and sobs of love and gratitude wafted through the Patio of Orange Trees. "Is it you, my lord?" "Oh you! I shall be your flag, lord! Staff me! Flutter me in war! Sacrifice me on you! Holy Trinity! Holy Trinity!"

Sor Angela leaped to the overused window grate. Rubbed against the pocks of dry rust till she bled. In the moonlight Aguirre saw the bare legs of the Girl-Nun extruding from the severe slag wall like tender young sprigs. A wild wind, a higher, indomitable destiny, held her sprawled against the iron grate. "Slit me! Splay me! Crack me!"

Aroused by her voice of fire (flames licking through the wretched little window in the fundamentally inflammable wall), Aguirre kneeled on the back of his mule, then stretched out his legs, slid toward the rump, and saddled the bars with slow, steady resolve.

La Endemoniada drooled with desire and satisfaction. Her eyes rolled back and she passed out: her legs ceased to quiver and fell still like the necks of sacrificial swans. Two Sisters of Charity managed to disengage her, pulling hard. Day had dawned.

Thus was a great love born.

*　　　*　　　*

The Sister of Bitter Mercies received him at eight. Lope did his utmost to conceal his everlasting love. He sensed great comprehension and sympathy in this compassionate nun who was open to life's problems and had learned to regard nature as a (primitive) extension of God's will. "I daresay there's not much to discuss. I will pass on your proposal to the girl, as you call her. But the decision is hers, and well it should be, as she's already fifty-six."

"Many thanks, Mother. We're almost cousins—we met in Guadalupe, at the Convent of Guadalupe, ages ago . . . !" The Sister of Bitter Mercies chose not to linger over the possible sense in the senseless chatter of this peculiar Old Man. Evidently once a soldier (his tatters smacked of the military), probably discharged for insanity. Surely a sex pervert, like most of them . . .

The formalities were brief. The Girl-Nun's yes could be heard in the Office, on the far side of the Patio. The Bishop permitted the interruption of his overdue bath to sign the authorization papers, which his envoy carried off at a run. Frothing up soap bubbles, trying not to pop them, the Bishop came to the realization that God, in his infinite if erratic and belated goodness (God is not bad; he's distracted, remiss), had miraculously rid them of La Endemoniada, a disgrace to all people of faith.

They strapped Sor Angela's valise onto one of the mules left in the care of Nicéforo. Her coif shimmering: freshly starched, warm from the iron. She straddled the withers, mannishly. Aguirre sat behind. Waving and giggling like children, they rode off toward Misti, never looking back at the desert of volcanic stones where Arequipa straggled.

"Where to? Jungle! Mountains! Where nobody can trouble our joy!" Lope was ecstatic.

Riding. Riding.

On the flanks of the Mollebaya hill, Lope plucked wild flowers and gave them to her. Nothing more eloquent.

One night, crossing the Confital pampa in moonlight, they mated almost without wishing to: crazed by desires that rose up inside them like other astral bodies. Muleback lust. But they knew not what they did; proceeded as before on a spiritual plane, oblivious to the canine transgressions of their bodies.

He adored her: she was more than his dreams. One night, camped in the desert of Tincopalca, Sor Angela drew two tiny circles in the dust; then she linked them with a line that stroked up into one circle and back to the first. "You see, darling? This is the mystery of the Holy Trinity: three beings in one, three persons in one. The primary Triad . . ." Her eyes blazed beneath her coif. Torrid, irresistible eyes. "The Holy Trinity? What drivel . . ." was all the Old Man would say, chivalrously concealing his healthy skepticism toward all zoological fantasy.

They also tried to overlook what happened that night. They had said good night, each on his own side of the embers of the fire. But their desires rose up and tricked them: they copulated wildly and Aguirre experienced one of those rare supererections *intra vas*, common among lesser quadrupeds. They stood and took a few steps, unable to disjoin, panting in pained pleasure. Then, merely pained, they sidled—a single entity—toward the shore of Lake Saracocha, whose waters are limpid and cold. By filling a boot with water, they cooled the incubus until they could part.

Over languorous suppers, Lope told tales of Imperial Cuzco: his first glimpse of golden Coricancha, the moan of Atahualpa. She listened in awe. She loved to hear him warmly recalling his old friends off roaming who knew where: Mancio Sierra de Leguizamo who had staked the Sacred Disk on a game of *mus*; the softhearted pirate Alonso de Cabrera, old Hernando de Soto who had squandered his youth in its quest.

In their amorous discourse *à deux*, that encapsulized realm of lovers (those oranges painted by Hieronymus Bosch wherein lovers travel, the Old Man had once glimpsed them in firelight!), the erstwhile killings, duels, and treachery seemed like silly capers: atrocities whose only present-day purpose was to amuse a sweetheart.

One evening at sunset, amid the rocks, still warm from the sun, where they had taken refuge from the chill wind that spills off the Andes, Sor Angela was nestling against Lope's chest as he told her tales (without hard feelings, in spite of everything) of his uncle the pork butcher (who had, after all, waked his hunger for America). When suddenly, roused by true love, she flung her arms around him and— as though breaking her vows—cried out, "I love you, my lord, I'm madly in love with you! Do with me what you will! I am yours, forever!" And she began to sob as hard as befits a woman who has cuckolded no less than Christ.

Something grand had fallen into the desiccation of his life. He felt proud and grateful. Rose sheepishly. "Now,

now . . . Sor Angela, my little girl . . ." Unsheathed his
sword and began pirouetting and feinting with overplayed
dexterity. Felt younger than before he was born.

Riding. Riding. League after league of pure love. Ever
more repressed, ritual, rarefied. For what dark love of suffering did they refuse to surrender to the dogs of desire?

Lovebirding along, they neared the Sacred Valley. After
low hills, they plunged into forest. Nicéforo, off on another
trail, caught up where the slope turned steep. Reporting
that the Expedition horde was within two hundred leagues.
"As lost as ever, Chief, lost as ever! Without you, sir, they're
nothing, and always were!" Reporting that the restoration
of Túpac Amaru Condorcanqui had lasted not even a year.
That his people were slain, but never humbled. Savagely
impaled. That Túpac was drawn and quartered in the Plaza
at Cuzco. Desecrated—like his great-great-grandfather. Like
someday his grandson.

They ascended along the Apurimac. Sor Angela, mar-
veling; she had never seen such a land. She laughed at the
sight of parrot feathers; feasted on soft, sweet fruits. One
morning she began to tremble with fear: she was sure this
river was none but the Euphrates and that Aguirre (incar-
nation of the Almighty) was leading her to Paradise.

The mules were perforce abandoned; Nicéforo lugged
the suitcase on his back.

Waterfalls. The most marvelous iridescences flaring in
the mists. Immaculate waters smelling of stone. Huge, happy
butterflies humming solemnly as they glided. Wild creatures
that watched with flicking eyes and fled.

Now Lope was led by surefooted instinct. He knew he

had to climb and climb. Into the Andean heart, toward those cities of which Huamán had once spoken, for the very purpose of concealing them.

Toward the secret, scaling. At times Aguirre sank into depression: Sor Angela was a new abyss. Desire to plunge, and fear of the abyss. It struck him that he ought to enter her with the gait of a mule (gingerly, without trampling on her privacy, as it were).

Vilcabamba. Rosaspata. Espíritu Pampa. City after abandoned city of white marble. They set their course by the peak of Salccantay. Crossed the fierce Urubamba near Colpani. Teetered on a long bridge of broken boards strung up perilously with lianas (woven in the decline of the Inca Empire). Sor Angela friskily rocking and laughing, swinging harder and harder, trying to touch the perfect curve of the rainbow wrought in the mist and spray of the raging river. "Ravishing! You're ravishing!" bellowed Lope, seduced by her delicious mischief.

They came to a plantation worked by a family of modernized Indians, the Richartes. Ate their fill, apparently had been expected. Nicéforo made inquiries: "We're almost there, sir! A big city sits at the crest. Huamán is standing by to escort you. Everyone knows how to enter: the Sacred Valley keeps no secrets."

They proceeded at dawn. Orchids rooting in tall trees, drenched in fresh dew. Ducally-plumed birds that the German scientists, always leery of the disbelief that greets marvels, were not to record until the age of photography.

Huddled together beneath the leaves of banana trees, they endured a night of torrential rain. Aguirre was contemplative. His life now seemed so far away. Something like someone else's mistake. "How can I have lived without love?" All as ephemeral as streaks of wind on water. "Without love, nothing, nothing!" Sor Angela fell asleep against his rib cage: bony as the chest of an old bird. Aguirre now felt that love alone held him, all else was a swirl in the stream—nothing but struggle and strife. "Cruelty is the sport of curs and widowers and bachelors." A revelation, as sheets of water rinsed his face.

At dawn they discovered a little *pirca* wall snaking upward, and followed it. Glimpsed in the distance the form of Huamán, garbed in a poncho. Climbed, vanishing into the pearl-gray vapor of clouds. At the summit stood a stone gateway with a little house attached; presumably a guard post. Huamán was seated on a stone bench.

"We have arrived, Aguirre. This is the city, the Cosmic University. It symbolizes Universe, Tawantinsuyu, Inca Empire. Joins earth and sky. Body and spirit. Night and day. Forges the amazing alliance of the living and the dead, as you shall see . . . Each structure is a lesson and yet also a mystery. This you will learn for yourself. There is nothing more to say . . ."

Sor Angela looked about with curiosity. From the gate, white stone steps descended. Beyond, a rocky hill in the shape of a phallus: Huayna Picchu.

"There you see Machu Picchu, Aguirre, or in other words, 'the heart' . . . You will ascend for your nuptials. In due time I shall assist you. Your servant. Here you'll unravel your knotted body! You'll regress! You'll relax! It's high time, Lope! Bodies were not created to be instruments of unhappiness, as your religion preaches—though you have renounced it . . . Have no fear, simply proceed. The steps

at times seem to descend, but indeed they climb . . . Goodbye!"

It was April 9, 1802. Meaning that they entered Machu
Picchu 109 years before the official discoverer for the white
race, Professor Hiram Bingham of Yale University, USA.

Arm in arm, the Conquistador and the Girl-Nun ascended the steps of the City where no one was (they felt
this).

The City was horizontal and vertical, alive in two
rhythms. Musically scaled. Seen entire from above, an open
hand. A powerful stone hand stretching toward ethereal
silence.

On the slopes, they passed more than a hundred cul-
tivation terraces. Then, still mounting steps that rose parallel
to a rivulet of water that linked fonts of carved marble as it
decended among the rocks, they came to the first edifices.
Superior to Cuzco in artistic conception, so far as Aguirre
could judge.

Sor Angela felt afraid and huddled against him. So great
was the hushed mystery and beauty of the place that when
they opened their mouths, out spilled verse. This was what
she said: "Streams of limpid, crystal water . . . Green
meadow with cool shadows rife . . . Birds that here strew
their laments . . . Lord, how this grandeur fills me with awe!"

Then Aguirre in solemn tones: "Final palace of the seen
world, periphery of the absolute. Celestial geometry that,
blinded, we once scorned . . . ! Here is a permanence of
words and stone. All life, a shock of stone petals . . ."

Suddenly Aguirre was struck by holy terror. Fell to his

knees. Kissed the earth. The Girl-Nun looked on with the horror of a woman who finds that the man she loves is capable of mystical transports. "What's gotten into my lord! For heaven's sake. Don't be like that or my soul will fly away!" In Machu Picchu, the numinous, the Conqueror had bitten the dust.

The city existed half in Heaven, half on Earth; by turns, heeding the unforeseeable rhythms of clouds and showers. At moments the sun shone hard; at moments it shattered amid flurrying tatters of gossamer clouds against the hill of Huayna Picchu. When a cover of clouds solidified overhead, Earth was supreme. When the cover dispersed, the City soared Skyward.

They came upon a remarkable circular tower, much like the famous Temple of the Sun at Cuzco, and beyond, as described by Huamán, a big palace with a sturdy roof. Abode of the King. All had evidently been prepared: dishes, goblets, aryballoses, baskets heaped with fruit, rugs, tapestries lining the walls. Behind a door, shockingly intimate, the great bed (large enough for two couples), draped with an ultrasoft pelt of white llama. At the sight, Sor Angela broke into a run. Bounded down the steps and came to a halt in the middle of the Plaza of Ceremonies, beneath the Temple of the Three Windows. She was quivering like a leaf.

The obligatory intimacies of the journey had gradually led them to comport themselves with strict formality, almost in the mode of Sicilian fiancés (the stronger the blood, the greater the formal constraint).

That first day, they parted: she to the Palace of the Virgins of the Sun; he to the Palace of the King.

At no time did the solitude of the City disturb or depress them. Not a lovers' problem: love is populous.

At Huamán's instruction, the Richartes delivered food every other day. On balmy nights, dinner was served in the open air, most often in the Temple of the Three Windows. After the grilled guinea pig, she refrained from sucking her fingers, and Aguirre graciously abstained from belching.

They talked and talked, calmly imbibing aged *chicha* from the cellars of the Lower District.

In showers and storms (common in the Olympian heights) they dined in the Royal Palace by the evocative light of Incan lamps, wrapped in vicuña pelts, which softened the roar of thunder. A delicious feeling, shelter in the storm. They toasted: suppers of pleasure and love!

Talking. Talking. Lope told tales of old hostilities: marauds and exploits of *tercio* and regiment. Recalled lost friends. Recapped some of his moments in power: "Whack 'em! Whack 'em! Crack their ribs! Better too many hanged men than too few!" Sor Angela beamed. Listened mesmerized to tales of fires crackling, teeth gnashing, blood burbling from slit throats. When she saw that her delight was beginning to show, she would lower her head and hear out his discourse with an immutable Monalisan smile. She kept her enthusiasm closely in check.

When her turn came, she recounted scenes from the lives of saints, with a hint of mischief not lost on Lope. When alluding to Christ, she achieved mystical tones. "In love for the Lamb our soul truly lives; in that tenderness. In the Lamb's warm fleece!" she theologized.

Now it was Aguirre's turn for delight: "Is what they say true? Do you really levitate, Sor Angela?" Then she, modestly: "It's not so much the levitation, my lord. Heights make me horribly dizzy."

They strolled through the City, mornings and moonlit nights. Learned to spot local creatures: the jaguar with the slanted stripe on his paw, the thieving boa with his home on the second slope, the bear clan. Passed discreetly by the mummies seated in the Royal Tomb.

Although they said goodbye, they never left each other's minds. Aguirre would often step out in the late evening and take two or three turns past the House of the Virgins, as though by chance. She was sleeping, or pretending not to see him.

Their courtship lasted almost two years, with little variation. They dined together Tuesdays and Fridays.

Huamán knew they were ripe for matrimony because the roars they sent out in their sleep seemed to issue from a cage full of jaguars. Unhurriedly and serenely, the preparations were begun.

For the ceremony they chose the last week of May, month of the Great Harvest (the ancient fête, *Hatun Cusqui Aymoray Quilla*). As in all festivals, the ancient dead of Machu Picchu and environs became a little more apparent. By dawn they were out and about in the workers' district, like smoke in the air. Dozens of hands patting *quesillos*, kneading *sanko* (the maize paste for the great fêtes). Hands of little girls tied two potatoes to each dried ear of corn: ornamental symbol of fecundity to hang over the doorways of homes. At sunset hundreds of feet rehearsed solar dances in the Plaza of Ceremonies.

Aguirre was learning that Machu Picchu counts among those few places where parallel worlds converge. Here the spiral of time narrows (in normal places the loop aperture is larger). A vertiginous unity (which men vaguely desire but can't endure the presence of) drives mad those who attempt a prolonged analysis without adequate initiation. Future and past hold their usual places and coexist—without claims to exclusivity—on the plateau of present time. For the novice, images of time past appear to be torn and strewn across a Waste Land: occurrences stray erratically like souls in torment among clouds scattered by a blustering wind. But no: a secret Harmony can be glimpsed (naturally not a matter of solemn Historicity . . .) if and only if no ingenuous attempt is made to capture it in that net of smoke known as human reasoning (minirationalism!).

Wisely, Lope knew how to avoid what he did not understand. He refrained from staring, even when what he saw was truly unsettling. This sporting attitude, which might be considered shallow, saved him from horror and philosophy. Thus he behaved, for instance, when he glimpsed—among a group of Incas who shuffled by tugging a quadrangular stone—a short pudgy man in a gray frock coat and French bicorne with his hand tucked between the second and third buttons of his waistcoat, mounted on a white horse shying from cannonshot. *"Murat! La carte! Murat, dépêchez-vous! Hélas Murat!"*

Aguirre endured days of hectic preparation. Came and went. His steps rang out anxiously on the stone steps. The anxiety of a man on the brink of fulfilling a long-deferred dream. "She! The Girl-Nun! The nape of her neck beneath her coif, in my arms, oh!" When he noted how immensely happy he was, he would kneel as though in prayer (if nothing else, he invoked his artificial atheism and this was worth more than many prayers). His heart like a gawky old bird: toucan transported in a narrow cage.

The trousseau: silver rings forged by the youngest of the Richartes from an Incaic piece contributed by Huamán. On his annual trip to Cuzco, Alvarez (brother of Richarte's brother-in-law) procured a length of fine nanduti for panties, bloomers, and mesh stockings. The essential acquisition was a pair of those red nuptial garters in those days sold only by episcopal prescription *ad usum matrimonialem*, to be mandatorily returned within the month to the offices of the Inquisition with an end to their proper incineration.

As the ceremony drew near, they met only once weekly to coordinate details, in Huamán's presence. Deported themselves with maximum discretion: when they dined, a reed miniscreen was set on the table between them, to intercept libidinous glances. She went about veiled like an Arab woman (her lips had swelled and thickened, like those of an explorer dying of thirst in the desert).

May 25th dawned rainy; later the sun felicitously shone. The bride, who for the preceding two weeks had kept out of sight (Lope investigated, fearing that she had fled in the grips of that terror known only to *toreros* before a fight), appeared at nine-thirty at the summit: gateway of the City.

Majestically she commenced her descent to the Plaza of Ceremonies, where Lope stood. Walked beside Huamán, who wore his white poncho with dignity and grace.

"Sor Angela, oh my God, Angel . . . !" Lope's voice came out like a whisper cracked by longing and tender lust. The Girl-Nun descended in a long, unadorned dress, a perfectly starched tube thrillingly and yet threateningly like an impenetrable metal pipe. Her back draped with a vicuña-silk *llicta*, a long cape. Her hair neatly coiled beneath her nunnish coif. The stylish detail was the placement of the waist of the dress (tube) just beneath the breasts, set off by a narrow pink ribbon: the Empire style, rivaling Madame Récamier in her famous portrait.

Aguirre enraptured at the center of the Plaza of Ceremonies, in a felt hat tropically plumed per his official rank (he would have preferred a simple, intimate ceremony). They had polished his steel breastplate with ash and mended his sword hilt. Nicéforo, proud to serve as witness, was robed in the habit of a sacristan, which covered up his twisted legs.

Solemnly they joined at the center of the Plaza and began the ascent toward the Temple of the Three Windows, where the ceremony would unfold. Richarte and Alvarez, with children, women and other domestic creatures, silently looked on from the terraces of the Lower District. In a clearing on the slope of Huayna Picchu, Nicéforo spotted the family of jaguars and the three bears: spying.

In the Temple, Huamán had lined up fifteen royal mummies; rather like a college of cardinals.

Upon seeing the perfect apertures of the three windows, Sor Angela murmured: "The Father, the Son, and the

Holy Spirit! The Trinity again." Aguirre pondered symbolic possibilities not quite so metaphysical.

Huamán officiated deftly. The ceremony was brief. Catholic formulae had been inserted in the ritual at Sor Angela's insistence. Consulted by the *amauta*, Lope said only this: "Fine. We must let women be Catholics . . . it adds spice." In his opening remarks, Huamán said: "You shall be alike in passion, for one must not be cold while the other burns." Then Catholicism: "Wife before the Lord of Lords, you shall be the sole receptacle for his semen and his spirit. Solely into you shall he pour himself. If he spills someplace else, you'll clip it off. For what the Infinite Spirit unites, solely he can put asunder. Always shall you choose boredom and death over infidelity!"

He directed them to exchange rings. She naughtily offered up her ring finger and held it exaggeratedly stiff. Aguirre slid the silver band the length of this incubus; when it reached the last phalanx, instead of leaving the ring in place, he drew it back toward the tip, then slid it again slowly to the base. Their breathing deepened. The Girl-Nun's eyes glistened greedily beneath her coif.

Then Huamán: "Now put on her sandal, sir." Lope, flustered, gave him an inquisitive look. Huamán pointed to the embroidered sandal resting beside the little ring pillow. Lope leaned down tremulously and lifted the hem of her dress. She offered him her foot. He slipped the sandal on and straightened up, his mind on the red garters: "Those darling little garters!"

Next the officiant and the newlyweds drank consecrated *chicha* from the same *quero*.

Then the unforeseen occurred: Sor Angela fell to her

knees, hugging her breast, as though struck by a ray of lightning. Sobbed bitterly. In silence they allowed her to unburden herself. Nicéforo burst out laughing, as though he had been choking it back for some time, and Aguirre gave him a kick that sent him off howling in pain to hide among the mummies.

The powerful spirit of Judaism, and in particular, of Catholicism (that pimply Jesuit spying on mulattas who sing at sunset) had bitten into the conventual soul of the Girl-Nun with the fury of a dying dog.

Guilt. It was Guilt. Sor Angela was sobbing and imploring the bloody Christ of the Convent of Arequipa to pardon her. For her betrayal and also for the future, for what was to come. "Oh Lord! Oh Lord! . . ." she sighed. But guilt and this morbidly Catholic grief had a perverse flip side: Sor Angela felt that she was calling on the Lord to look upon them. And when the Lord turned His eyes toward them (from His presumed cosmic distraction), He would then transform into the Supreme Voyeur, the offended third person, the excluded third party presupposed by all coupling of human bodies. The Lord would have to prowl around spying, suffering with every moan. And to sniff painfully at the tiny cracks (so perfect was Incaic architecture that a knife's slim blade could not be slipped between the stones).

Calmer now, she got to her feet with the aid of Aguirre, more a hindrance than a help (aroused by her tears, the Old Man slid his hand down the side of her thigh till he could feel the faint edge of the nuptial garter through the stiff cloth). "What God has united no man shall put asunder," he murmured with salacious hypocrisy.

Huamán suggested that they continue upward, toward

the Intihuatana: solar collector, place for the conjuration of Chaos. The ceremony was in essence complete.

As they mounted the topmost steps of the City, they heard the exquisitely strange music of the heights. Machu Picchu is known to be a giant stone flute, and also an Aeolian harp.* Only rarely does this music of ineffable beauty reach the ear.

The great carved stone of the Intihuatana culminates in a short, thick quadrangular little phallus, which, as Professor Coltrane has pointed out, could *also* represent an erect, swollen clitoris. After circling this suggestive monument, both symbol and astronomical gauge, they returned— more relaxed, jesting quietly—to the Palace of the King for the ceremonial banquet.

Guinea pig stuffed with chili peppers. Doves in cherry sauce. Legions of potatoes, Huanca-style. Papaya with rice. A roasted male llama kid. Aged *chicha*; maize liquor. Delicious corn on the cob. Pineapples pulped in their syrup. A basket of fruit reminiscent of chestnuts (making Lope wistful).

They ate informally. Sor Angela, annoyed by the extra-broad rim of her starched coif, rolled it up like the brim of a homburg hat. They drank deep. Huamán did not forget the mummies: he climbed up and smeared

---

*It is curious to note that the poem "The Heights of Machu Picchu," by Pablo Neruda, omits these two musical instruments from its ample sequence of seventy-six objects that serve as metaphors for the City (presumably those recalled by the poet as he composed): reef, foam, shovel, towering shadow, grapevine, belt, iceberg, bubble, sea bride, scarred moon, teeth, black-winged cherry tree, equinoctial quadrant, manacles, blood level, etc.

their faces with *sanko* and wetted their lips with royal *chicha*.

"All that I have been and done, what was wrong and what was right . . . All, all. What was cruel or dolorous, lost or won, all, all . . ." Aguirre could find no words to express it. Softened by the wine, he launched into flights of grandiloquent rhetoric. "All, all! And all to attain the shore of love, the peace of love, oh God!"

In the Plaza of Ceremonies, a parallel celebration: hundreds of feet hopping to the *way-yaya*. Two steps forward, one step back. Now with serenity, now with frenzied joy. "All to the plaza, no one at home" was Aguirre's maxim for the wedding day.

The Alvarezes felt that an Iberian prank was in order. One of the children turned up with a gift box for the bride. Sor Angela removed layer after layer of wrapping: the precious object within was a long, wrinkly sweet potato whose tip had been dipped in red ink. Hearty laughter. Sor Angela sweetly stroked the boy's head and offered him a caramel bonbon.

At four in the afternoon, they were at last alone. Riveted in the silence and solemnity of profound desire (every remark, every word sounds false). Center of desire within vortex of silence: like the eye of a storm (all sailors tell of this).

They experienced a sort of deafness (as though their ears had turned desirously inward to listen to the heavy beating of their blood). They had the impression that the animals had deferentially retreated or that the birds were flying higher than usual. Something wave-like swells from the strained desire of bodies, dashing the humdrum objects of everyday relations, and sweeping away the trivialities of time present.

It stands to reason that the travails of love were painful and Homeric. This was eroticism of unparalleled intensity, for Aguirre was denuding a body not merely covered since birth, but intractably clad for nearly two thousand years. He was possessing not only the Girl-Nun but an idealized vision of the Girl-Nun the nape of whose neck he had glimpsed on that memorable October 17, 1525: an image that had haunted and hounded him for close on 350 years. All this meant fervor, mad heat.

Moans, shrieks, supplications, and heavy silences that are merely the lull before the final howl; flight and fierce pursuit.

Aguirre must have felt proud when he saw that the force of his passion could stand up to entrenched religio-erotic fantasy. More intuitive than rational, since its forms—like those of poetry—are not achieved through effort but discovered in the motions of bodies.

On the seventh day, when Huamán padded down to the second cistern to deliver fresh food, he found a red garter strewn there, as chewed and mangled as the rib of a lamb carried off by wild dogs.

Whereupon Huamán began to fear genuine danger: the plucking out of an eye, for instance.

*   *   *

On the twenty-first day Lope turned up, walking as well as ever, and went down to the lower slopes. Evidently the worst was now exorcised. He set to discussing tomato plants with Richarte. He probably did not know that he wore the face of a man who has fought hand to hand with a young bear.

7

A Grim Arcanum:
La Maison-Dieu
or
La Tour abolie

Beyond the barrier of desire. Matrimonial eroticide. Everyday life. Aguirre comes down off the peak. Visits the fledgling Marañón Republic. New ethics and hierarchies. Colonel Carrión and Bishop Alonso de Henao. Soirée chez doña Elvira. Doña Inés. Lope's irrelevance. Resentments.

SAID HUAMÁN: "Here you'll unravel your knotted body! You'll relax your nerves and muscles! Only love can do it for you, Lope . . ." No easy triumph for a warring man.

All visual and tactile angles, all violence of love: limber tumble laced with the urgent nerve of desire. Bodies lusting for tangle and furrow. Destroyed to rise again, exultant and alone. Always like more than two bodies.

Came that memorable morning after more than two years. She was soaking, drowsy-eyed, in the great cistern at the foot of the Tower of the Sun; lost in the water's ineffable tale as it tangled with her raveling hair. Lope, wrapped in a white tunic, was watching her. With new desire, thus. He caressed her from behind: a surprise. Parted her hair; with languid passion kissed the nape of her neck, wondrously dry like the inner feathers of a duckling adrift. Sipped warmth from that secret cup, from that small valley guarded by tendons; quintessence of her femininity.

Lope felt his head reeling. Reaching out, he braced his hand on the sacred fountain. Then he rallied; wrapped her in his tunic and lifted her. A strange force rose through him (and kept his legs from flying out beneath him like the stilts of an overladen stunt man).

They retreated into the Royal Palace and did not emerge for five days. Unforeseen nuptials within nuptials. (Lope felt like the runner who tears in puffing and panting, with ankles bleeding from the rocky trail, and suddenly discovers the bliss of strolling barefoot on cool grass. Why hadn't this happened sooner?)

Those five days, one immeasurable, incomparable moment. The hours had not passsed. Five times the sun had not risen, five times the sun had not set.

Marvelous incessancy. All those kisses: one long quenching and quenchless kiss. One breath. Surrender to tenderness reclaimed by assaults of fresh desire. Flaming passion plummeting into soft tenderness.

One of the great surprises of the Old Man's life: the secrets of the skin held this! Nothing compared, nothing. Not the shocks of his lives, not the turmoil of war, not treachery or villainy or betting on horses or gambling at cards (self-inflicted terrorism). "Nothing like it, girl! Such magic! But fine, enough talk!" He saw that he was truly in Paradise. "This is El Dorado, Paytiti, and all Peru! And you're all the Amazons, all the soft boots and dry beds in the world!"

Love as war had been supplanted by love as alliance: of bodies and souls. Enlaced, they rose in symmetrized desire, until, smiling, they attained the highest height, a flash of lightning. The shadow of a smile, drooping eyes, and they sank into the folds of a velvet lull.

As had occurred from time to time during those years, Sor Angela broke suddenly into verse. In the secrecy of love she protested silkily: "You left me whimpering and wounded; I rushed out crying for you, but you had gone! Try not to do it again, darling . . ." Then Lope: "I was un-aware, I swear . . ."

And she later: "Finish now if you wish! Rip the fabric of this sweet tryst! Oh, lamps of flame in deep caverns of feeling!"

Days, nights. Mornings consuming long afternoons. Time as one. How distant now was that war of bodies! Tussle and mount and triumph, primitive eroticism, requiring tor-turer and victim.

Several seasons of pure love ensued. At sunset, in their white tunics, they strolled arm in arm, languidly. Savored the air, the feel of the stone, the grass caressing their ankles (they didn't know that they were poets).

Love, tenderness, rapport rooted in affection; all this they had. Nor did they speculate on how long it might last, although the standard matrimonial contract wrongly decreed that it should last all their lives. Love as a single self with a double soul. One can die old or young, from catastrophe, constipation, or shock. Nobody sensible speaks of lasting.

Many important things happened in America during those years. Aguirre, who had acquired the knack of interpreting the images that fleeted through the sacred realm of Machu Picchu, knew that these were extraordinary times. Now and then he heard the Richartes or the Alvarezes chatting as they checked the tomato stalks (hardly minding that the Old Man was listening; somehow he had ceased to seem foreign): "Bolívar landed at La Guayra, on the *Avon* . . . Now things'll really get ugly . . ."

Hate swept the streets, in full flower. *Corregidores* and *alcaldes* had lost their *joie de vivre*: subversion spoiled the party.

One clear night, the unlikely semblance of an ink-black negro accoutred like a French *maréchal* glided over the face of the great ritual rock at the foot of Huayna Picchu: Toussaint L'Ouverture.

Subversion found its voice. People knew the name of George Washington. The *corregidores* could not comprehend how the consumptive workers of the mines of Potosí had come upon those three grand words that had already begun to cost them their lives: *Liberté, Egalité, Fraternité.*

Suddenly one morning, Aguirre felt the air thicken: objects regained their usual weight; life ticked routinely away, hour upon hour. Something had departed on tiptoe, with the tread of a cat. Married life had come to seem hollow beside those remembered days of lofty love. His spirits sank.

He felt lonesome: he alone was aware of the descent from the land of poetry. Sor Angela seemed not to notice, or hid it rather well. In any case, he kept up the display of tenderness, the habit of happiness.

Lope began to smoke too much. Went walking at night without joy or desire. At times, if the moon was up, he would climb to the ledge where the mummies sat and settle in between them, in lotus position, to meditate and contemplate the night, the distant snowy peaks, the phosphorescent glaciers.

At Huamán's suggestion, the children (Alonso, Gonzalo, Angela, Numancia, Andresillo, Torcuato, Mercedes, and Felipe II) were reared with the large motley litter of Richartes and Alvarezes; the *amauta* frowned upon raising children at a remove from the realities of other families. But Sor Angela chose to keep the last two, Bonifacio Octavo and María Estuarda, at home; she said she had grown fond of them.

This signaled the end of a great season of love. The ceremonious peace of lovers, requiring constancy and style, crumbled amid the informalities of family life. Shrieks, spats, diarrhea, colds, indelicate lunches. Sor Angela gave herself wholeheartedly to mother love; her husband forfeited exclusivity. He reverted to sulky early breakfasts, souring the sweet chirimoyas. Grumbled openly to Huamán and Nicéforo Méndez, as bitter as a Windsor: "To think that I abandoned my Empire for love!" He and Nicéforo teamed up and challenged the Richartes to *truco*. They drank too much. On Saturdays they went back to carousing. Conjugal duty began to be neglected. When reproached, he was heard to protest: "Damn! A man can't make love with the mother of his children, and under the same roof! It's incest, it's indecent . . ."

Many months elapsed. Aguirre opined that it was solely an excess of intimacy.

One morning, when Sor Angela went to the stove to heat her curling tongs, she found this note beside the milk kettle: "I need to see people. Don't worry. Lopecito." (This unpleasant pet name accompanied the general abuse of familiarity often occasioned by marriage, to say nothing of the dirty diapers.)

Huamán tried to calm her: he had seen them depart at dawn with a pack of mules. Lope had promised to perhaps return before the November rains . . .

He found the region once again rebelling. This time it was the *cacique* Mateo Pumacahua, bearing the flags of the Inca Empire. They had stormed the city and shot General Picoaga. Drunk on *chicha*, linking hands, day and night they danced in the Plaza of Huaypata. Padre Muñecas, soused on transchristian mysticism, had apparently entered La Paz leading a mounted band of Indian rebels.

Said Aguirre to Nicéforo, thinking aloud: "Thing is, the mantle of God always trembles. Never stops. Sometimes the earth trembles, like the quake that flattened Quito last year. Sometimes men tremble, and then everything gives. But so it must be! Kings must flee with their strumpets and silverware! Cardinals must flee impersonating nannies (this happened in Haiti . . .)! Do you see?"

The Old Man felt that he had come to be more tolerant. It was as though he had ascended Spanish and descended

American. A sort of lazy neutrality, a live-and-let-live. Almost a preference for fate over will. A sort of collusion with ignorance and failure.

In two months they arrived. The horde was republicanized in a fertile valley beside a great river, under optimal geopolitical conditions, only 12,144 kilometers from Paris, as marked on the arrow at the crossroads of Plaza Libertad. Not the tropical jungle. Nor the moonlike monotony of the Pampa of Dogs. A "little Switzerland," in the words of Senator Roberto de Coca.

Upon greeting them, Lope felt no nostalgia, fear, regret, or gratitude. He intended to pay a no-stress visit to the Republic, like a visit to a sick aunt with no hope of survival.

The city was plainly prospering amid the revolutionary spirit of the day, despite pressures from European commercial agents, who were attempting to monopolize foreign trade (Morgan, Bahring Bros., Rothschild, et al.).

The horde received word of his arrival without elation or great surprise (it was as though he had never left). Carrión, now Colonel of Cavalry and Commander-in-Chief, proposed that the Junta render him a formal tribute, as befitted a visiting ex-Head of State. A civilized Republic could permit such gestures . . .

The ceremony took place in the Plaza Mayor, where a bevy of maidens from the Voltaire School, appareled in crêpe uniforms, awarded him a set of symbolic keys to the city. A glass of wine was served in his honor at the Casa del Gobierno, in the presence of not all members of the Junta. The Bishop (Padre Alonso, that is) let it be known that he would receive him "tomorrow at ten." "Hell! Upstarts! Just who does that Priest think he is . . ." Though Aguirre was furious, he knew at once that he would have to adapt to the new etiquette. This did not have to be read as a breach of respect. Apparently when they became republicans they tried to repress the natural hierarchical tendency, which ranks men, renders a peaceful life, and does not pretend that the Bishop's spayed cat is the wildcat's equal.

They lodged him on the upper floors of the Hotel Paris in the room with the balcony. The manager, Ayala the eunuch, came out to greet him garbed in an impeccable tailcoat. "Looking good! From troop barman way up to *maître d'hôtel*. Go-getter! Watch there's no anaconda beneath the bed . . ." "*Monsieur* . . ." was Ayala's sole reply. Ceremoniously he bid him follow along down the hall, as though he had never heard the insolent comments.

When Lope saw the bed, he was amazed that there could be others like it in other rooms. It resembled the bed of Pope Clement VII, El Intrigante, on which, in 1527, during the sacking of Rome, he had raped a malevolent Belgian nun who spoiled the climax with this remark: "I forgive you as your own sister would."

They drew him a warm bath, reminiscent of Flemish brothels offering underwater services. Same, but better, except without a girl. The Old Man drowsed in the irresistible mixture of wistfulness and warm water.

He was alerted by a buzz that he, who had listened to virtually all the buzzes and noises of the world, had never heard before: housekeeping had slipped a printed sheaf beneath the door, it was the evening paper, *Le Commerce (des Arts et des Lettres)*. Nicéforo passed it to him tremulously.

Although he did not understand the exact words, over

the centuries Aguirre had learned to grasp the general meaning of signs. He might be defined as quasi-illiterate.

An essay from Buenos Aires by Mariano Moreno, "Independence and Law." An account of an attempt on Bolívar's life in Kingston, Jamaica. "Pétion Supports Bolívar." "Setbacks for General Belgrano." "Sipe-Sipe." "News from Tarija." The feature piece appeared in French and Spanish: Sablon, the editor-in-chief, had translated an article about the Inquisition from Voltaire's *Dictionnaire*. Transcripts of decrees from the Assembly of the United Provinces abolishing "slavery in the womb" and instruments of torture. "Taurine Chronicle." "Births and Deaths." Then Aguirre cried out in shock: "You're not going to believe this, *negro*! Will you look at this!: In the social column: 'Tonight *doña* Elvira Aguirre y de Gutiérrez will host a musical *souper* for her friends *chez elle* . . .' What do you think of that! How do you like that! How about that Girl! Turns out to be a satisfaction to her old man, no? You think she still has that butterfly collection?"

He ventured a cynical appraisal of journalism: "You read it and throw it away, what a waste! Tomorrow, when the next edition arrives, this one'll stink like rotten hake, ready to toss! They'll go mad, nobody can digest so much news all at once . . ."

Evidently America was going independent, from the United States to Patagonia. At first it had sounded preposterous, the brainchild of cretins, cranks and misfits (like everything that changes anything in this world, from Christianity to the French Revolution).

"That King Ferdinand is a loser, Nicéforo! Never mind

that tippler Pepe Botella!* The Empire tumbled down
around them, just like I said it would, I put that in a letter
to his great-granddad! If the Marañones weren't stupidly
wasting their time on that Republic, now would be the moment long awaited! But it's hopeless! They know nothing
about international politics, they'd fall on their asses!"

In fact, the Old Man was feeling vexed about the marriage of *doña* Elvira. Though it was a good marriage, the
Girl should have consulted him. He had always thought the
Scribe a pitiful, miserable intellectual, and even so, he would
not have objected: for a spirited woman, better a fool than
a brute. In his view, the Scribe would be helpless in the
hands of the Girl, like those tiny river fishes she loved to
feel dying between her breasts.

They left the Paris. The night was clear and calm. Despite republican spectrality, push and progress (English commerce and the new commercial doctrines) were clearly on
the up-and-up. But the specters were still playing tricks: a
battalion of bedraggled Spanish soldiers, led by the Marqués
de la Pezuela, trudged across the capital, strewing a horrific
stench (which they themselves could no longer smell). To
everyone's good fortune, they camped out of town, on the
riverbank. A German Romantic roamed into the Plaza
Mayor with his mules, tents, maps, theodolites and note-
books: it was Alexander von Humboldt, togged in quaint,
Zouave-style leather trousers and pouting drolly as he struggled to light his long-stemmed plaster pipe. At dusk he lit

*Translator's note: "Joe Bottle," a nickname for Joseph Bonaparte.

a bonfire to brew his coffee and to drive away beasts—
ignoring the fact that the Plaza was milling with mirthful
citizens who preferred his antics to the blare of the local
band.

A tallow lamp marked the doorway of the colonial-style
home of *doña* Elvira Aguirre y de Gutiérrez. Tall, grated
windows looked over the street; vines spilled down luxu-
riantly from the roof garden where long conversations were
spun on summer nights. Young men chitchatted with the
young ladies of the house. Beyond, the great parlor shim-
mered in candlelight. Little black servant boys came and
went through the parlors, offering beverages, *empanadas*,
slices of salty fried sweet potato to stimulate the appetite.
Long gowns, tall arc of tortoiseshell combs, languorous
flourish of fans painted with Venetian landscapes, rustle of
rich silk skirts. Men in big black frock coats, ever so decorous: as good as gelded by the decorum of the new age.
And military men whose stars and bars bespoke a great
pining for glory. Some poufed-up gilded hairdos in the mode
of European gents.

His entry was met with muted curiosity: no crowding
around or tasteless cries. The stupendous *doña* Elvira
awaited him in the vestibule, where her French perfumes
mingled with the fragrance of jasmine flowers. All grace and
smiles, she kissed his cheek, dispensing with formalities.
"How handsome you look! So handsome! You've been away
too long! Come in, come in! Blas was just asking about you,
how we've longed to see you!" And taking his arm, she
steered him into the parlor. Delicious to feel, beside him
once again, this girlish body on the brink of womanhood.

And furthermore, there was a hint of coy calculation in the tenor of her voice, the twinkle of her eye. Somewhere between innocent immodesty and luscious perversity.

In that instant, as he crossed the parlor, the Old Man rediscovered the sophisticated joys of the good life, of pleasure and well-being. Joys of frivolous friendship and urbanity. He quaffed a glass of cool *carlón* wine.

Life had evidently altered the ranking system, but Lope, obtuse to change, clung to obsolete hierarchies: a common phenomenon in reunions of former students or fighting men. When he saw Blas Gutiérrez posing as a solemn, sober lord of the manor, he lit into him indelicately: "Pastyface! Where've you been! Penpusher!" Obviously no way to treat a respectable member of local society. A man who sent his poems to Moreno and Echevarría. "Don't just stand there, slug! Get 'em to pour me a proper glass of wine. These thimbles are for prissy whores." *Doña* Elvira laughed, and the splendor and allure of her mouth was like the whisk of the cape that distracts the crazed bull in the instant of danger.

"*Doña* Inés, *doña* Inés!" Seized by emotion, he kissed her hand; at that instant the trio of blind Indians—rigged in makeshift black tie—struck up a sentimental arrangement of "Für Elise." Ethereal hand of *doña* Inés; please do, don't. Quite the lady, leaning on the piano with a sniff of disdain for some late sorrow. Veil of saint or empress trailing from the high arc of her comb.

Then he went about greeting them: Rodríguez Viso, Nuflo Hernández, Roberto de Coca, Sánchez Bilbao, Antón Llamoso, Colonel Carrión in his tropical stars and bars, Custodio Hernández. All stretched out their hands with the hubris of gentlemen and equals. He felt an urge to shout

out: Hey, Marañones! But there was no point. Senator! Sir! Colonel!

Lipzia showed up in heavy gray sideburns. He looked older. His greeting betrayed his feelings for Lope: admiration for his power, fear (of the pogrom), affection, abhorrence of violence and caprice, the desire to sell him something (Belgian weapons, swords), the desire to emigrate once and for all to a city safe for commerce, like Amsterdam, for instance. "Jewboy! Damn! I'll wager that if I tipped you over, all those ingots you've hoarded would crush my feet!" He embraced him. Lipzia was not all that effusive because they had noticeably neglected to invite his daughter (the usual prejudice).

Liberated from colonial dominance, evidently they could now devote themselves to business (those who were businessmen, naturally). *Bon ton* of the European salon, ceremonious, sedate, and solemn: with that insistence on convention that always lands the bourgeoisie in an infinite yawn. "You're doomed to boredom! That's what'll kill you, boredom!" To avert contagion, he drained two glasses of cool *carlón*.

They were crowing over Rodríguez Viso's triumphant election to the presidency of the Club. "Must build a fittingly grand building, in the English fashion! So tranquil you'll hear the tread of a cat!" said Rodríguez Viso, vowing to accomplish this memorable act of glory.

One of the Englishmen, in a flawless frock coat and a wig the color of old gold, was none other than H. H. Wildcock, the man who had divulged—or deftly guessed under stress of torture—the whereabouts of the land of Paytiti. Though he now wholesaled cloth, he did not neglect his contributions to the Royal Geographical Society (a form of undercover work in the guise of scientific and travel essays). He reported that in London the word was that Minister Pitt and *don* Francisco Miranda, the "father of subversion," had agreed upon the future form of the United Provinces: an Inca Empire controlled by constitutional parliament, or in other words, an English-style Incadom: two chambers, one for commoners, the other for *caciques*.

"Pitt's mad, mad! He wouldn't say the same thing today! Look what the Indians did when they got inside Cuzco! Look at Mateo Pumacahua, what do you do with people like that! Drunks . . . dancing . . . ! And how about Padre Muñecas? Folks like that make us look bad! We'll be the joke of the Congress of Vienna!" They seemed sincerely ashamed of the people around them.

The fervor and turmoil of politics was the passion of them all, the passion of the day. Flushed and radiant, *doña* Inés requested a moment of silence to impart the news: Mariquita Sánchez had sent her a beautiful song from Buenos Aires. Blas Gutiérrez arranged his tails on the piano bench, and the blind Indians struck up a tune, at once martial and subtle.

> *Hark, mortals, the sacred cry!*
> *O liberty, O liberty . . . !*
> *The Inca tosses in his grave*
> *and fire kindles in his bones*
> *that stirs his sons to resurrect*
> *the ancient glory of the Land . . . !*

Gentlemen and ladies clapped wildly. "Long live the Independence of the American nations! Hurrah!"

The house quivered with *joie de vivre*. The party at its peak. Orchestra playing popular rhythms: waltzes, minuets, Gongoresque *vidalas*, Versaillesque *pericones*. Black boys came and went with trays, by now their buttons had come undone. *Empanadillas*, fried *torta*, *ceviche* of pulped pejerrey with a touch of lime. From tubs of ice on the dirt-floored courtyard came bottles of *espumante* from Cuyo with rivulets of seductive sweat slinking down their sides.

All was discussed: the dangers of Artigas's politics, the San Martín mobilization, the ups and downs of Bolívar.

The Girl approached him once again and took him by the hand. With irresistible, contagious gaiety. Led him to the second courtyard to show him the birdcages she personally tended. Great wire mosques bristling with parrots, toucans, goldfinches, local pheasants, cardinals, and a very rare bird that was neither quetzal nor bird of paradise. A little monkey in a sailor suit stared worriedly at the gleams of light from the parlors. "Why do you want a caged monkey, daughter? You had so many in the wild . . ." "It's the fashion, Daddy . . ." she coyly replied.

From the back porch, they looked into the last courtyard. Tips of cigarettes glittered like fireflies in the gloom: smoked by negresses sitting on the quebracho door sills of their rooms. Phosphorescence of petticoats and teeth. "They're free, Daddy! Free! Now they're equals, see?" A touch of zestful defiance, of justice triumphant, in the voice of *doña* Elvira. "Good evening, citizens!" cried the Girl, waving vigorously; a few sly snorts were the sole reply.

When they stepped back inside, she—as brazen as ever—wished to show him her bedroom. Aguirre felt shy. A vanity with beveled mirror. Antique dressers. A huge canvas of an immodest plump pink woman painted by a Cuzqueño Indian with commercial taste: *Maja in Veils*. Dangling on the wall between the two beds, a rosary with giant beads. Above the night table, a bronze medallion of Aguirre in profile, minted on the occasion of the third commemoration of the Marañón Empire. Two monastic beds, long and narrow like Carmelite nuns sleeping barefoot. Over them sagged the mosquito netting, like wispy sails becalmed.

Gazing into her eyes, Aguirre whispered: "You're not cross at me, daughter?" He eyed the two sizable beauty spots just below her throat, the paternal punctures. Stirred by the wine and the agreeable ambience, the Old Man succumbed to tender sentiments: "Maybe I haven't been the best father . . . I don't deny it . . . and as for what happened . . . But the situation, life . . . Now that you're a bit older, maybe you don't love your father like you used to . . ." The Girl stared at him with unsuitable intensity; spoke in an overly intimate, undaughterly voice: "Daddy, my daddy . . . !" Aguirre quite nervously inquired after his little grandchildren. Then she: "They *are* yours, Daddy darling, but you shouldn't fuss about them or ask many questions." And as though she had suddenly opened the window and aired the dangerous darkness from her voice, she added resolutely: "Blas is a good man, Daddy! You knew him only under your command, never in private. He's a beautiful person and I'm very very happy!"

In the front parlor, spirited dancing. Out on the sidewalk, sunken in Goyesque shadow, a throng of Indians, ne-

groes, and mulattoes stared at the party barricaded behind
the colonial grille.

Lipzia brought him up to date. At the time of the An-
dahuaylas quake, El Dorado had vanished—as if by magic—
and never was found again. On that spot—by all reports—
a volcano rose up, brimful of swirling gold: molten, as on
the first day of Creation. H. H. Wildcock interrupted: "Gold
means nothing nowadays. Sugar, cattle, and wood! Gold
comes in pounds and marks . . ." The gringo's partner was
Parish Robertson, another traveler. Aguirre spoke: "You'll
make a killing, gringo, and you won't have to hoof it like
Waaterral! Free trade, just what you needed! Now's your
big moment: every Indian'll wear a patent-leather shoe!"
Then Lipzia: "That's progress, Aguirre, sign of the times.
Sooner or later equality catches up with us all . . ."

No sign of the Indian contingent, not even *caciques*,
amautas or headmen. Not Mamani or Kunturi or Chacón.
The Girl explained it: "They're so shy! They wouldn't enjoy
a classy party, why make them uncomfortable? They're very
equal, I don't deny it, if a trifle unrefined. And besides, with
the new piece rate, they work when they like and we mustn't
deprive them of the liberty to do so. They work at all hours
draining the marshes, driven by ambition. Times have
changed, Daddy!"

By now the aristocracy was set. One spoke of *the* Rodríguez Visos, *the* Tirados. There being little they could do
to upgrade their own blood, they at least energetically pur-
ified that of their Shorthorn and Aberdeen cows, from the
finest English pastures.

These people desired a constitutional monarchy, but
the notion of Indians acceding to the Crown was intolerable.

"Can you picture Mamani as the Conde de Paucartambo—
what would we come to?" "Bolívar will restore the Inca
Empire only if they name him Inca."

Carrión—Colonel Carrión—ambled over, as pompous
and decorated as a bakery cake. Puffing on a hefty cigar.
His position was secure; he had proceeded shrewdly. No
sooner did he get word of the May Revolution in Buenos
Aires than he scooped the forthcoming proclamation of
1813. In the newly inaugurated Plaza Libertad, with unction
and fanfare he incinerated a crate of irons, whips and straps
whose use and care had been delegated to him by the Holy
Inquisition via the Priest. He spoke with the insolence of
those who hold the weapons of others and do not mean to
give them back: "San Martín, Bolívar and Miranda will wage
the great battles. They may defeat Morillo and La Serna.
But that will be the moment to remind those gentlemen of
the cultivated voice of the cities, and to dissuade them from
heeding the cries of the rabble . . . Heroes write merely the
rough drafts of reality. . ." he wound up ceremoniously.
This remark was diligently recorded by Clerk-Sergeant Sal-
días.

Aguirre rather nervously noted that much passed between Carrión and *doña* Inés. She had migrated over from
the piano to listen to his oily, despicable voice. They glanced
at each other quickly, as though fleeing the scene of a crime.
Doña Inés eyed him with that injured and yet secretly col-
lusive pride she could not conceal when ravished by true
love.

The men of *Le Commerce* (Blas Gutiérrez, Sablon, López
de Ayala: champions of colored peoples, ardent revolution-
ists) looked fearfully upon the phalanx of powerful land-

owners that to Carrión's mind embodied security and peace. The latter had been admitted to the Club at the business meeting that prior Tuesday, after eight years of blackballs, with the stipulation that he could maintain his membership only so long as he remained in active service and refrained from bringing his wife to the New Year's dances. After sporadic, tormented seasons of sinful cohabitation, Carrión had taken to wife la Perticari, unpresentable in those starched red silk frocks that never matched her black-and-blue eyes, inflicted by the Colonel himself, who could not forget the past. The scenes were so violent that on more than one occasion Padre Alonso had had to come dashing across from the Cathedral, whip in hand, to explain to him that the Lord's benevolence embraces the past in the case of genuine Catholic repentance. Carrión, weeping in despair: "Bullshit, Padre! Bullshit! No divine mantle can cover up a woman who's spent a lifetime with her ass in the air!"

Neither gold nor glory can salvage a woman's past. As they strolled around the plaza waiting for the orchestra to play, barbarous cries rose from the darkness, reminding poor Greta of services rendered long ago: for the rabble does not believe in change. And they had no choice but to seek shelter in the bar of the Hotel Paris, where they drank grenadine in dense, oppressive silence. He loved her with deep, true, unhappy love.

A squat zambo in tails with a bushy mustache à la Nietzsche not quite concealing his ample lips. The negro Nicanor! Patiently he had enhanced the lighter tones of his skin, and he wore a false bald pate to forestall all talk of kinks. (Every three days his sideburns had to be trimmed, for on the fourth the invincible fatal curl began to show.

The Jew was tired of selling him Solingen scissors.) He made his excuses: had been detained at a luncheon at the Archbishop's for the chargé d'affaires of Austria. He was Minister of Foreign Relations. Of all of theirs, his had been the most versatile and virtuosic career. He greeted the Old Man with pointed decorum, maintaining his distance through the exaggeration of etiquette. Greeted him as though he were a partisan of the *ancien régime* the Revolution had not managed to purge in its most brutal days.

Accepting a glass of *espumante*, Nicanor Olindo expertly set forth the issues under debate at the Congress of Tucumán. Nowadays when speaking, he would allow himself to toss in a few words of local French, learned, one might conjecture, in his erstwhile contacts with Sablon, when during a sultry night in the jungle they had merged to form that dissectable quadruped the dewy-eyed mystic Diego de Torres had once believed was a Unicorn expiring in the darkness, dehorned by some immortal dealer in ivory.

"Although independence is a *fait accompli*, we must tread carefully—Rivadabia said as much in a letter to me. It would never do to cross swords with the Congress of Vienna. Europe will not brook Bolívar's plan for a continental union ... As for Belgrano, who could think to *refonder* the Inca Empire in the age of the Holy Alliance? Good God! Who would dare propose such a course to Prince Metternich?" Roberto de Coca broke in: "Not only international but also domestic issues must be assessed. A Napoleonic code is imperative! One cannot be too clear as to where the rights of others begin. A Land Register! A reliable Register of Cattle Brands!" Blas Gutiérrez, one of the founders of the Liberal Party, declared that he agreed with Minister Olindo. Good relations with Europe would foster good immigration. His remark that America should be a melting pot implicitly and irresponsibly extolled bastardy (*sic*).

The gentlemen were getting solemn and boring. *Doña* Elvira, genially nudging and smiling, herded them toward the piano. "Gentlemen, *clericot!*" The little black boys brought in a silver platter from Potosí and a huge cut-glass pitcher. With naughty and delicious poise, the Girl stirred with a big spoon, poured in several cups of cognac, and tasted: "Needs sugar! Sugar!" It was then that she leaned forward and her hair slipped glittering like flame over her brazen mouth. Before them arose something like the flanks of two little colts yearning to leap a fence. And once again that silence known to all. Silence laden with pain and no hope of redemption (as when she bathed in the rivers, so long ago!) "One, two, three, lit-tle spoonfuls," she said. The silver serving spoon sank into the sugar and rose up like the squawk of a dove pierced by an arrow. An utter silence closed around them as she stirred and stirred. To some, she even seemed to be singing. Though the orchestra had been playing all the while, there was no sound. The three blind men were furiously cranking out czardas or Turkish marches, and yet there was no sound.

By and by, when the *clericot* was served, all began to wake from the spell. Weakly, as though from the depths of a tunnel, the piano of Blas Gutiérrez began to sound; he was the only one thinking about anything else, it was a melancholy theme, quasi-Chopinesque.

Furtively Aguirre tried to take the hand of *doña* Inés, but she was standoffish. She even looked vaguely annoyed.

Their group sat down again. Under discussion was the plight of Fray Juto Santa María de Oro, who had failed to reach Tucumán for the Congress. Dogs had pursued him relentlessly through the desert. Beyond the Tinogasta post-house, spy dogs. This side of Hualfín, in the gorge at La Ciénaga, the attack. Hundreds of wild dogs! Devouring his horses and an Indian driver. Mad with thirst and hunger. All-out war, renouncing forever any hope of harmonious coexistence among the species. Padre Oro spent two days on the roof of the wagon, and was forced to sacrifice not only his kid boots, but also his much-thumbed Bible: the dogs savagely gnashed it to shreds, from Genesis straight through to the Apocalypse, when he was rescued by a caravan of cart drivers. The frightful Pampa of Dogs!

The Old Man was starting to feel out of place. The evening, which had started off with such zest for life, was spoiled by this feeling of exclusion. He resolved to try again with *doña* Inés. But she: "No, friend, no . . . please!" And Lope: "But why? Have I changed? Come on! Let's make something delicious of this night, meet me on the river-bank . . ." But *doña* Inés: "No, it cannot be. I'm not as free as I once was. My social obligations are quite demanding. And besides, I must confess, I myself am not the same . . ." And she went off to help serve the *clericot*.

Aguirre prowled around the parlor. "These bastards are making me feel abnormal!" He felt not anger but fury on seeing this splendid woman ruined by the new etiquette. "Refusing pleasure! Assholes! All that breeding makes 'em sour as Catalonians when their shoes pinch."

Doña Elvira and Blas Gutiérrez rushed for the door. Monsignor Alonso de Henao, arriving for his "pastoral"

visit. Over from the Bishopric preceded by two black boys
fitted out in Vatican colors. Matters were still irregular: he
performed as Bishop only from ten to eleven A.M., and at
social functions of note. The better part of the day he was
still a priest, and could be seen, broom in hand, grumpily
sweeping the nave and grumbling about the lazy sacristan.
Anxiously he awaited the overdue arrival of three Italian
priests (Padres Porcapottana, Sostanziale, and Zampaca-
vallo), who would enable him to savor his rank to the full.
Apparently in America men of true calling were scarce, and
although the clergy commonly fed upon the dregs and rubbish of society (drawing therefrom that power of resentment
required for the propagation of Christian sorrow), it certainly did not wish to call upon the Indians. That would
mean falling far too low.

"Just a pastoral visit, madam. I thought it proper not
to grudge you my blessing . . ." The evident scarcity of re-
sources and staff dictated the use of a sort of portable baldachin, a capacious bronze-handled purple umbrella. In the
vestibule they were lining up to kiss his ring. The zambo
Olindo, Carrión, Captain Martín Pérez, Admiral Juan
Gómez, Llamoso. The liberals were in no hurry.

A pack of urchins gathered on the sidewalk, pleading
for coins and sacred medallions.

Escorting the Bridesmaid of the Lamb had not been
easy. Before Napoleon, the priesthood had been gravely
endangered by scientistic and liberal atheism. But it now
colluded with the revolution. Monsignor Alonso had seen
fit to denounce a number of Spaniards and to speak out
about "corruption by the Crown of Spain of the most fundamental Christian principles." But he had recently blun-

He held out his ring

dered: on learning of General Morillo's massive campaign, launched from Spain, for the reconquest of Venezuela, he had hastily dispatched an effusive greeting: "To the hero who will restore the Catholic Faith now under threat from atheistic riffraff and the Masonic liberalism of men like Bolívar and San Martín." Alonso called for a premonitory repression of all importers of ideologies inimical to "the sentiment of our peoples and our Christian concept of family and State."

How did this come to be known? Diego de Torres, the contender for sainthood, managed the Post and Telecommunications Office (those falcons coached to run messages to the Creator in the upper reaches of Heaven were out of date; obsolete ligation technology). Reportedly it was the handwriting that led him to mistake this vital missive for the one *doña* Inés mailed to Carrión every Friday. Some construed the error as a subversive act on the part of the mystic, who now spent his days underlining Saint Thomas's *Compendium of Theology* and who believed, with the fanaticism of all sectarians, that it was imperative to transform Earth into a vast City of God, a compulsory municipal pre-Paradise. In sum: the letter reached Colonel Carrión, who put it to good use by rekindling an old conspiracy. He took the liberty of summoning the Bishop and ceremoniously incinerated the text over the ashtray for his monumental cigars. "Keep this close to your chest," he said mafiosally.

Proceeding beyond the vestibule, Monsignor Alonso saw Aguirre. He held out his ring to be kissed, as he had often imagined doing. The gesture served to stoke Lope's vast and virulent hatred. His blow was backhanded and possessed "a devilish force that did not match his years" (claimed those nearest the deed). The Priest tumbled across the vestibule and landed in the dusty street, entangled with the baldachin and one of the black boys.

They rushed to his aid. *Doña* Elvira sobbed. Blas Gutiérrez, the liberal, and master of the house, offered apologies on behalf of all. It was a dark moment. "Some of us do not wish to acknowledge historical change . . ." the Bishop sighed as he got up from the floor. Then he etched a cross in the air with insufferable priestly pomp, more or less toward where he thought Aguirre might be, and sang out in his tenor voice and second-rate Latin: *"Ego benedico te et absolvo tibi, filiiii . . . !"*

To heal the breach, someone roused the orchestra, which struck up a festive Neapolitan march, noisy and raucous. The Old Man slunk toward the back. *Doñas* Elvira and Inés hurried after him with teary-eyed maternal purpose, perhaps to soothe him as one might a dotty old grandpa who had exasperated everyone. Aguirre was mortified and incensed by his plight.

He hid in the second courtyard and sulkily inhaled the scent of jasmine flowers. Reminiscent of the time he took cover in the perfumery of the Sultan of Aleppo's harem and listened to angry eunuchs clash their scimitars. But somehow the blow had vented that unbearable feeling of bitterness. "All would be perfect now if only I could screw *doña* Inés!" But it could not be.

He perused the birdcages, those skeletons. Opened the hatches and shook. (Most of the birds failed to take note of their freedom; it was as though they had been born in captivity.) The sailor-suited monkey let out a conspiratorial screech and scooted into the eaves. Aguirre slipped out through the negroes' door.

In the street he was accosted by Nicéforo, gloomy because his black brother the Minister had balked at recommending him for a spot on the republican police force, his only means of rounding up the security he needed to marry and renounce the roaming life.

On the far sidewalk they mixed with the blacks and Indians gazing toward the radiant parlor. A line of dancers now festively snaked to the beat of a saraband cut with rumba. Sweat-soaked, shirt unbuttoned, the zambo Olindo led the line, bobbing like one of Goya's puppets and squeezing the waist of a girl from the Voltaire School.

"We'll have to mobilize the monkeys! Muster Vallaro's blacks! The blacks of Peru! The Jívaro! This must not go on!" The Old Man felt injured. "Can you believe it, *negro?* They treated me like a nobody. From Marañón Emperor to mere paterfamilias—if that. But they'll go to hell. They're stupidly republicanized. Already dying of boredom! They talk sideways with their kissers stitched. There's no authority! No dignity! No leadership! The one indulgence they won't permit themselves is guts!"

All night they toiled in the marshes, where the new suburb would rise. With bare hands they dug up the putrescent mud and filled the pails. For each full pail, the foreman marked a cross. They were paid by the pail; children earned half. Wrapped in rags to fend off the ferocious mosquitoes, they looked like Turks in turbans and baggy trousers.

Mamani, who supervised the Chancas, sidled over shyly

but fondly. "Where've you been all this time, sir?" Then Aguirre: "I was in love, Mamani! Love!" "Then you won't be needing them boots!" said Mamani matter-of-factly. "Why don't you give 'em to me?"

Aguirre found his first pair of sandals exceedingly comfortable. Mamani pulled on the battered boots and with crazed joy danced a *huaino* to the sly violin of Traverso, the leper.

8

Unnumbered Arcanum: The Madman, the Raver, or, the Infinite, the Vast

Aguirre roams revolutionary America. Meets desiccated Pizarro. Historical detour: Ayacucho. Goes home. Failure of a marriage. Again the Voice and an abominable rhetorical act. Huamán: amauta *and* guru. Ayahuaska *and awesome visions of liberation. Lost Unity. The Vast, until Hiram Bingham (officially) discovers Machu Picchu.*

*H*E ROAMED with no wish to return, dreading his return. After swaying the mule, which hankered to return to the hills, they headed coastward.

Furious at the Old Man for failing to land him that job with the police, Nicéforo Méndez brashly confronted him: "I've been nothing, I am nothing! Everyone else got a better deal! What am I? Take a look at Olindo, sir! He's a Minister!" Then Lope, calmly: "He's light black, not dark black, he played his best hand at the right moment, and scored . . ." Nicéforo went on bitterly: "What about Adhemir, who's conductor of the City Orchestra?" Then Lope, in a useless effort to soothe him: "His case is different. You have to admit he always had a gift for singing scales. Remember how he whistled to drive away the shrieking monkeys?" "I'm nothing! Zero! I'm the only fool who got nothing from the Revolution!"

But Aguirre felt his own inconsequence. The frustrating sense that he had failed to accomplish his Imperial manifest destiny. He was fleeing his past, his people, his wife, his future. He fled joylessly, lamenting his bygone fiestas of treachery.

Months of dreary marching. Drought. They drank the water from cactuses. Ate prickly pears and spat out the spikes dreaming of imaginary Biscayan hake.

Nights of dry, naked desert. No way to hide from the vision of stars and galactic clouds frightfully whirling. Vertiginous threat of Chaos. What to do? Cold sweat of terror on Aguirre's face. "I'm standing here alone in the middle of the desert! I might be scum, but I'm the only one! The only one watching! What if God died of a heart attack? What would I do?" (Aguirre returned circuitously to one of his old fears: God was powerful and irresponsible, like the son of a Catalonian publisher. He presumed that He paid little attention to His Creation.)

After reaching the sea, north of Chala, they hiked northward by fits and starts, dallying in green valleys that offered respite from the dry desert. Feasted on stolen figs, peaches, fresh eggs, and hens. Ventured forth only at the hour of the siesta, under the shimmering sun. Only then were they almost invisible. The packs of hounds went wild when they found they couldn't sink in their fangs. Baffled by the barking, the foremen (astride walking horses, sporting panama hats and brandishing whips) vented their fury on the backs of the blacks and Indians crouched in the cotton fields; accused them of unproductivity.

They slept in abandoned cow sheds; by now most were pissholes or snake nests.

Noon on an empty beach, Nicéforo noticed that the birds were committing suicide over the sea. From inland they flew in sloppy formation, soared up, and then plunged like books off a tall shelf. They burst on impact, *boof!*, and floated away, not upon the sea but in eternity.

"It's mass suicide. The animals are fed up!"

Two leagues beyond, they spotted a whale beached on a shoal. It was expiring there peacefully, beyond reach of the sharks that would exploit its decline.

Black signs. Dark times.

In Mala, on a promontory over the sea, Lope suffered a ferocious attack of existential melancholy. Spent several nights on the Hill of the Dead, gazing at the sea: that symbolic infinity, the Sea. But for the first time he had no wish to sail. It was a terrible sign of spiritual fatigue. "The inner sea, the inner sea . . ." he said again and again, hypnotically.

On the 16th of August, a Tuesday, they made their way into Lima, feeling no nostalgia and no desire. Little was familiar. They found lodging in a flophouse beneath a bridge, frequented by cholo traveling salesmen and bookies.

Lope spent two weeks sprawled out in bed while Ni-

céforo played *dinenti* on his knees with five peach pits.
Aguirre with his eyes on the ceiling like a painter who knows
not what to do with his white canvas. Rumble of toilets,
reek of fried food (heart *anticuchos*, sometimes even the
hearts of dogs), nasty, noisy quarrels about evictions, theft,
and debts. At night, when the clientele returned from the
Cockfight Coliseum, the winners lined up feistily before the
Spiderwoman's door. It cost half a sol and she did it only
two ways: French or Puppy-dog.

They began stepping out at dusk: befriending the modern city. Invariably they headed toward Miraflores and Ba-
rranco, where they could watch the calashes of the city's
rich entrepreneurs. Ladies in capelines, French governesses,
sailor-suited boys like toy admirals. *The* Riva Agüeros, *the*
de la Puentes, *the* Torre Tagles. One lucky day they caught
a glimpse of Monteagudo with María Abascal, his teenage
conquest: their calash whisked by, strewing her glassy gales
of laughter.

They also observed extensive troop movements. Blue-
blooded young officers said long farewells before darkened
grates; thus Cornet Christoph Rilke cached a rose petal in
the secrecy of his military coat. The final battle drew near.
La Serna marched toward the sierra, and toward a gentlemen's defeat. Emancipation was felt to be fact: company
agents spent all day in the hotel composing letters in English
infinitives.

One day he shook off the funereal gloom. Set out early.
Headed for one of those public scriveners in Jirón de la
Unión and dictated an energetic letter to General Belgrano.
He assumed he would be attending the Congress of Tucu-
mán, and was the indicated individual to wield his influence

or moral authority in the form of a petition. The epistle was the product of long contemplation. He fervidly recommended the restoration of the Inca Empire, and adjured the General to hold firm in opposition to those who wished to appoint a European Prince to the Crown of the United Provinces. Thought up a brilliant line: "The Congress of Vienna, or in other words, those who advocate restoration, hopes to defeat us with diplomacy, knowing that they cannot defeat us in the field." Quoted Bolívar. But the effort miscarried. While the scrivener was reading back the letter, an Italian commission agent, a man cordial and refined, worked his way through the cluster of onlookers. Remorsefully he informed him that Belgrano had died, defeated and all but forgotten, in unspeakable poverty; that the Congress had dissolved; that Laprida, its President, was sure to die in the gutter. "*Mi dispiace*," he said, and ever so deferentially withdrew, waving his pearl-gray top hat.

Aguirre slipped back into gloom like Monday on a government job. He walked out through Chorillos, ate shellfish, walked back through Miraflores. He felt that nothing was so dark and deep as the anguish of the modern city, where our solitude and anonymity are myriad in the thousand unknown faces that pass us on the street; one mirror of indifference.

On an impulse he headed for the Cathedral; the façade was no longer familiar. Before closing time, they hid in the second confessional (not in demand: *Man Spricht Deutsch*). They watched the last worshiper shamble out, a widow without children or cats. The Mongolian sacristan shut and bolted the door, snuffed the large candle dedicated to Saint Rose, and came shuffling up the central aisle. Crossed him-

DAIMON

self, and then masturbated handily before the little statue of Saint Joseph of the Eternal Threshold. Donned one of those purple cassocks penitent females wore for the procession of the Lord of Miracles (October is the purple month!) and vanished through a side door.

Then the Old Man moseyed over to the glass casket where *don* Francisco de Pizarro lay. He looked much thinner. Yellow as parchment, and speckled with dried mushrooms. Hollow beneath his suit, which retained his shape. The hard, dry, frowning face of a pork butcher remembering a bad deal in his moment of death. "Son of night, you went begging from door to door. Twice or thrice weekly you suckled the udder of a compassionate sow. Conquistador, Marqués, who more than you deserved a marquisate? But naturally the pure-blooded counts and marqueses shunned you. They took everything, don't you see . . . ?" He gazed at him for perhaps an hour, until the light faded and Pizarro dimmed away in vacuous ecclesiastical darkness.

As they left, Nicéforo softly sang some old tunes:

Almagro pleads for peace
The Pizarros cry for war
All those men shall die
And others rule the Earth . . .

Aguirre gave him a kick and the negro lurched away yipping like a dog. They met again that night in the hotel.

After a lot of random roaming, out beyond Huancavélica they spotted some merchants from Lima on the road.

The latter had set out for Ayacucho with laden mules and carts full of trinkets, not solely to witness the historical last battle that would mark the end of Spanish rule in America, but for the promise of excellent sales: nobody spends with more gusto than a soldier on the eve of battle. Booths selling cold beer and *anticuchos*, sacred amulets and Belgian bandages, lye disinfectant, laudanum-based sedatives, pouches of coca, scapularies incorporating a tatter from the cloak of Saint George, old sabers as souvenirs for those that conquered no one in battle, portraits of Italian and French chorus girls in the buff. The major companies kept booths on both fields.

Down toward Cangallo, they watched the patriots march by, General Sucre at the fore. Mariscal *don* Antonio José de Sucre, splendid in his gold-frogged blue frock coat and bicorne trimmed with African white ostrich plumes. Aguirre noticed that though outnumbered by the Iberians, they glowed with the unmistakable aura of victors.

Lope had no interest in entertainment, sacred or historic (if anything repelled him, it was History). Despite the protests of Nicéforo, who would rather not have missed the spectacle, they ambled on toward the sierra. The Old Man was in terrible anguish. He kept himself going with shots of *pisco* backed up with black pepper and gunpowder. This bolstered his spirits, at the price of severe intestinal disorders (Aguirre had never been much of a drinker). At times he looked like a sleepwalker astraddle his mule. Down months of trekking, if any course was kept, it was only the whistling of Nicéforo to guide his master's mount.

"This is the worst, Nicéforo, the worst. When there's nothing left out there but you don't die either, no, nothing happens! Nor is there life or hope . . . In the vapors of the soul all the trails tangle up like a nest of vipers. If you plunge into death, you don't die. If you plunge into life, you don't live. Nothing worse than the worst . . ."

He looked like a stray drunk. Nicéforo had never seen him so bad (and yet, he was to see him much worse, for a man who believes he has hit bottom is only halfway there).

Intensely they lived the first days of their reunion. This is when love imitates itself and searches and searches in the sacred dusty attic for the great erotic icons and lost sweet nothings. They said how happy they felt, how they loved one another more than ever, how they had come to understand one other through separation. But this was outright evasion of fact: their bodies, like two laggard burros, refused to imitate the aforementioned great icons. It was all imitation fire. Gush of romantic novels. The poets they had been (in the days of truth), had become writers of prose, or worse: journalists of forsaken love.

The weeds of tedium sprouted back. Sor Angela ironed her coif with extra starch, but due to humidity or other unknown causes, the wings at once lost their prior proud stiffness and flopped over like wet wafers, dripped onto her shoulders like the colorless wax of a snuffed candle.

Further, the castle of love was no longer private. Shrieks of children climbing up from the Lower District. The groaning board: remorseless pork-and-bean *pucheros* and *guisos* that necessitated long nightshirted siestas (calling for confession as well as prayers). Fights. Recriminatory disputes of an investigative nature (matrimonial police). "Who left the turkey on the fire?" "Who didn't smell the milk boiling over?"

Suppers nobody hurried to conclude because the ravenous ants of desire were no longer active (*Formicae pubicae*, Linnaeus). Stifled belches punctuating sentences; wine more soporific than seminal.

The depths of their eyes did not glisten, words feigned heat. Many words extolled "the marvel of such love," but their purpose was to conceal a yawn.

Moreover, Sor Angela had abandoned theology, one of her greatest charms. No more subtle interpretations of the Trinity, or mystical paradoxes of the soul lusting for the Beloved, or titivating matins when Aguirre surprised her kneeling naked in the middle of her room. Not a vestige of levitation.

She began nagging Lope; she made him feel irrelevant and defeated: "You should've looked after your Empire! You should've stuck to your guns! What good is what you did? The Republic didn't even give you a seat in the Senate! You missed your big moment when you-know-what happened to Ferdinand VII . . . All the crowned heads are coming back, you told me so yourself that time we were talking about the Congress of Vienna, all coming back except you!" On other occasions she would point to the shrubbery in the distance and cry out: "You see, you see? The dead are crouched out there, getting brasher by the minute, and here you are doing nothing!"

She was putting up stewed tomatoes and mango jelly for winter. She carped, her eye always on the vats, stirring, adding sugar, her coif drooped around her shoulders. Aguirre could not abide her yammer, more accusatory than encouraging. He went walking in the Lower District and didn't return to the Plaza of Ceremonies until almost time for supper.

Two rather tense years, of matrimonial inelegance.

She reverted to her daily rages because one after the other the children were turning into lefties though from birth they had been instructed to eat with the right. When the news reached her, Sor Angela would scramble down the hill in a fury to rant in the home of the Richartes or the Alvarezes—depending on where the child had spent recent months. First to fall was Gonzalo, then Alonso, the oldest, then María Estuardo, whose mother said it was only to be expected, then all the rest. Sundays, as they feasted on ravioli, all hell would break loose. Furiously she railed at the speechless chorus of lefties. Wept helpless torrents.

Rebuked Lope as though he were directly responsible (Lope treated them as would an uncle; in his opinion it was late in the day to act like a real father).

"You do nothing! You sit there listening as if it didn't matter! Take the bull by the horns! Teach them a lesson! Smack them! Shut them in till they learn! They all know you're their father! None was born left-handed, don't stand for it! The Family is falling apart."

Months later, jealousy. Sor Angela, like all wives who allow their waists to widen, began to suffer from that obsession Saint Thomas calls "Seminal Exclusivity." "Why did you dally by the tomato plants when that hussy Lucía Richarte bent over to pluck weeds from among the melons? Do you think I didn't see you?" Or: "I saw you! You spent almost two hours with the mummy Virgins of the Sun!" The consecrated semen belonged to her and would go on belonging to her until the end of time. She would not permit spillage or deviation of any kind.

The most frequent and serious incidents were caused by Ermelinda, the youngest Alvarez. When Aguirre returned, she had been a mere slip of a girl, eight years old; now she was a grown-up woman of eleven. The Old Man appraised this fresh, Hellenistic display of the eternal force of life with tenderness and reborn emotion.

When the woman, who still played like a little girl, clambered up the stones of Huayna Picchu, Aguirre gazed at her with dumbstruck pleasure. Life! Life! But Sor Angela was lying in wait and pitched stones to scare her away. "What has that little hussy got that I don't?!"

Sor Angela's life had soured. She distrusted every motion, inspected eyes: in every sneeze she saw a sigh. She invented an imaginary erotic monopoly. Agonized. Wept at night.

Dry days of mere survival. Conjugal love had become as arcane as conjugal love advocated by papal encyclical.

Matrimonial eroticide had been achieved. Their bodies had lost that enigmatic distance that bodies require; they were as familiar as the spoon and the pot dangling over the unlit stove.

Aguirre watched Sor Angela plod back from the terraces with her basket of fruit and greens: her feet sunken in the earth, absurdly heavy, leaden. At times he feared that the abundant flesh of the Girl-Nun (she had let herself get fat, weighed 122 kilograms) might overstrain her slight frame.

At around that time Lope began to note that it was not

merely immoral to go to bed with the mother of one's children: it was monstrous.

This withdrawal magnified Sor Angela's furies: she threw stones, she shattered plates and Incaic ceramics that Hiram Bingham might have taken back with him to Yale.

Lope noticed that the big kitchen knife had disappeared several weeks before. He found it Nerudanly interred among the rosebushes, no doubt put out to rust for the violent perpetration of some septic wound. Sor Angela was certainly plotting castration, if not murder.

On the 31st of December, they were feasting in the open air at the Temple of the Three Windows. The evening elapsed without grief or glory. At midnight she lifted her goblet, yawned, and said: "New year, new life." Then she resumed the topic of her varicose veins, complaining of the cost of slippers. In that instant Lope believed he heard a voice distinctly calling him. He withdrew without a word and walked toward Huayna Picchu. Laboriously ascended the so-called path of bears, to the site where the mummies sit facing Vast Space. Humbly fit himself in among them, in lotus position. And then meditated, gazing at the snowy peaks phosphorescing in the night. Again heard the voice, which seemed to emanate from one of the princely mummies, the faint, afflicted voice of a mummy: "Oh, it is you. You it is." But the voice was too weak. "So speak! I'm listening!" It was only a murmur: "Is it you? Let us go."

The Fiend had the almost inaudible voice of a drowning man. A cicada crushed under the seventy-six volumes of the *Encyclopédie*. The century had been dreadful for the Evil One as well as for the Almighty; both were reeling from the blow ringed by archangels and little devils fluttering about with damaged wings.

Aguirre made his utmost auditory effort. He was thrilled to hear the Voice after almost sixty-five years of silence. Only a buzz. The Fiend was perhaps resorting to one of his other well-known tricks and speaking tavern Finnish; it wouldn't be the first time.

"Help me, Lope. *Help!* We're on the verge of destruction. A hand, a hand will do!"

But Aguirre did not understand. He thought the first word was "Hello!" He thought he was beginning to hear him, though communications with the Other were plainly damaged. "Yes? Hello! Yes, I read you loud and clear."

With the first glimmers the Voice dwindled out completely. The mummies emerged in the light of dawn, dozing peacefully like skinny Buddhas in a concentration camp.

Aguirre descended. He found the kitchen knife in its damp sepulcher, beneath the rosebushes. He tested the blade, uneven, notched, but good for the job. Though seasoned now in domestic hatred, the knife retained the lost aroma of joyous stews, of basil and garlic.

It was easy to cut the snore through the skin of her throat. The convulsions were no greater than those of the big hogs his uncle had slaughtered on Fridays, back in the glorious lost days of his childhood. The deed he committed seemed rhetorical: she had died some months before.

He dragged her across the deserted City (the City Bereft of Angela), laboring like the triumphant wasp that drags the vanquished female spider. When he heaved her into the chasm of the fierce Urubamba, he was shaken by convulsive sobs. He had given her to the thousand dogs of the torrent corraled and snarling at the foot of the precipice. But life was like that.

He wandered for two years. He was his own ghost's ghost. Viscerally he knew how hard it was for Western man to destroy what he most loves. At moments he yielded to romanticism: to guilt and cowardly regrets. Laments, lots of liquor, a protohistoric hint of the tango.

Huamán watched over him. Nicéforo Méndez patiently endured his insults, rubbish, and other emissions.

What was and is no more, lost love, forlornness, *nessun maggior dolore* . . . and all that.

An exceptionally melancholy autumn commenced. Aguirre accepted Huamán's counsel. Back and forth they ambled across the Plaza of Ceremonies, speaking in modulated tones, trying not to stumble into, or trample on, the images that tumbled from the past and future (Huayna Capac bathing with the Coya; the High Priest weighing the testicles of marital candidates; the great Pachacutec presiding at a military parade).

Huamán, always circumspect, stood firm on several important points. "Is it worth it, Aguirre, to try to conquer the world again? What's it worth? You always believed limits and barriers were outside yourself . . . All you undertake will come to the same end, because the walls are inside you, Lope, believe me! You and all Christians suffer from an incurable ill: that of nonbirth . . . You *do* because you cannot *be*. You kill for fear of life. You scramble over land and sea because your inner life is scrambled." It was not a sermon. Lope could listen without rage and this was a promising sign of maturity. In the past (as Huamán knew) he would have refused to entertain the topic, he would have reacted badly. It was different now: Aguirre no longer felt that healthy old passion for blunder and folly that had lent such glamor and stupid horror to the History of his race. Great weariness, deep discouragement (like a clown out of work), led him toward the mature tedium of wisdom. He accepted Huamán as his guru.

For two weeks he performed ritual ablutions at the Fountain of the Inca. Fasted; meditated upon his nullity. Serenely he began to understand that he needed to be born. "Wasn't that all, a refusal to be born?"

Huamán bowed his head slightly to show that he had heard. He did not wish his opinions to sway him. Aguirre was finding the way on his own (with blankets and rugs they had transformed the Stone Throne into a comfortable divan where Lope could physically and metaphysically relax). He recalled scenes from his childhood. The time he had senselessly gouged out the eyes of the cat that napped among his aunt's woolen underpants; the time he had inexplicably offered his father (who was sprawled on his mother) the pot of scalding liniment for the rheumatic horses instead of the requested butter. Sometimes quite minor moments and things, suggesting trends in the fog of his soul. Inexplicable connections.

Aguirre feared the drugs that the Indians so artfully consumed. Huamán insisted: "But why? What are you afraid of?" And Aguirre: "I'm afraid of losing my mind for good . . ." Huamán smiled for the first time since the days of the death of Atahualpa, three hundred years before.

DAIMON

He broke him in on coca tea. Weeks later, he casually gave him some to chew. Lope saw that he lost nothing; instead he gained a certain zestful loquacity. The *amauta* taught him how to hold the quid tucked in his cheek, and to forget that it was there. The barrier was down: they could proceed to greater experiences.

"You must destroy your Imperial dignity, which is like a coffin, you're enshrined in your own rank . . . You must learn to move your body as everyone else does, you must give up the eternal posturing of dignity . . ."

Aguirre obeyed: he breathed in *vilca* powder with a nasal inhaler made of two tiny eaglet bones suitably perforated. Felt exultant. Did liberating writhes and twists. Tried to leap.

Huamán taught him to disdain received wisdom: "You must break the links, Aguirre. You're chained to an old chain you found at birth, which has always seemed utterly natural . . ."

Making the most of his enthusiasm, Huamán taught him to shout at the top of his lungs, something the Old Man had never done. Now he yowled like a wolf, then at once felt a sort of relief. "I should have done this long ago . . ." Ancestral howls entombed from the time of the cradle by a culture quintessentially aberrant (which is the true voice of man the animal?).

The *vilca*, administered in mild but stimulating doses, released him from his habitual inhibitions. He ran naked, danced as best he knew how, heeded cryptic rhythms he claimed were intuitive, laughed for no reason. Sobbed his heart out.

Aguirre slept hour upon hour, deeply: nerves frayed from attempts to defend the fortress of lucidity and reason. He collapsed into his bed. All day he had been embroiled in a frantic struggle to repress a sort of inner chimpanzee striving to burst his skin from within. Huamán, always obliging, helped him sleep by applying cool compresses to his overheated temples. It was worse than giving birth.

The *amauta*, in a quiet persuasive voice: "You have direly separated from nature. You are degenerate beasts, wretched *doers*, you and all yours! There's no simple cure, you must have patience, Lope."

One drizzly morning they ground and boiled the *ayahuaska*. "We'll work gradually," said Huamán.

For two months Aguirre bravely imbibed the small doses the *amauta* provided. It was galling: he was forced to endure the depression without elation of any kind. He sank into the terrifying territory of the Bottom. Panted; gazed dementedly; sobbed; woke shrieking.

"Hold on, Lope, hold on! The worst of the Bottom is your fear of it. Hold on, nothing ever happens, you'll see!"

The *amauta* was not alarmed: Aguirre had succumbed to the allure of the Bottom like a little boy determined to see the guts of the fuzzy spider. For the moment there was no exit. His body battled: vomit, savage attacks of eczema, diarrhea. He was endeavoring to eject the *ayahuaska*'s slow, gradual intoxication through every pore. He retched deeply but only expelled a delicate dribble of greenish phlegm.

"I'm bare, I'm bare! I'm as naked as a peeled banana!" he shouted in horror. He groaned, and then inquired: "Am

I at the Bottom yet?" He pleaded, but the *amauta* had no reply.

He dreamed that they wrenched off his breastplate and with it the skin of his chest, which had stuck. With abhorrence he gazed on his chaste pink nipples pasted to the corroded steel.

Another day he claimed he was utterly desolate, and dug himself a cave, which he covered with leaves and branches. Trembling, he burrowed like a frightened mole.

At last, after a long trajectory of horrors, he reached the Bottom and saw to his surprise that he was not shattered. Not burst or squashed. The Sun had not fallen on his head. His sobs tapered off. The Bottom—he was at the Bottom and nothing appreciable was happening. It was a memorable day. His contorted muscles went slack, and he lay down in tranquil submission on the bed of the Bottom. Fell off to sleep undisturbed by mosquitoes or drizzle.

Huamán watched him sleep for nearly two weeks. On waking, he requested a big breakfast. Peanut butter, coffee, guavas, strawberries, juice of mango and pineapple, orange marmalade. "What's up, Indian?" he brayed. "What's going on? Hey, could you fix me a dozen partridge eggs, no more than three minutes please . . ."

Lope recounted that the worst thing about the Bottom was feeling like nothing: mouse shit, grain of sand rolling in the Urubamba, dead dog on a trail forsaken even by buzzards. Huamán declaimed: "He who has really visited the Bottom is unlikely to feel frightened of what happens here . . . He understands that all is a gift, that life is a wondrous gift, and you never look a gift horse in the mouth, eh?"

*   *   *

He prepared a new batch of *ayahuaska* concentrate with superfresh roots. Mixed it half-and-half with *pisco*. Serenely Huamán determined that for a man like Aguirre it would be dreadful to get hung up halfway, quasi-deanimalized.

Lope drank it and sat down on a mat. "Nothing, for the moment, nothing!" he said. Then Huamán: "It's a sizable dose, Aguirre. You clearly must shed your remaining defenses." "What defenses?" Then Huamán: "It's as though you saw everything through a window. But the window is nonexistent and can be suppressed by the mind, in which case all things unify . . ."

"You're a stone *intihuatana*, that's how I see you," Lope said calmly. "You're an elongated stone, but no: now you're a tower of orchids turning into bees, a cluster of nasturtiums and seething wasps . . ."

The Old Man went rushing away with dilated eyes. He was fleeing from his vision. He might possibly attempt suicide, but Huamán had prepared for every eventuality: posted groups of Alvarezes on the dangerous precipices over the river. Aguirre returned huffing and sat down on the mat. "So be it. Amen," he said.

Submissively he allowed that the colors had begun to drip on their respective objects, but without spilling. They ran down within a strange and limited and indestructible infinity. Huamán's white poncho was now an ivory-white winter landscape by Breughel the Elder that he recalled having seen in a Flemish castle during the merry, barbarous age of the *tercios*. But the snow was snow, falling in tiny flakes that piled up softly like granulated Cuban sugar. He felt impelled to suck on Huamán's sweet poncho, but he could not get up. He said, "You have at last fried me in your frying pan, I'm at the End of Substance."

End of Substance. Only the eye believed in substance, only the hand. "Look over there, Huamán, there's the big kitchen knife, remember it? Restored at last to its place in space. And substance no longer exists: no blade, no steel matter. Only a gleam stabbing at the air, drops of water fanning open in air . . ." He bellowed. "So be it, so be it! Amen and hallelujah, hallelujah, amen."

The All at Once rose up. A huge monster, hidden until now. How had he failed to see it before? Great roaring horde. Siamese elephant singing as it climbed out of a tiny mirror with the slow shamble of an elephant.

All at once now. Harmoniously the gleam of the knife pierced the hide of the elephant: gray, muffled explosion. Huamán etherealized upward and then horizontally, like a long brush stroke, but he was still Huamán. "I'm off, I'm off!" the Old Man shrieked exultantly, but he was also weeping in despair.

It must have been a terrible moment: a dry hand, the parched hand of the Old Man, began to swell. "Who's swelling me, who?" His skin stretched like latex. Extremely elastic rubber slime. Five fingers, five balloons soaring toward the peak of Salccantay, which also was swelling and spilling icy infinities that never fell.

"The window! I want the window, for the love of God!" But he was shouting in a storm. Besides, on the deck of the galleon all were dead. A gluttonous turkey buzzard winked at him as it thrust its beak into the helmsman's swollen belly. He glimpsed the gigantic balloon of himself in the mirror of the icy northeastern flank of La Verónica. Relocated his nipples, his invariable navel. His balls were like dried figs in a goose-pimple pouch.

Five huge shadows with supersharp blades gathered around him. He saw the eyes of Almagro and Orsúa. "Get ready, Lope. We're going to slit your sotted, jaded hide. You'll spill, but you won't be lost. The Universe will enter you, purely!" He ran as best he could; with dark rapture he resisted surrender, defeat. Plaintively invoked his mother, whose name he could not recall. Swore that he feared nothing more than loss of identity. "This is death. Worse than death! No!" he pleaded pathetically.

But it was too late, craftily the little blades skimmed his skin with a swish like grazed silk. Not blood ran out, but soul. Truly nasty, vomitous.

He felt relieved, as after bloodletting. His soul had been pressuring him from within like the hollow of a ball. "Filthy soul, supreme bother!"

Trickily the ultimate effluvia blended with essences: essence of table, essence of stone, essence of Huamán. They ranged far but were never out of sight; slunk back after a while like tired obedient children.

Then world began to ingress. Still bleeding color and vibration, the rims of things filtered through his wounded aura. A chair cumbersomely entered, first legs, then back. With the crescent circling of waves. Of song. There was no clogging. At no time did he feel overfilled, like a sewer on the day of a storm; much less a toilet. But nor was it a pleasant sensation (question of temperament). "All vibrates inside of all else: the bee in the sunken snail shell, the nun's foot in the sultan's navel. There's no cause for alarm." He urged Huamán to make a note of his words, but the Indian appeared to be napping.

Air upward, there was a sort of center, but the thing was unclear because the texture of reality is labyrinthine: it could well be mere optical illusion or possibly the texture of things did densify at a given spot. He preferred not to investigate. What for? A good story? Torture on student exams? Something to brag about? Whether the Sphere did or did not have a navel no longer concerned him: Adam had no navel and Christ no canine teeth, by sheer theological logic.

He let himself roll, happy, happy; like a fat man tumbling in the open air. The things that came and went, and his own coming and going among pyramids, hills, and galaxies, did not tire him. A sort of secret central equilibrator prevented indigestion.

Things collided and caressed and (those that could) combined. But without bustle or boasting, ever so natural. Thus Jupiter flattened Saturn's satellites like tortillas and stole them one by one. The moon came and went, shallow, spongy, and frigid: spinster in a ballroom.

Feel like going farther, Lope? Farther into being? Then the voice: "Beyond. The Magellanic Cloud, Libra, Scorpio. And roll back from the other side where 'hens feed' in celestial fields." Then Aguirre: "Worth the trouble?" The voice: "As a matter of fact, no. Old men are of Limited Mind. Their configurations recur..." "Then let's consider it seen," said Aguirre, who had always found the innovations of sameness more original: the sometimes faintly perceptible variations on familiar things, the shocking surprises furnished by what seemed predictable.

He came back to Machu Picchu. To the mat on which he lay. Huamán was smiling.

"From above, Earth actually looks round, slightly flattened at the poles, rounded out at the equator," Lope explained placidly, as he relaxed on the mat. "Odd not to have seen the turtle that holds it up . . ." Then Huamán: "What turtle?" "The one with its paws on the four columns, holding up the plane of the world," said Aguirre, who suffered from the medieval impressionistic rationalism of his youth. He went on: "Not a speck of disorder. No chaos or anything like it. Amazingly tidy: not a leaf out of place! Perfect synchrony, impossible not to mention the Supreme Clockmaker . . ." Huamán was obliged to refute him: "But that *was* Chaos. What you have seen is in fact Chaos, or if you like, the order and laws born of the blast . . ."

"Huamán, Huamán! What a sick imagination! It was a sweet dance, a vast and simple silence, fresh air without a puff of wind . . ."

"But it is as I say, Lope. All falls away into inconceivable distance. Reality spreads open in space like a stream of spit, like a sugar cube crumbling in air!" The *amauta* spread his fingers and his hands floated before his face with slow majesty. "Human beings measure only some of the rhythms of motion: the solar calendar, the Venusian calendar (which I prefer). There's also the calendar of the green Pygmies of the Sierra de Parima, where each day contains eleven thousand of your years; they therefore live life lamenting its brevity. They say: no more than an instant and *poof*, you die! They feel bitter, profoundly resentful. All because of an overly pessimistic calendar. This explains why they're cruel and cook their enemies over a slow fire . . . Man invents his own torments, Aguirre . . . But the fact is, we're the inhabitants of the blast, which may last four or five seconds or four or five thousand millennia . . ." Then he fell discreetly silent, he did not wish to burden Aguirre, or sway him. ("No one can live life for you, my boy." These were Manco Capac's words to Huamán as they waited for Pizarro's men to behead Atahualpa's fourth concubine.) He also knew that in the face of any confusion, Westerners tended to retreat into morbid pieties.

"Tell me the truth, Indian, am I being born?" Aguirre inquired with torment in his voice. And Huamán: "Yes, you're being born. But don't get your hopes up . . ."

The Old Man tried to stand, but his body felt like a vast plain vanishing beyond horizons. His struggle was as futile as that of an ant attempting to lift the wet sheet laid out to dry under which it has paused.

He wept like a little boy, and Huamán reproached him sternly. "Weakling!" he said, and went off disgruntled to piss. Evidently he was in no mood to indulge him.

The space, the sheet, was filling with blood. Thick, recognizable blood: of an Indian. The blood swished as it rose. At first he shrieked in horror, later felt calmer. He did not feel regret; nor did he feel that fury that had once kept him battling the dead. After a while it even felt pleasant, not too warm or too cold. He began to slosh about. Found Sor Angela's coif adrift.

He lay outstretched and still. The world floated in and out of him continually, but he did not feel distressed. Nor did he fear drifting too far out, sometimes to terrifying distances. "I've wasted so much time under roofs," he sighed.

*   *   *

He lay still until October. Huamán decided to give him another dose. The effect was instantaneous: Aguirre asked to be sewn up, so his spirit would cease to eke away. But Huamán explained that it was unnecessary, and he yielded with unwonted docility.

"Why do you want your skin sewn up?" Then Aguirre: "To get stronger inward, I must, I can't keep trickling out . . ." He inhaled deeply, like a deep-sea diver. Squeezed his eyelids shut as though his inner fluids were too salty. Invoked Orpheus and sank into a stupor that lasted hours, days. When it began to drizzle, Huamán and Nicéforo slid him beneath the eaves, still on his mat.

Aguirre rummaged in his inner basket. But the one he sought retreated: was not to be found in the usual places (between kidneys and groin). He floated on his back in his blood, always watching alertly out of one corner of his eye. Swung from vein to vein. Lay in wait at the coronary artery with the patience of a hunter. Nothing.

Arduously he descended again to the intestinal labyrinth. Inadvertently he stepped on the gallbladder; out shot a squirt of bile, with the exact squeak of a toad peeing.

"Fiend where? Where Fiend?" But the echo of his voice was the only retort, a twangy echo imbued with bowels and dampness.

Valiantly—for he could slip—he sidled through the ballsy scrotalia, a spot that seemed obvious. Nothing.

With the skill of a Madrasi yogi he cleared out the impure Atman, which left no room for the Other, by means of a lengthy fart. But nothing, not a trace.

Discouraged, he opened his eyes a slit. It was then that he saw the sucker in the white tunic with the fair hair and reddish beard of an English con man. The fellow gazed for a dismayingly long time without blinking. Aguirre shook with fury. Then the man in the tunic spoke: "Do what thou will, I shall forgive thee. So it's best not to bother . . ."

"Damn transvestite!" Lope roared. "If you are who you look like, turn this stone into bread!" And the bearded fellow: "No, for man lives not by bread alone." Then Lope: "Leap off Huayna Picchu and coast down to the riverbank." "Thou shalt not tempt the Lord thy God . . ." the man answered with irksome calm. Aguirre, on the brink of losing his temper: "Show me that you can feel joy and pleasure and worldly glory." The man in the tunic vanished instantly, without reply.

Aguirre was convulsed by a shudder of horror. Almost two thousand years of fraudulence! His suspicions had been confirmed. He shouted at him: "Swine! You opposed socialism, aeronautics, pleasure! Fraud!"

As he dozed in stressed fatigue, he understood that the Enemy was near defeat; that henceforth he would merely scrape along in the throes of death.

Nobody seemed to have noticed his titanic inner battle. Huamán was cutting *ayahuaska* to be boiled. The Old Man fell proudly off to sleep, snoring rhythmically.

He waked with a start, dragged himself over to Huamán, and clung to his poncho. "Don't leave me here like this! I'm helpless! I beg you! Don't fuck with me, Indian! I beg you!" The *amauta* emancipated his garment with a neat yank and scolded him vexedly: "At your age, Aguirre, it's unbelievable, but you act like a child . . . !"

The Vast

Aguirre was arriving unawares. Step by step, led along
by the marvelous force of nonwill, which softened all his
intentions. This firm victory of nonwill demonstrated that
his urge to *do* was broken at the base. His Southamericanness
was almost complete.

He floated through time without preset plans (fortunately no hint of that high-flown "eternal feeling" dwelt on
by certain Hispanic poets). He was seen in the Plaza of
Ceremonies, resolute but purposeless, like a horse, mane
to the wind, savoring the breeze and the mere fact of being.
In winter he could spend a week or so in the kitchen, loung-
ing near the ovens with the utter indolence of a dog, maybe
even a woolly sheepdog. He attenuated in time; hours and
days bore him onward without a jolt. He could spend two
weeks without sleep, planting tomatoes for no good reason,
and then give them away to the Richartes and Alvarezes,
lugging his laden basket to their shacks with the earthy,
ample stride of a Portuguese washerwoman who sings all
the way home.

Aspects of the Vast. Men of the Christian West had
deified the gridded structure of time and now were impris-
oned behind its bars. By means of *ayahuaska*, Huamán had
induced the zealous *doer* within Aguirre to surrender to real
time, in which day-night and month-year are merely indices
unable to conceal or supplant temporal totality.

The Old Man felt that the future no longer wrenched
him from present time. He dehistoricized. He merged with
the substance of day like root in soil, like branch in air, like

the copulating dog (jaw slack, tongue out, drooling with blissful abandon).

"The earth is One! Absolutely One with the world!" he shouted joyfully. Huamán approached him: "You're clearly in the Vast. At last you've landed in *being*. You'll be as we are: you'll degenerate some, but you'll live deeply."

It was true that space no longer halted before his eyes. Things were not there to be measured, used, appropriated, altered. Things were, as he was. Here. It was a great novelty and a great wonder (for the usual rational categories only serve to color the pure surprise of being in inferior shades of gray).

"What's happening, Huamán? What's this?" And the *amauta*: "Those are the colors of paradise lost (by your people). You didn't have far to go, Lope. You've returned to your primitive animalism, but it won't last long: you retain many of the bad habits of manness. When the *ayahuaska* wears off, you'll see less. You'll have to make do with a copy of Paradise, but you'll be quite far ahead, quite far ahead . . ."

The time ran long, without hindrances. He dwelled in instinct. He spent weeks hunting, stalking his prey on the wooded slopes. Cooked and consumed his victims only for hunger. Sometimes, for the sake of fairness (not dirty charity), he gave the birds back to the air. Fought with the jaguar clan over the mummy seat, because it was there that he loved to lounge peacefully in the cool night air.

His desires were brief, and never went stale. Mere initiative, reflex, urge. He obeyed them in the bud. Thus he rashly threw himself on Ermelinda Alvarez, the nymph who had been the cause of so many scenes in his married life. He struggled with the beauty, there were shrieks. They surrounded and subdued him like a mad beast. Her parents made threats, vigorously protested, but he only laughed. Two days later he received a bouquet of hyacinths wet with dew. The beauty smiled at him from the Lower District. Love was born, almost, again!

Years, eons, in refound nature. The miracle of the Vast.

July 24, 1911, dawned rainy.* They had made preparations to relinquish their land to the discoverers. Huamán had filled his bag with fine garments and precious *quipus* and was waiting in a foul temper. Aguirre was thoroughly oblivious.

Melchor Arteaga, a relation of the Richartes, had divulged the site of the sacred City to the gringos for thirty minibottles of Guinness stout. At the sight of the City, Hiram Bingham tipped him an extra ten soles, with these words: "Look here, Arteaga. Nowadays with ten soles you can buy a dollar."

Arteaga remained below, drinking Guinnesses with the Richartes. In spite of the heavy drizzle, the gringo headed doggedly uphill with Arturito Alvarez and a police officer lent—in the name of no one—by President Leguía.

---

*See "The Discovery of Machu Picchu," by Professor Hiram Bingham, in the April 1913 edition of *Harper's Magazine*.

"The gringo! The gringo! *Concha'e su madre!* The gringo's here to discover us!" the children shrieked. Huamán went to the lookout and saw him there: gazing upward through binoculars. Fitted military breeches, knee boots, safari coat, stetson.

"So, and only so, must it be," the *amauta* murmured, dodging the binoculars. "Douse the fire. Leave all as is. We will not spoil the gringo's discovery. Let him find the past," he decreed.

The women and children went down first, into the valley, Alvarezes, Aguirres, Richartes; Huamán's serene ceremonial Virgins.

Nicéforo gathered Lope's things and rounded up the mule, which kicked rebelliously after so many years of grazing the hills.

Huamán and Aguirre said their goodbyes at the fortified gate, above. The *amauta* gave him a llamaskin pouch full of gold nuggets and aquamarines. "This will stand you in good stead, Aguirre, times have changed! Nowadays if you want to roam America, you must pay your way!" Then Aguirre: "And what about you, Indian?" "Now is not the time. We must wait for the Black Sun to set. I will merge with the people, perhaps in Pisac. The people are the Vast too, Lope . . ."

They said goodbye solemnly. Went off in opposite directions.

Professor Hiram Bingham arrived, his eyes moist with scientific and economic emotion. He was grazing the lofty wing of academic fame (he simply had to take detailed photographs and send off the material to the National Geographic Society). In his famous description of the discovery, he remarked:

It fairly took my breath away. What could this place be? Why had no one given us any idea of it? Even Melchor Arteaga was only moderately interested and had no appreciation of the importance of the ruins that Richarte and Alvarez had adopted for their little farm . . .

9

Arcanum XV:
Le Pendu,
the Hanged Man

Wandering through deserts and woe. The sertão. *The jungle and voluntary slaves. Hell of rubber forests. The Manaus boom. Enrico Caruso and Galli-Curci. Pola Negri. Carrión and the great world. A blow to the heart and belated jealousies. Gloomy assessments by men and animals of the jungle at the Congress of Chachapoyas.*

*T*HOSE YEARS of descent from the mountain are dim. Years almost without a trace. In the vicinity of the Vast, Lope wandered vaguely (a pure and simple life, almost the antithesis of documentable, externally memorable historical life).

Evidently he once again crossed the jungle toward the desert. The hot, parched *sertão*. Crust of hard dust. At around the hour of noon, the traveler may see fabulous cities rise and sink into nothingness; if given to contemplation, he will expand upon the birth and death of civilizations, Spenglerizing. If merely thirsty, he will spur his horse toward illusory cascades of cool silver water that are no more than a flutter of reflections wrought by the hot air rising from fissures in the parched red earth.

In the local newspaper, *A Voz do Jeremoabo*, he learned of Zapata's entry into Mexico and of the massacre of gringos and *hacendados* in Durango and other states. It can be deduced with near certainty that years later in Itapicurú he read the news of the triumph of General Huerta in the name of "the restoration of civilized life and the rule of law," on the model of the great nation to the north. He must have learned of the tragic demise of Madero, who died with the bewilderment of fair-minded and compassionate men when surprised by the stubborn treachery of thick-skinned louts. He parched in the parched, impalpable dust. He learned that in this savagely planetary land, the life of the traveler, of the man on horseback, was decidedly undesired by nature. An intrusion that the shimmering glare of day and the oven of dry vapors would try to waste to skin and bone for the beaks of caracaras. In these horrific realms, only Portuguese traders naturally prospered, with their samples of calico, buttons, and medicine; or priests en route to take possession of parishes registered in the Vatican with a question mark beside them, sometimes two or three hundred kilometers from the actual site. In its infinite experience of men and power, the Church reserves those spots for sincerely devout young Sicilian priests with a pedagogical mission, or for degenerate friars certain not to be followed by mistresses and cardsharp cronies.

Every two or three days he crossed paths with lost

caravans of ascetics in rags. Starving stick figures with hair of straw and glittering eyes. Wretched apostles of Antônio Conselheiro, the visionary. Within Christian orthodoxy, there was no stricter denial of life: a preference for fasting and even a certain suicidal inanition intended to prevent "wicked urges"; a firm faith in the end of the world, or in other words, in the destruction of the vale of tears, site of temptation (the indisputable sign of the imminent end of all things was beyond doubt the founding of the Republic: demoniacal institution which began by declaring all men free only to end by enslaving most).

In villages along the way, Aguirre found them building shrines and churches with fierce medieval fervor. They toiled day and night; they gave birth and died stacking sacred bricks. The local priests (dictators of faith to the peasantry and sole managers of the mystery) felt attacked and mocked where they were weak: not this time by liberal Masonic atheism but by mysticism. Sensing that they lacked sufficient conviction to protect their flocks from the appeal of the prophets, they requested military intervention. In Canudos, Colonels Dantas Barreto and Sampaio had already put a stop to unproductive mysticism and subversive zealotry.

Those were sad times. Years of defeat and drought. Sometimes 50 percent of the population of these forgotten provinces died of starvation. Men became animals; children were born the size of monkeys.

Fleeing the Republic and the tyranny of primary education, the *jagunços* sought sanctuary in the wilderness, and were routed time and again, relinquishing lands to be auctioned in black-tie soirées at the Ritz of Bahía.

On the banks of the river Vasa Barris, Aguirre saw a band of guerrillas—*cangaçeiros*—probably including Tatarana and his friend Diadorín, brewing coffee in the open air beside mounts and blunderbusses.

Beyond, caravans of sick negroes fleeing the *senzalas* of the mills to form peaceful workers' cooperatives in heretofore unexplored valleys. Singing their dusky, melancholy blues as they traveled, invocations to Xangó.

Battered, broken, lost for all eternity, they chose to die of love. Pure, lofty semen wed those wounds. Act of defiance: the revenge of endurance; demographics; last jeer of the wretched before vanishing. Worrisome statistics had turned up in the Ministries. Educated modern urbanites were not merely a tiny minority: they were reproducing at a reluctant pace. All for genteelly curbing their appetites, for not blazing and burning like tigers, for mating out of marital duty and thus isolating their refined lukewarm sperm (produced by legal transaction, not by savage lust). But the fact was, the country would be mulatto verging on black and this roused incredible malevolence in the ministries and military.

The corporations were tightening their grip. Zucker und Trust Gesellschaft, Transamazonian Lumber, Gazel Mining Incorporated, Northeastern Sugar Co.

Tribes now craved secluded valleys, and the cover of the jungle. They were the antithesis of the Bandeirantes, or better: crushed nations begging permission from clans of monkeys and snakes for a spot well out of the sun, on the floor of a habitable ravine (it would be hard now to convince the animal kingdom of their good faith).

Despite the Vast, the Old Man felt that to linger in the

sertão was to belabor a lost battle, and he had always dreaded treading on a lost cartridge, and dying, after the battle.

He went looking for the great rivers. Those avenues that lead us from the luminosity of shores to the depth and anonymity of the forest. Journeyed hard, against the current.

He turned up in Xingú among the execrable contractors of rubber, the new riches of industrial progress (pneumatic tires, electrical insulators, footwear, condoms, raincoats, elastics of every sort). Great interests at stake. War of economic dominance, diplomatic intrigue, devious deals. Overseers remiss in the service of Free Enterprise and Free Contracts. Overseers armed to the teeth with straps, cartridge belts, bandoliers, Mauser rifles. The production police. Recruiters of voluntary slaves.

The recruits followed them into the jungle, singing their ceaseless, sorrowful songs. Knowing they would be lashed to the giant gum trees. Knowing they would be forced to wound those grand, peaceful trees, and to catch the latex drop by drop. At dusk, when mosquitoes drank blood from their backs and leeches sucked blood from their feet, the tappers would roll the rubber into a ball, a sticky gob, and lug it back along the trails to the scales, which stood in front of the sheds where they would be confined till dawn, for resignation was not permitted before the expiration of the contract.

Aguirre moved among them, half-seen. In the sheds at night he heard their moans of love. They mated and multiplied despite the knowledge that their children would be sold from camp to camp.

He saw worm-infested negroes and Indians, dousing kerosene on the larvae that fed on their flesh. He saw beri-beri-infected citizens despair at the sudden discovery that a leg or arm was peculiarly weightless and painless, like some rubber prosthesis. They pricked themselves with needles, held the insensible member over the flames, and at last wept disconsolately for the unfeeling flesh; some in a wild fury tried to amputate their own limbs and died of ugly wounds.

Calm syphilitics compared the progress of their deaths. Whispering with the humility of the damned, they seemed to evoke distant nights of love.

The lepers self-segregated, heads encased in sugar sacks. Died for years, devoured by an indolent vulture that preyed beneath the skin; years feeling their flesh turn to fetid clay and fall out in hunks. Cursed the noble human heart that sustained their horrific lives, beat after beat. Were fiercely resentful: their sole desire was to slip into the kitchens and molt their wounds into overseers' stews.

Now and then the Old Man was recognized. Now and then the boughs of some grand old tree gestured. Now and then the wind or some bird of night whistled, for him alone.

After some weeks of traveling in heavy rain, he came to a spot that looked familiar. Here the Great Quebrachera Company, Inc., in fact a subsidiary of Michelin & Moët Chandon Reunis, stationed its central office and sleeping quarters. But Lope sensed something else in these tranquil woods. At dawn he woke with a start and ran toward the main scales, which sat at the foot of a blackened stone. His heart pounded: the phallic monument of the Queen of the Amazons! And naturally, beyond stood the Lake, miserably polluted by latrines (for tappers and overseers), and by in-

dustrial waste from the manufacture of rubber. More than
two hundred years! Queen Cuñan, what style! And the princesses! Here and there mere traces of temples, stone walls
rising from the brush. The limpid waters of the Lake, spoiled
forever! Aguirre began to pine; for several days he lay
sprawled, refusing to eat; the mule sneezed from the cold.

At nightfall he watched the tappers returning on the
forest trails, bent beneath the latex balls, which ensnared
their hair and gummed their eyelids almost shut. The yield
was weighed, meticulously recorded, and subtracted from
the debt. But the Debt was invincible: one day of food for
a small child cost three days of work, in the best of circumstances. The workers protested: for some, seventy-seven or
eighty-three years would settle their debt and set them free.
"Business is business, friend!" said the overseers to the malcontents.

Aguirre suffered from nostalgia, mixed with the de-
grading, infernal reality of exploitation. He decided to part.
"What matter the Amazons anymore? What matters any of
that anymore! Distant days, love, memoricity!"

A man who has spanned existential abysses and verified—via terrifying space-visions—that the Magellanic
Nebula tapers and stretches toward the voluptuous buttocks
of the Andromeda Nebula every three million years is no
longer inclined to be all that moved by the realities of mi-
crocosms: not lost love, nor ordinary tragedy, nor the torment of lepers, nor the chorus of maiden orchids singing
almost inaudibly at dawn.

At times he loathed his forays into the Vast and his
resultant capacity to *be* while others took *do* to its ultimate
consequences (mercilessly exploiting the weak and igno-

rant). He would rail at Huamán and his jungle recitations: "You've cut the balls off my soul, Indian!" At times he judged his wisdom to be something akin to the good-hearted daftness of fools. He felt healthy horror at the prospect of turning into a saint, a compassionate professional pardoner and spiritual vegetarian. He shrieked, he raged, but it did not last. At most he might shout for the Devil from time to time, as one calls to an abhorrent but necessary enemy or an inexplicably indispensable power. "O Fiend, O Evil One! What glories we would reap were you beside me!" But it was simply a reaction to great pain and injustice, and was forthwith forgotten.

Evidently around this time he came down with a raging fever, which he did not tend in time (*being*, so lauded by poets and antidevelopment philosophers, does pose some suicidal risks). He drifted in a *jangada* for days. Presumably was fed by compassionate clans of monkeys that chanced to remember him, by Homopuevas who were unaccountably good to him, by defeated jaguars, or by time-honored enemies of the pale men, like Campas and Carijonas, who ceased all hostilities at the sight of this strip of dried hide lying forsaken on a tree trunk.

In dire conditions (fever) he drifted through the lands of his lost Empire.

His senses in part restored, he turned up among the Jívaro, who amicably presented him with the tiny head of the harquebusier Matías González, whom they had shrunken many decades before. Lope mustered the strength to bury him on a hill over the sea, with no emotion whatever: his downed soldier was a talisman devoid of power.

The Jívaro offered him cassava bread and turtle tamales.

Urged him to learn the technique of body shrinking; had evidently gone quite commercial. "It's easy, Aguirre, you use infusions of special herbs and hot sands . . ." Informed him that export was expanding. "Just think, they're even marketed at the Tivoli in Copenhagen!"

One evening, adrift on a tributary, he passed an endless row of huts resting on piles. The wretched riverine slums of mighty Manaus.

He saw a sign in glowing lights that blinked on and off: MANAUS RUBBER CAPITAL. A little doll wearing tails and clasping a cane tipped his top hat, off, on, in greeting. Aguirre had never seen anything like it. The far-famed electric light. He gazed intrigued at the hundreds of little electric orbs of the sign.

He felt an irrepressible *joie de vivre*, but he knew he had barely the strength to climb off his raft. He was a rag, a relic, a has-been.

Night of the Grand Gala: *La Traviata*, starring Enrico Caruso and Amelita Galli-Curci. Such magnificence. Splendid, sparkling people rolled into the Opera Plaza in luxurious open *voiturettes*, and their liveried chauffeurs bowed to them. Sugar magnates in pure white suits of Irish cloth, newly arriving from Bahía and Río de Janeiro. Foreign managers with exotic mulattas. The Prince of Herzegovina with his luscious, picaresque *travestie* Lulu Saint-Jacques. Somber, sweat-drenched Portuguese in tuxedos with pious, pudgy wives swathed in black and nubile daughters wrapped in vaporous white like virginal laundresses who take lessons in piano and French.

The Old Man was jostled at the foot of the marble steps. Guards brandishing clubs kept order among the poor onlookers. Life! Splendor! How such a social phenomenon could occur was beyond his comprehension. He was dazed. Loudspeakers alternated heroic music and popular ballads ("Manaus Capital of the World My Love").

Up drove Pola Negri in a dual-carburetor Düsenberg to the cries of the crowd, wearing a tiny black, fringed silk dress that bared her back down to an anatomical spot Aguirre could never have imagined exposed. Long ivory cigarette holder, two Pekinese pups, deep, dark rings under her eyes, and hair cropped close like a Prussian youth. Apparently she was the guest of Rodríguez Menezes, of La Forestal.

Someone attempted to break through the police cordon. It was Arturo Cova, endeavoring to deliver to the Colombian Consul (a fastidious gentleman in white sporting a *canotier* and a malacca cane) his thick, well-documented report on the barbarous enslavement of the Colombian tappers. Cova was skin and bones racked by hallucinations and beriberi. He struggled but fell at once among the horses' hoofs. Battered, bruised, rebuffed yet again, he returned resignedly to the bars on the riverbank where his wife offered herself for coins to ex-foremen.

By showtime the Plaza had emptied. Through the theater's high skylights rose the supple, spherical sounds of Caruso, the smooth, hyaline tones of the amazing Galli-Curci.

Unsure why, the Old Man began to follow a stray dog. Alike amazed, they threaded among parked cars (carriages with horses on the inside, Aguirre had heard). The dog peed, without hostility, on the white stripe of a Goodyear tire. They paused before the spectacular steel-blue Rolls-Royce belonging to Max Oberon, King of Tennis Balls: the indomitable self-made man famous for the palace he built of Grecian basalt with gold urinals and gold toilets (perhaps to exorcise and exalt the memory of his drunken, irascible father, who had always missed when he did his duty in that lewd, squalid shed during the brutal years of his childhood).

Six times (six) Galli-Curci repeated "Addio del passato." Three times Caruso repeated "Libiamo ne' lieti calici" (and withdrew in a huff, declining to provide statements to the international press). General Funes Barreto da Costa, head of the local garrison, conferred the flowers, the emerald brooch, and the check. Sweat pooled around the boots and patent-leather shoes of public officials. For thirty years past and thirty years to come, the voice of Galli-Curci would be the sole refreshment in this breath-of-woolly-dog air.

At Maxim's and the Greco, bottles of champagne popped open to cool the throats of arriving guests.

Drunk on cultural fervor and spiritual ferment, people crowded the nearby bookshops. Purchased sound recordings of the voices of the heroes of the evening; perused shelves displaying spines of books in several languages. *Le Disciple*, by Paul Bourget, debated by all with fierce passion, sold dozens of copies.

In wretched dives near the market, the downtrodden passed around a greasy photograph from the front page of the subversive (and illegal) weekly *A Revolução*: Lenin in suit and vest, and both tie and worker's cap, leaping into the air over Red Square with legs spread and arms outstretched, celebrating one more anniversary of the seizure of power. At his side, Trotsky in leather overalls and dentist specs. Beyond, an unknown with Neapolitan whiskers.

The Old Man had lingered in the parking lot. And it was there that he suffered one of the rudest shocks of recent times: in a Bugatti convertible glutted with power (the driver was fiddling with the starter with thunderous, and startling, results), he spotted Carrión in a glistening red uniform trimmed with sugary braid. The Old Man's legs quivered as he uttered the name of the woman in the passenger seat. *Doña* Inés! He felt a sort of burning in his ankles, shrunken now into two pale ceibo toothpicks connecting the tatters of his trousers with his shaggy espadrilles.

Doña Inés! She was stupendous: broad white capeline with blue tulle sash caught at the chin, long gown spangled with mirrored sequins, stole of Siamese albino ostrich feathers. Though she did not smoke, she was stylishly fingering a long, delicate mother-of-pearl cigarette holder with an unlit Camel in its tip. *Doña* Inés de Atienza: grand lady!

Carrión wore a fierce Prussian helmet with a bronze spike, a sort of rhinoceros or unicorn horn threatening to ram the free clouds. He impatiently stroked his whiskers, as stiff as the bristles of a wild boar. She (no doubt fearing an explosion of fury due to the delay caused by the explosions of the motor) caressed its wings, with the grain, naturally, so as not to get pricked. At last the *fumata bianca*: the car revved up. The driver, a black man attired in starched coarse white linen and the epaulets of a Danish admiral, positioned his glasses, squared his shoulders, bobbed his head, and requested authorization to depart. "Au Pied du Cochon!" Carrión barked.

DAIMON

The limpness that follows a violent blow, then indignation. He notes that this is probably the first time in his lives that he has "understood" and tolerated love, and in particular, her love for another man. He feels wisdom sever impulse. He wavers! What went wrong? In former days he would have obeyed his impulse, he would have leveled Carrión with a mere look! His voice would have thundered! (But he sensed that had his voice emerged in time, it would merely have squeaked like a trampled guinea pig!) He was diminished, shrunken.

As the automobile drove off, the Old Man ran as hard as he could, sandals flapping. Colonel Carrión, who saw only a pitiful beggar, tossed one of those new copper coins (he is generous with the down-and-out and prefers not to be indifferent in these fleeting days of amorous flight, of partial liberation from the unsoaring ordinary life provided by his lawful wife, the vulgar, tyrannical Greta Perticari). The Old Man studied the coin (wet from the pee of his friend the dog): on one side an image of the Republic and the word "Liberty," on the other Justice with breasts exposed and eyes bandaged (the converse might almost have been better).

Au Pied du Cochon, which offered peasant and provençal specialties, was an elegant spot made fashionable by a number of chic people who dined there after the theater. Carrión had chosen it because they prepared for him, by special request, a bean *guiso* with feet of pig and mutton. After hours of cooking, the hoofs turned creamy; when seasoned with garlic, parsley, paprika, and big rounds of onion, in the opinion of the Colonel, this warm gelatin was an unforgettable dish. (With the tolerance of lover not hus-

233

band, he permitted *doña* Inés to order an *omelette aux fines herbes*.)

Through the tall windows, Aguirre watched him eat. The Old Man missed his lost teeth and Sundays in the home of his uncle the pork butcher. Carrión had removed his magnificent dress coat, and draped now over the back of the third chair, it occupied a space equal to that of a minor official awaiting orders. Carrión dined with the poise of a leader, spooning out just the right amount of *salsa* for each bite; now and then a well-chilled glass of Veuve Clicquot, swashed around his mouth two or three times before swallowing, was the best substitute for the *sémillon* and soda he had often drunk at feasts in the mess.

Aguirre saw it clearly: she worshiped this crass, bloodthirsty beast, her social opposite, who was wiping the grease of pigs' feet on his wide regulation suspenders (yellow with violet stripes).

On his way back to the riverbank, he was forced to endure two or three scenes invented by his ripe erotic imagination (he could not resist the temptation to picture the lovers alone together: this weakness constituted the rhetorical essence of modern cuckolds). In the Negresco Suite with its view over the Amazon, naked, or sheathed solely in tulle, she slinks backward. Leans on the white piano. Whimpers (her ravager is stark naked save for the Prussian helmet). They roll on the downed mosquito netting. *Doña* Inés struggles, scratches, but her sex systoles and diastoles with the disquieting hiss of a suction pump. She resists, she struggles, but her defeat is that much the greater!

Misery and the music of lament reign in the bar where Arturo Cova sleeps with his head on the table as he waits for his wife to return from her little "stroll." Two melancholy guitarists accompany an impersonal singer whose voice emanates from a gramophone perched on a wicker chair. This was a new tango: "Mi Noche Triste" (in those days called "Lita"). The singer on the record was very famous: Carlitos Gardel.

This was Aguirre's first encounter with the tango, and it was a bond that would last forever.

No friends or acquaintances. No imperial ambitions or women to sweeten the horizon. No lost art. No money or youth and not much desire for survival. He ascended westward from Manaus along the veins of the great rivers; always preceded by the progressive push of the pioneers of the great corporations, men in pith helmets with theodolites, carbines. North Americans, Japanese, British; spiritually guided by German ministers and protected by fierce, swarthy inspectors.

Men from the Mining Corporation, from Bunge & Gildemeister, partners of Signor Matarazzo, seekers of gold and precious stones on commission for Stern & Lipzia International. A handful of businesses funded by local capital, always imperiled by inflation: Menéndez Lumber, Inc., or Marques, Janez & García, wholesale exporter of jungle feathers and exotic freshwater fishes.

But beyond, beyond the central sierras, all was as it had been at the beginning of the world. Lope came across places of ancient solitude; remote provinces of his Empire he had long since delegated to his captains, Coca and Rodríguez Viso.

There he learned, from the Chavantes (from the horse's mouth, as it were), that an important meeting would convene in the jungle of Chachapoyas, in regions unblanched by white men, near the great Circular Cities.

Aguirre's presence would be welcome. Apparently they no longer considered him Iberian, or his hispanicity had been assimilated into the continental catastrophe. He deemed it no small honor to participate in a Congress that would gather together all the sorrows of the dispossessed.

Heteroclite delegates converged. He was ferried up the Ucayali by a cordial group of Baré Indians piloting an immensely long lapacho pirogue hollowed with the usual precision.

They reached the designated spot before most other representatives. Aguirre settled in at the top of a huge round tower appointed with condor and jaguar heads in stone. He could sleep up there in the open air, where mosquitoes never ventured, above the green roof of the jungle—a vast, luxuriant pampa traversed by warm breezes. Nicéforo saw to carting up food, and palm leaves to repair the roof when torn by the brief but furious downpours.

As the days passed, word came of the new arrivals. The Carijonas! The Otavalá delegation. *Cacique* Pincén, Jr., and his blood-and-yolk-imbibing warriors.

Not only men. Also animals. Bands of jaguars, snipes, pampean pumas, the heads of ancient and venerable monkey clans, delegations of wild dogs from the Pampa of Dogs. With the characteristic discretion of the animal kingdom, they prowled on the outskirts of the Circular Cities and communicated through translators: Carijonas or Uitotos or

Campa medicine men who still retained the ancient secret, or power, of conversing with animals and plants.

An assembly of such varied company could not avoid quarrels. The incorrigibly cannibalistic Caribs seized a Portuguese who had strayed westward off the route by more than 250 leagues while traveling from Lisbon to Manaus to spend Christmas with his immigrant brother: he was slain, spitted, roasted, and eaten, despite the firm objections of local Arawakans who wished no further disputes with the Federal Office of Indian Aid.

People like this fostered the black legend that defamed the natives, in evolution since the advent of the Spaniards.

The Tehuelche were fierce, arrogant, and liquor-swilling (ever since the days when their *caciques* permitted themselves to be corrupted by the authorities of the province of Buenos Aires, who plied them with demijohns of firewater). They rigged horse races and fleeced the elegant Otavalá, who never refused to pay. They made immense roasts of old mules, drank toasts with their blood, and fell into a clumsy drowse.

At the time of their arrival, the Uros, led by Urón XXIII, announced that they could not allow ordinary creatures to look at them, as they had not mutated and had thus maintained themselves at an evolutionary stage predating the degradation of humanity; they claimed to belong to the race of the Founders. But despite repeated requests by the organizers, they were not only brashly looked at, and in the face, but were the object of obscene, abusive gestures. To no purpose they explained that their blood was a different temperature (a little lower, 35.7 degrees Centigrade) and

their hearts larger than normal because they had never descended from the level of the altiplano. They were deemed
pompous fools.

The de facto inauguration of the Congress occurred at
dawn on the 27th of October, when the birds held their
pre-announced protest. They spread across the sky, sweeping in circles and singing backward, or in other words, per-
forming their usual scales in reverse; descending them
(musically) or drowning harmony in the loud, blunt sym-
metry of beginning composers. The effect was appalling.
The widows of the great chiefs wept disconsolately and
dusted themselves with ashes. It was the end of the world.
The air of life wrinkled, and filled with perverse pins and
needles. It was the apotheosis of noise.

The delegations were officially announced. A band of
runty misshapen white men with blond manes and peculiar
blue eyes seized the first seat. They were haughty; grumbled
about administration and service. The anthropologist Agus-
tín de Mahieu had assured them that they were of Nordic,
Viking blood; that in the tenth century a Scandinavian vessel, misreckoning the route to fair Vinland, had run ashore
on the coast of Santa Catarina (forcing upon them this sad,
irrevocable deed, the discovery of South America); on foot,
following the sun alone, they had reached Paraguay. These
braggarts pretended to know Icelandic words and runic characters. They were excoriated, but all this only went to show
that the Congress would come to naught.

Elegant straight-haired Otavalá in long tunics paraded
by. Tupí-Guaraní who never ceased their eternal mystic
dance (the continual swaying dizzied the monkeys, which
fell from the ceibos like ripe pears). Piapocos. Guahibos.

Banivas. Uitotos. Campas. Even a group of Morochucos speaking a Cervantine dialect, in from Peru. Some whose skin was tinged with mysterious colors: deep inky black, chalk white. Many ceremoniously introduced their invisible demons.

One last pair of giants, whom Aguirre believed he knew, came forth with great dignity; he was mistaking them for the Tiahuanaco idols gunned down at his command to mollify the Church. These were two huge, blind, gloomy men of a certain age, homosexuals by necessity, who nurtured each other with cordial concern.

The widow of the last Ona stepped forward and for two days her story bored them all: dreary ballads detailing the history of a ruined nation. Silently the last Mohican filed by (he resided in California on a share of the royalties, administered to him by the heirs of James Fenimore Cooper).

The predictable handful of whites and mestizos attended, in the role of dignitaries of the debacle.

At around eleven each morning, a lugubrious six-horse carriage rolled by under the blazing sun, driven by six headless gauchos. This was that spitfire General Quiroga, displaying pride in death.

Surly and hostile, drinking maté alone, the gaucho Martín Fierro (legendary advocate of urban anti-progressivism) listened to the meetings while plaiting and unplaiting a rein rubbed soft. Now and then the gaucho Cruz turned up and together they silently sipped maté, doubly bonded in loyalty: for if Cruz had saved Fierro from the blades of municipal violence, Fierro had rescued Cruz from death with eight neat verses.

Agapito Robles, the rebel from Rancas (unaware of his own death), sought recruits for a decisive battle against the Cerro de Pasco Corporation. Fervently he described rampages through the high desert, mass shootings, the cool cruelty of Judge Montenegro.

Several citizens in suit and tie: a certain Erdosain, who sparred all day with La Renga, a high-strung, lame-legged woman with a cigarette dangling from her mouth. Walking the trails, he tried not to muddy his black Porteño shoes; she teetered in those spike heels stylish in 1938: they debated endlessly as though plotting (or excluded from) some conspiracy.

Now and then, *don* José María Arguedas, who had applied for a license to commit suicide at the University of La Molina, looked in at the hour of dusk.

Aguirre thought he spotted, among those who spoke Portuguese, the famous Conselheiro, with the long locks of a visionary and the blue habit of an itinerant saint.

In the early sessions, homage was rendered to Caupolicán (brief and deeply felt by all parties) and to Tabaré (owing, actually, to pressure from the Charrúa delegates).

The information presented was known to all. Some delegates belabored statistics (prestigious, arithmetical form of rhetoric) with the meticulousness of Amnesty International.

Nurandaluguaburabara, the *cacique* of Tapajóz, summed up the state of things: "The whites have Mausers, railroads, cardinals, liquor, syphilis, Bibles, geographers, dogs, Portuguese, whores, dollars, trinkets, Foreign Trade, foremen, bosses, League of Nations, shoes, snakebite serum, blond tobacco, the academy, Yankee preachers, theodolites, and above all, trained colonels." All was said.

With the aid of the Campa delegation, the plants delivered a long, detailed report on their grievous circumstances. They had been cruelly transcultured. Commercial incentives of the crudest sort had altered the vegetation of the ocean shores and of the fertile lands of the interior. Pears, grapes, olives, cotton, wheat, exotic vegetables. The traditional species had lost the battle. It was certain that subtropical orchids would not survive the proliferating air pollution. The lust for lucre had substantially modified original divine harmony (the plants' report confirmed their known mystical inclinations).

When the representatives of the Tawantinsuyu ascended the platform, they were greeted with controversy (Yankees! Romans of the Southern Hemisphere!). The Tehuelche exploded into a disgusting chorus of buccal farts, and taunted them for having allowed themselves to be crushed by "three hundred grubby Galicians." But the representatives of the Inca Empire, among them Huamán, understood that this was no time for idle revisionist digressions, much less to inflame the historical resentment of nations that had never assumed the burdens of civilization. They presented a clear and systematic critique, with solemn expert witnesses, some of whom had been educated in the universities of Cuzco and Lima.

The situation was clear. In the temperate zones, across the Southern Cone and the northern nations of North America, the occupation was total. They unfurled a diagram on which large blacked-in areas attested to the above. Provided a brief historical overview: Custer, Little Big Horn, the Conquest of the West. Exhibited a photo of Sitting Bull in the doorway of a New York tobacconist, garbed in feather headdress and mantle: he was employed by the Lucky Strike Corporation. Discussed Rosas, who had convinced his gauchos that Indians were enemies; and General Roca, who invented the "raid the raiders" technique. Demonstrated, with precise data, the *fazendeiros'* "deforest and denativize" campaigns. The exposition about fences, property codes, and checkpoints was brilliant: unless you took the road, you were continually requesting permission to proceed.

They displayed immense diagrams of the South American highway and railroad network. Quoted Scalabrini Ortiz, and recommended that participants read his texts. Mentioned Lisandro de la Torre. Generously commended Haya de la Torre, while deploring his cowardice. Their judgment of Getúlio and Perón (upon hearing his name, Araucanian sots pounded furiously on mule-belly drums and sang out a march, "The Peronista Boys") was harsh but not hostile.

The demographical report was heartbreaking: of the ninety-one million natives in existence at the moment of the discovery of Europe, only eleven million pure-blooded natives remained, bereft of power and glory; the remainder Civilization had eliminated.

At the ninth assembly the *cacique* of Aparia concurred with the *amautas* and Mexica seers (*peyotl* eaters): "It's the Black Sun. This is it, all right. Black Sun. They triumph, they shall triumph. Shit. They shall triumph. Their triumph shall be their doom: they'll end up swimming in their own piss. They'll have to go to Venus to see a natural landscape.

But it'll cost them! They fucked us and they will be fucked, that's the punishment! Nobody can stop them! It is written! They will proceed! But they'll take the last step over their own dead bodies! Same as Spain: ravaged by riches, ruined by religion . . . Our disappearance was foretold by the stars. It was known that pale men with beards would come to destroy our alliance with the plants and animals. And the worst is yet to come. They'll buy us out. Dress us in gray suits. Give us pensions."

The self-criticism sessions were merciless. The representatives of the Inca Empire were perhaps the most ruthless: "Damn fools! Somnambulists! Ninety-one million sold in a snap! And then from bad to worse. Exclusion, excluded from everything. We should have known how to finesse misery! We should've been Marxists, for instance, and fucked 'em with their own philosophy! But nothing. Nothing . . ."

Some of the more politicized delegates read out a detailed history of the Long March. The audience listened with great attention. But evidently most of them no longer believed it was possible to normalize the link between man and nature. They were prone to a certain fatalism that coincided with the message of the great Aztec sages. They preferred to believe that the cycle of destruction—the Black Sun—must be carried to its ultimate consequence. No hope, but also no despair.

It fell to Huamán to deliver the report on science and technology. He said that since time immemorial the men of America had known of the hidden powers of matter. The unleashing of this potential would severely alter the lives of men. He quoted Lord Rutherford, and Enrico Fermi. Against all expectation, the conquerors of nature would in the end be its victims.

A group of extremists broke into shouts: "Yes! Yes! Let 'em fuck themselves. Let 'em do it, let 'em! They'll be neutronized!"

Evidently nobody had summoned the courage to produce a concrete plan. Deep down, they knew the battle was lost. They surrendered to Destiny, to the sacred texts. Prayers and melodies rose in the night. Nobody presented a concrete plan, simply because they no longer believed in plans.

Bitter pride got the best of most. They clapped when the *cacique* of Aparia said, "What does it matter that they land on the Moon if they have not yet come to Chachapoyas!"

It was the rhetoric of ruin.

Early one morning Aguirre went to wake Nicéforo, who was lying beneath a ceibo. He said to him: "Let's get out of here! Make all preparations for departure! We have no business here. Leave it to the anthropologists and the dead!"

10

The Sun:
Eternal Force of Love,
of Life

The modern liberal age. Aguirre lost in the big city. End of the dream of civilization: the coup. Cardinal Alonso and the Generalísimo. Suppression of breasts and books. Belisario Sepúlveda, torturer, and the essence of pain. A weakened, but life-saving, Devil. Another amazing meeting. Love and power and a good flowered shirt. A prosaic chewing accident, probably fatal.

*T*HE LIBERAL republic and its civilizing destiny! The capitals had grown wondrously in those years. Beacons of euphoria rimming the coasts. Río de Janeiro. Caracas. Lima. Santiago.

Marvelous English railroads crisscrossed the deserts, with fragrant *boiserie* and beveled glass windows against which thousands of juicy local insects splattered unforewarned. The International Postal Union. Great multinational fleets had rounded the Continent, and now Cádiz and Vigo were within thirty or forty days (at the news, the Old Man was incredulous, and with the face of the immigrant who can't surmount homesickness and failure, he stalked into the Ybarra Agency to substantiate this madness).

The Grace Line, Moore-McCormack, Deutsche Südamerika Linie. Up and down the Pacific Coast glided the *Reina del Mar* to the rhythms of great rumbas in the tropical dusk: "Siboney," "Perfidia." Dolores del Río, Carmen Miranda, Negrete's scampish gunfire. The *Rex*, the *Andes*, the *Principessa Mafalda* crossed the Atlantic. Champagne froth in the almighty sea. People appareled "palm beach" and disks scooting on first-class decks. Iced daiquiris. Broadbrimmed Italian hats soaring away amid trails of giggles.

Allure of Río de Janeiro, republican and yet imperial: *fin de siècle* mansions whose decorous English gardens verged into the irrational tropical intimacy of palm and banana trees, lianas and flowers. Little black maids scurrying naughtily at the hour of the siesta, in that torrid heat that stills the hummingbird in flight. And at dark a rustling of palms (which might be mistaken for the granddad senator leafing through *O Jornal do Brasil* behind a thuja tree in the aforementioned garden) announces the first breath of wind from the sea, blowing in past Ipanema and Copacabana.

Barrio Norte. Flamingo. San Isidro. Grand aristocratic homes with French libraries and German billiards. Boys in sailor suits scorching in the white flame of precocious (noticeable) eroticism, chased around and about the garden by the hysterical English governess who only suspects that they are dangerously igniting matches from the box that vanished from the kitchen.

At spirited *soirées* in these mansions, zealous democrats,

institutionalists, and principists debated, until dawn, the commas in an article of the forthcoming Penal Code, citing Savigny and von Jhering. Senators as stalwart as their fathers, and generous, Masonic, constitutionalist admirals solemnly delivered their opinions.

Brilliant times for corporate progress. They had at last struck upon a solution to the Indians' ineradicable cult of *being* and the negroes' magical dancing abandon: immigration, solid reinforcements for the white wealth of America.

The aforementioned ships landed with their holds full of Neapolitans as stubborn and strident as mules; sly Genoese; wizened Welshmen ready for the coldest climes; Galicians ready and willing to be jailers, fishermen and grocers; Basque milkers impelled by a dark Celtic yearning to raise up monsignors and generals; bewildered Poles; battered Jews fleeing pogroms and the anticapitalist revolution (by way of his connections to Baron de Hirsch, Lipzia assisted in the creation of agricultural communities in the desertic Pampa of Dogs). They came in droves, with a hostile hunger for achievement. They stormed America, as had the Conquistadors before them, to do and be all they never could.

New York. São Paulo. Buenos Aires. On summer nights, nasty musical squabbles. Invasion of sound spaces: the tarantella fraternizing with snips of Hebrew scissors. Irish and Galician bagpipes playing their invincible, infinite tunes. "O sole mio."

Numerous families whose last names always superabounded in vowels or consonants. From this mass arose Kennedys, Mattarazos, Frondizzis, Leonis, Uriburis, Finocchietos. Surgeons, charming chorus girls, anticonstitutionalist colonels, literary and scientific autodidacts.

Liberalism accomplished a miracle in one generation: that urchin in tatters secretly commands the sword of the anti–San Martinian general or perchance the revenge of a victorious scalpel!

The home of Senator Rodríguez Viso stood in Barrio Alto, on a ridge that overlooked the limpid waters of the lake (of the malodorous swamps no memory remained but the coughs of the workers that had drained them) where sailboats from the Yacht Club softly skimmed like wings of swallows.

The Old Man waited for morning perched on the gridiron fence of the Tudor mansion. At the crack of dawn, he watched the Catamarqueña maid carrying food to the dogs, each in its individual minicastle. Next the milkman, who in liberal societies is known to negotiate the dawn ruffling no one's sleep with fears of criminality.

The newsboy left a copy of *El Comercio*, the magazine *El Hogar* with the social pages, and *Rebelión*, the anarchist mouthpiece whereby the Senator kept up-to-date on doings in the unionist Left.

All morning the house was besieged by deliveries. What did they receive? Choice fresh meats, fresh bread and those tasty Chartrain half-moons for the gentlemen's breakfast; a set of Maxpower golf clubs that had at last arrived on the *Andes*; a crate of lobsters thermidor special-ordered from Paris for the reception that evening; assorted correspondence, handwritten invitations, bill collectors, the singing teacher, the Sisters of Charity collecting used-clothes-for-the-poor.

DAIMON

At nine he watched Rodríguez Viso and his wife la
Schneider step out onto the front balcony (the same from
which Monsignor Pacelli had waved so long ago) for their
breakfast in the sun. The Senator was probably reading a
précis of Anatole France's lecture in the Montevideo *Odeón*;
or Blas Gutiérrez's cogent lead article "In Defense of the
Republic," warning of the totalitarian leanings of certain
failed intellectuals fascinated by the symmetries of fascism
and by its success among certain ranking members of the
Armed Forces who "seem to forget the ideology of the
framers of the Constitution." A clear allusion to Carrión
and Baltasar Salazar.

Vasena, the malleable manager of AgroBovine with the
whiskers of a shop boy, waits in the downstairs drawing room
with a salver stacked with telegrams and pressing company
bills. Victorio scrubs the sumptuous Bentley, scheduled to
drive off punctually at ten forty-five.

At the eleven A.M. meeting, Rodríguez Viso will accept
the modified contract per the recommendation of Anchor-
ena and Patiño and confer with Lipzia as to the role of Prado
and Gilmeister vis-à-vis Sugar Growers, Inc. He will come
to see that in the matter of export quotas and the maintenance of price parity with Amsterdam, he must deal with
George Raft, of Havana.

As for the murky question of Spinola, the Genoese,
and the entrenchment of the Italian group, he will feel constrained to conceal the fact that the automobile smuggling
is a screen for "tax-exempt" sales to the top brass. But he
favored this method with the military: "Better to lose one
hazelnut than the whole sweetroll . . ."

The Senator was not overly alarmed by the student

protest led by Diego de Torres. The sole inconvenience was
entering the Club (shattered glass, tear gas). The wild-eyed
Diego de Torres had not simply vacated his position at Post
and Telecommunications after a brief interval of two years
at the Seminary of Saint Michael, but had thrown himself
headlong into revolutionary mysticism. It was he who had
organized the radical action groups in the university and the
unions. He was studying Quechua to foment unrest among
the Indians.

Lost downtown, Aguirre got into some unpleasant
scrapes. He had paused to recover from the swirl of traffic
and fumes on the incomprehensible corner of Florida and
Garcilaso de la Vega; and suddenly his espadrilles were spat-
tered with coins. Those forgetful bastards had taken him
for a beggar!

Later, while perusing tourist ads in the window of
American Express, he was accosted by la Salduendo (nowadays a gushy, snobbish matron, as stupid as ever, wife to
Roberto de Coca and *Presidenta* of the National Charity
League), her charity ladies, and Padre Squarcialuppi (the
young Jesuit who was the darling of them all and the "cousin"
of Cardinal Alonso). They were philanthropically endeavoring to hustle him into a police car, destined for a Home
for the Elderly. "Come on, Gramp! They'll treat you royally!
You'll feel right at home, Gramp!"

Their charity was overpowering, brutal, irrefutable. The
Old Man tried to work up the strength to scream at her, as
when, ages since, he had caught her coquetting on the trail
and it was time for her turn in the whorehuts. But his voice

failed him. It was scarcely a creak, a chirp. "Don't you see, Gramp? Your cold's so bad you've lost your voice! But the nuns will cure you!"

He ducked into a vestibule; fortunately it was teatime at Harrod's, presenting Oscar Alemán's jazz band and Liberace at the piano.

Never had he felt so small and insignificant. "Fuck wisdom! Fuck the Vast!" He felt very desperate, but fortunately he still believed his being was as indestructible as steel; though at the moment he could not tell what it was good for.

Utterly undone, he spent almost two hours warming himself in the hot, stale air that rose through the grate in the ground from Subway Line B, newly opened. Built by a German consortium.

The headlines of *El Comercio* were incredible (the first time always seems incredible): ARMY COUP. GENERAL CARRIÓN AT THE HELM. "In the early hours before dawn today, troops from the Viña del Este garrison . . ." Large photo of Carrión embracing Colonel Baltasar Salazar, both in fatigues. "We shall protect the fundamental principles of our Nation from subversive activities bred by liberal mismanagement." "At 08:47, the last indecisive garrison, Pajas Blancas, fell in with the Movement." Resistance from several groups of unseated legislators. Admiral Juan Gómez rejoins his Staff aboard the destroyer *Emiliano Zapata*. "The forces of Air, Land, and Sea unite in this patriotic decision."

The Old Man was standing on the corner of Arequipa and Callao when he saw the column advancing on the Casa del Gobierno. The newly promoted General Carrión rolled by in a La Salle double-phaeton behind beveled bulletproof glass, his mustache as groomed as in Manaus. Waved. Accepted preprogrammed clusters of carnations. Kissed the tot in blue frills "lifted in the arms of her worker mother, symbol of the revolutionary ardor of the masses" (sappy voice of the official broadcaster).

Outside El Molino Bakery, a group of liberals dared to insult Carrión. Lugones, Cardozo, and other militants, incognito in the crowd, silenced them with cruel gusto— newly unleashed by extraconstitutional impunity. Mounted cadets strutted by with bamboo lances raised, drawing behind them Krupp cannons recently donated by Siemens Panelectric Aktiengesellschaft.

To the warm, steady applause of progressive, principled downtown people, the troops turned onto magnificent Avenida Laranjeiras and marched beneath lofty palms on which shoeshine boys shinned like sad little monkeys spying something that shimmers. They paraded by the Mint and poured through the Plaza de Armas to the portal of Palacio Pizarro.

Appearing in the photograph, from left to right: Senator Rodríguez Viso; Dr. Nicanor Olindo (likely pick for Minister of Foreign Affairs); Dr. Diego Tirado, President of the National Court of Justice; His Eminence Dr. Alonso Cardinal de Henao, Primate of the Republic; Generals Martín Pérez, Baltasar Salazar, Nuflo Hernández, Julio Argentino Rofocal Aguirre, and Aníbal Fleuretty; and Colonels Rabufetti, von Rezzori, Aguirre Bormann, and Mastrolorenzo.

Carrión delivered the predictable speech on the balcony that looks over Laranjeiras. In regalia, and thus the helmet with its single spike, which released diamantine sparks in the sunlight. At his side, la Perticari, First Lady of the Republic, with a high and rather architectonic coiffure. One step beyond, Cardinal Alonso, solemn and swollen. More than manager for the Lord: almost his brother-in-law.

Carrión dwelt on spirituality and the need for purification. Had the Christian ideal been realized? What were the true values? He spoke of the lofty heart of man and of the destiny of the West: the sublimation of the desires of the flesh. And yet a vast and wicked worldwide conspiracy sinks us in materialism, in ideologies foreign to our natural sensibilities. Deviancy: liberty of the press and libertinism; liberal lifestyles and lack of decency. All the *laissez-faire laissez-passer* of liberalism . . . But no more! The Armed Forces crusade for the moral reconstruction of the national fiber!

By now the tough preplanned crackdown was in progress. Mastrolorenzo, leader of the nationalist colonels, outdid himself. *El Comercio*, the hallowed liberal haven, was ransacked. Blas Gutiérrez and a group of loyal writers resisted to the last inkpot. They were detained and tortured. Cardozo and Sepúlveda (Inspector Belisario Sepúlveda) shone among other less imaginative torturers. Blas Gutiérrez and colleagues were dunked headfirst in a tub full of excrement of common criminals (not even that of political prisoners).

This was the fate of Blas Gutiérrez, his mission, his ambition: the Old Man knew it. But he feared for the Girl, and took off at a run toward El Alto. The house in a turmoil: they had been up all night, seeking news of Blas. The black cook wept and combed the children's hair. Sablon glowered at the airmen sprawled on armchairs in the parlor. The family was to be exiled within twenty-four hours; such were the orders. *Doña* Elvira, as coquettish as ever, was packing her plumed hats and her best capelines. The Old Man noticed with tenderness that the butterfly collection (what remained of it: dried wood with a symmetrical hint of color, the mere spirit of the *Morpho cypris*, of the spectacular *Telea polyphemus*) was with the baggage. He plumped down on a sofa among her petticoats; she was pretending she did not wish to see him. Humming and fretting as she filled the suitcases. "Impudent thug! Mean bastard! Torturer!" She soothed the two maids, who were weeping in each other's arms: "Don't fuss: every cloud has a silver lining. At last I'll have my chance to study in Rome with Renata Torregrossa, opera has always been my true passion, I was born to be far more than simply a wife . . ."

While *doña* Elvira was searching for her nanduti slip, the only one that went well beneath her sheer dress from Balmain, their eyes met for one short instant and in spite of herself she murmured, "Daddy!" But just at that moment Sablon, who had never wished to naturalize, came in to report that he had just received his requested safe-conduct from the French Embassy. He stood in the doorway gazing at the tangle of feminine underthings with that liberty and complicity admissible among pederasts. It struck the Old Man that despite his contemporary clothing Sablon looked as eighteenth century as ever. Even in the sixteenth he had managed to look impeccably eighteenth: there was no denying it. With the squawk of a petulant parrot, he declared that he would travel to Paris via Montevideo and never return. His power of reason had indubitably cracked, but he would depart with his mind fertilized by the eternal seed of Lautréamont.

How had he failed to foresee the consequences of the coup! Lope felt the usual erotic urge, but it was barely a hint, a touch. Now was the moment to run off with the Girl! And to take paternal pleasure in her playful intimacy!

He saw there was no room for words; that this span of silence united them more than could any conceivable declaration. It was a communion, an ancient affinity, a magnificent and delicious crime, the memory of something grave and intense. He fell asleep among the petticoats, which smelled faintly of lavender.

Few could have foreseen the force of the crackdown that followed the coup; even the North American ambassador (H. H. Wildcock) was bewildered. Evidently Carrión and his staff had fully expected that in South America the Great World War would assume the guise of internal strife. For some time they had been stockpiling arms and training military personnel for this mission. The new armor-plated MX77s, demonstrating their maneuverability, coasted along factory corridors and through construction sites. Astonishing rate of fire: workers fell like flies. Likewise in the University battle the new "Echeverria" rifles proved remarkably responsive. Hundreds of subverted students were seen lying lifeless on the steps of the Plaza de las Dos Culturas.

Diego de Torres and his rabid student rebels (among them the ambidextrous Jesuit Squarcialuppi, a government infiltrator) expended all their strength exhorting the union throngs to renounce the wretched present and build a redemptive paradise, the paradise of the future. Nobody much listened, though Torres ended all his orations in textbook Quechua. To Mamani and the other foremen he was the same old pious prig. Priest-slave of his own church.

For Colonel Mastrolorenzo and his Rehabilitation Brigades, whose task was to extirpate the ideological cancer attacking national sentiments and traditional property rights, these were days of frenzied activity. Tortures, disappearances. At dawn they washed up on the shore of the Lake, hands severed, eyes plucked, bodies singed by electric goad: the mild poets in gray suits, the meek unionist literati from the suburbs who had unwisely entertained a preference for socialism. All of them disingenuous architects of anticapitalist subversion who had innocently imagined that the revolution would mean murder exclusively of others.

But the Armed Forces were not interested solely in the present. They launched a long-term campaign with a zeal that rivaled Bouvard and Pécuchet's (and in fact General Pécuchet was at the fore of this one). It entailed removing civilians from many responsibilities key to the organic life of the community, and as such directly linked to the eminent notion of National Security. Sections of the three branches of the military actively studied: cardiovascular surgery, comparative literature, biology, foreign trade, computer science, philosophy of law, meat export, municipal planning, futurology, higher mathematics, tennis, contemporary painting, oriental philosophies, physical oceanography, geopolitics. It entailed no longer depending on civilians in the many fields in which they had garnered prestige. There was a gap to fill: was not peace too grave a matter to be left in the hands of civvies? These spheres of human activity would be revived with absolute good faith, total commitment, and the traditional vigor and discipline of the military. A case in point: the committee made up of First Lieutenants Espronceda and García Venturillo, and Commodore Rubinatti, which had assumed the task of writing a vast "historical, social, and metaphysical" novel (in the words of their ratified Project, to be entitled *On Marches and Cosmogonies*).

A *Te Deum* would celebrate the inauguration of the new Government. On the eve, Cardinal Alonso closeted himself in his cathedral fief: young stones, with medieval aspirations, sprouting gold papier-mâché saints; altars like Turkish cupboards. Alone there, he fell to his jungle ritual: preparing sweet-potato wafers for the morning ceremony. He grated the vegetable into a dried manatee tongue, a savage scrap of animal hide he had kept stashed in a chest in the sacristy since time immemorial (and whose origin perturbed the young Italian priests, who were prone to believe only what was believable). He hummed with a lilt of femininity, a hint of domesticity, like a fat cook. He pictured Generalísimo Carrión at the thanksgiving mass: kneeling on the red cushions of his special prie-dieu, enthralled by the Godhead, a docile canine gaze in his half-shut eyes. Hound of Faith. Eucharist. Carrión parts the bristly pasture of his immense mustache. Between teeth stained brown by barracks nicotine, his tongue extrudes: a pink bed, warm with amniotic saliva. With a sudden and distrustful reptilian flick, it seizes the sweet-potato Host and slips it *ad inferos*.

Once more the enactment of the sacrifice. Once more the weaving of the old alliance, the ancient complicity. Once again Carrión and the Priest lock legs and spin before the unwitting eyes of all. Again Carrión under the metaphysical umbrella. Again the Priest empowered to wage the ancient battle against the body and its vices. No more youth kissing in the parks at dusk! Down with liberated breasts! Outlaw everything! Mulattas must button up even at the hour of the siesta (ban those slithery, outrageously sexy thighs trying to scoot away like tuna fishes)! Law and order! For the supreme Judaic Unity. Repression, productivity, submission.

Grand religious Gala. At the fore, beneath a baldachin, General Carrión and the First Lady, la Perticari (and Carrión cursing under his breath because she had washed and starched her Dior gown—special-ordered in emulation of Evita—till it was stiff as a board). And Senators, Ladies of Charity, high officials, members of the Diplomatic Corps. La Schneider de Rodríguez Viso, la Quesada.

Cardinal Alonso kissed a little blind girl who represented orphans. Then he washed, with detergent and overplayed humility, the feet of ten grubby parish urchins he customarily made use of during Holy Week, and last he ascended to the pulpit for the predictable sermon. ". . . From this high podium we must not omit to comment upon nonviolent political change . . . Neither corruption nor chaos can find allegiance in our Christian hearts . . . our allegiance to the new authorities, which with the aid of Providence will govern the fortunes of this Nation . . ." (and so on, trite, the same as ever).

Aguirre held an archaic, aristocratic notion of Power; he had forgotten that all power, his own included, derived from villainy and theft. At the sight of his people gathered in the Cathedral, he felt rage and a stab of envy: it wasn't easy watching the enthronement of this second-rate bastard! ("Breed bastards and they'll steal your throne," said Julius

Caesar.) Then came that sudden shove that thrust him into the aisle of the central nave. Though he took it on the shoulder, the hand seemed to have shoved him from within. Envy of Power is greatest in those that have wielded it savagely: the Old Man supposed that conditions were right for a daring coup, an 18 Brumaire, a crossing of the Rubicon. To the amazement of all, he leaped onto the altar stair and shouted out: "Marañones! Marañones! I've come to take my place at the prow of the Empire! A glorious destiny unites us! I've come only to reclaim the rank you always conferred on me!"

Openmouthed silence. Someone in the back called out, "Speak up!" This was fatal (microphones sat on the main altar). The acolytes closed in around him like *peones* subduing an impromptu *torero*. He lunged at the Cardinal, intending to administer the usual buffet, but he lacked the strength. He was much diminished: he saw that if a man was to succeed in these things, he must not be contaminated with wisdom of any kind. "Carrión, you bastard!" he shrieked. "Padre, *hijo'e puta!*" The acolytes were those pantywaists that played on the parish rugby team. "Sout Americca, how barbaric, to think that only two months ago I lunched at the Vatican with Monsignor Puciarelli!" sighed Padre Alonso in his most priggish voice as Aguirre was dragged away.

All had recognized him, and all pretended not to understand his words. "Extremist! Agitator! No God! No Home! No Country!"

Nobody likes hearing his father scream out that he's a bastard. Much less when he's a public figure at the highest echelons of leadership, as in the case of Carrión. And even less when all know it's the truth, for Aguirre had never concealed the facts of his conception: one saturnalian night in Lima he had mistaken an Indian goatherdess for a Dominican in the employ of the Inquisition. On riotous nights in centuries past, Aguirre, mirthfully reporting the facts, had pointed to the young Carrión and demanded: "Tell them if your godfather speaks the truth!" The boy had stared at the ground in mortified silence. It should come as no surprise that when he enlisted with Antón Llamoso at the age of sixteen, and was asked what military specialization or post he preferred, he had grimly replied, "Executioner."

This may explain his interest in Aguirre's treatment. First he assigned him to Inspector Araluce, but the latter excused himself for reasons of jurisdiction (citing Article 78, Clause 8, of the Code of Penal Procedures). They had no choice but to transfer him to the "Special" section, under the command of the promising young Inspector Belisario Sepúlveda.

They pulped him with sticks. Made him eat excrement from Hospital Muñiz (Infectious Diseases). Fêted him with salt herring, and when he whimpered with thirst, served him a basin full of feverish urine, from those virus-ridden mules used for vaccines. Performed the "telephone," smacking him with the huge cupped hands of Sergeant Palomo. These horrific blows opened his ears to spiritual spaces he never knew he had: out of nowhere he heard the husky poetic bells of the Church of Oñate, forgotten two hundred years before.

Interminable sessions with the electric goad in which one minute equaled one year (Einstein says so distinctly). Goad in the urethra, testicles, gums, anus, and in pain-distributing ganglia, which sly Sepúlveda knew like the back of his hand. They doused him with bucketfuls of water so that the electric current would surge more devilishly. And last, they peeled back his nails with pincers, like rolling open the lid on a can of sardines.

The Old Man then knew what we all have sometimes thought: that as far as torture goes, Christ got off easy. Considering what takes place in South American jails, crowns of thorns, nail punctures and cross-bearing are kid stuff anyone would choose over *pau de arara*, electric goad, and dogs that chew on testicles.

They hung him from his balls with a cord made of steel threads; a hundred times hoisted him and dropped him on an overturned chair. This was Sepúlveda's invention; it was called *pau de arara* squared (to the second power). He explained to his young students at the Saint George Academy: "Watch that the cord—use a slip knot or a double *ballestrinque*—doesn't tear the scrotum as it closes. Or you'll botch the whole thing. Watch and don't let the knot take even one testicle—let me warn you they're as slippery as drops of mercury—because the pain will drop 50 percent, a useless waste . . ."

One night as he dragged himself across the cement floor of his cell, he recognized the hoarse groan of the Scribe (whose moans he had so often heard amid the ups and downs of life). "Scribe! Scribe! Are you there? Is that you? Pastyface!" But only moans and maybe a literary quote or two amid his ravings. Aguirre learned that he had been badly tortured in a barrel of icy water sizzling with blond snakes of electric shock. And this was not the first time they had stuck a handful of nettles up his anus (the terrifying *Hortigae gassets dolorissime*, Linnaeus).

On a languid rainy day Sepúlveda, who was especially vexed by the postponement of the National League Games, attempted to locate the Old Man's ultimate pain centers (nothing worse than a miffed torturer on a soccerless Sunday afternoon!). He applied the goad at maximum strength so relentlessly that the Old Man's eyes glowed like one-hundred-watt bulbs.

Formally, Sepúlveda was awaiting the confession of a Great Unknown Crime. The greatest crime, justifying the severest torture. But the Old Man only confessed that he had committed all the crimes, every last one, and he went on to enumerate the well-known atrocities of his life. But Sepúlveda was sure that there was one last vast Great Crime that the Old Man would name only under the direst pain.

Lope panted heavily and felt himself succumbing. But he plunged as far as he could into the depths of his being, searching for some possible lost tooth of the Fiend's. It was like a miracle. Despite his swimming head, he could hear the Voice: "See, Lope? The *good* people . . . Do you understand? Hate, Aguirre! Hate! So long as you crave revenge, you will live . . ." At first the Old Man believed it was autosuggestion. "Is that you? Really? Was it you who gave me that shove in the Cathedral? Since you're who did it, listen . . ." And the Voice: "Hate, Lope. So long as there's hate, there will be life. You long to kill, therefore you're alive! Strength! Clench your teeth, hurl insults! The hell with turning the other cheek! So long as you hate, nobody can claim he has defeated the man behind your rags! Man is no more than his own rebellion, Lope, his own wrath . . ."

The Old Man was gnashing his teeth and spitting: a fit of fury. Sepúlveda assumed that the deponent had lost his mind. He spat at him scornfully and went to the refrigerator to take a swig from a chilled bottle of Quilmes beer. The session was over.

The Old Man was almost without presence anymore. He would never know how long he lay in the trough of the junior officers' latrine. They thought he was a rag plugging a hole to keep out the rats or to keep piss from spattering boots shined with Prussian zeal.

It was perhaps months later that he came to and found himself in starched white in an infirmary bed. Each morning a short, pockmarked nurse came in to take his temperature, and she invariably inquired in a shrill, hostile voice, "How's the sick boy?" Then without lubricant of any sort she inserted the syringe tip; enemas of boldo tea had been prescribed by Dr. Rosatto.

Before his release they filled two cavities (in observance of prison regulations), returned his rags, which had been meticulously inventoried, gave him a bottle of Chofitol tablets, and strongly advised him to avoid heavy food. He should take two pills after each meal.

Nicéforo, who had still not swung that job on the police force, was waiting for him. He explained that all vacancies in the public sector had been frozen at the behest of the International Monetary Fund.

They headed out at random and little is known of where

they wandered. Probably they struck south and inland across the Pampa of Dogs. Could Aguirre be that "sloppy crass old man" described in the indictment that accompanied Juan Moreyra's nephew on his travels through Lobos?

Aguirre was understandably very diminished. On the brink almost of nonexistence. Almost without presence. And to top it all, sick and tired of this depersonalized ghostliness: at noon he could scarcely make a shadow. He wanted to resolidify, he presumed that his time and potential were not altogether spent, but he had very little strength for the task. Almost a breeze: one of those lakeland *ignes fatui* at the sight of which pampean crones cross themselves and say three Ave Marias. Wind within wind, water within water, dust within dust.

In fact, little is known of those years. Presumably he now felt close to the Great Buddhist Extinction.

Motivated by nostalgia and wonder, he returned to Cuzco. His presence was noted in the chocolate shop around the corner from the Garcilaso residence (Cuzqueño chocolate was one of Aguirre's weaknesses).

It was on leaving the chocolate shop that he encountered, propped against a wall, the leprous gypsy girl draped in veils who offered to tell his fortune "a sol a card." She was part gypsy, part chola, but rolled-up jeans showed at the ankle below her layers of gaudy skirts. "Fortune, old man?" she said invitingly as Aguirre passed.

Foraging in his pockets (the least-used part of his rags), he found one lonely sol, minted in the days of the dictatorship of Sánchez Cerro. He paid her.

DAIMON

The card that came up showed a little man hanging from his left foot. "A damn bad card, old man. Bad! All I see is misery. You must really have suffered. No? Bad! They'll lend you a cot in the Unzué Shelter. You'll eat Salvation Army soup curdled by pious hymns. I see you in a line of beggars waiting for a spoonful of cod-liver oil. Evita gives you a ten-peso bill . . . But wait . . . I see you sleeping in the station lobby and a band of hippies steals it . . . Such bad luck!"

Aguirre listened worriedly. "There's more?" She explained almost joyfully: "It's *Le Pendu*, the Hanged Man. You're alive and well, but you're hanging from a noose, not by the neck, see, but by the left foot. Doubt. Torment. Your dirty locks fall away from your brow. You stare lucidly. You see, but you can do nothing. Old Eagle Eye! It's a horror, old man, I wish I'd thrown the Reaper, better to be cut down, excuse the expression, than to suffer . . ."

The leper girl's voice was brazenly youthful and happy. Aguirre found himself staring at her flowered skirt, which topped several others. And yet a force, a fullness surged from her thigh. As though someone had tried to conceal the head of a fighting bull under the cassock of a Jesuit. His mind wandered from the elucidations of Destiny. "Do you hear me, old man? I said I wish I'd drawn the card of Death!"

Nor did her voice sound leprous. An ardor, an ancient fire was rekindling. His right hand, a desiccated, wizened crab with only three fingers, slid daringly up the side of her thigh. To distract her he said: "This thing about the Hanged Man could be true, but it sounds long past, not future. What can you say about the future?"

The gypsy girl looked furious. "You don't think I'm

going to keep reading for one sol, do you? Get your hand out of there and scram!"

No mistaking her: the Moorish girl!

He tore off her veil with a sweep, and there, in the body of this delectable fifteen-year-old sham, glittered the ineffable furious embers of her eyes. Miraculous hussy!

Now his heart was pumping energy like a mad machine. Thumping. Tumult of love and desire. She would not let herself be kissed. She laughed and shrieked. "I'll give you an aquamarine, as big as this, as this! But don't bite, bitch!" He rummaged and found the stone. "Look, look at this aquamarine. Didn't I promise you more or less this?" The same weakness as ever: the Moorish girl and her feathers, her cameos, her gems and gold necklaces!

She stepped back. As she repaired her unraveling braid, she gazed into his eyes with that familiar sardonic gleam. When she had finished neatening herself, she said: "We could drink a cup of chocolate at *doña* Rita's and chat and get acquainted. I like older men and fresh fish!"

As they walked along the Avenida del Sol, Aguirre felt very uncomfortable: his reanimated sentiments showed through his rags like a worm that has swallowed a screw.

On reaching the sacred plaza of Huacaypata, they changed their minds and headed for the Roma. Sat near the wall of the parlor of the Inca Pachacutec's palace in the very spot where Aguirre recalled playing *mus* with Mancio Sierra de Leguizamo, Orsúa the Frenchman, and others.

They talked and talked. Drank lots of wine. Laughed. She brazenly divulged that she was working to pay for her lessons and to meet people: the fact was, she was studying piano and French. Delicious crook!

Aguirre was amazed: here he was once again, in the midst of life, treading firmly, and the Moorish girl across the table. Who would believe it! He caressed her with his bare foot and kept talking. He sank his foot deeply between her hot thighs, squeezed tight in jeans. The waiter, a priggish cholo, alerted them: a busload of Dutch tourists, and what they were doing was obvious.

The Moorish girl with her laugh as fresh as ever! The Moorish girl available and always aloof! The Moorish girl falling in love! The Moorish girl in love!

"I wouldn't dream of returning to Spain . . . ! Things have changed so much! And do what? Raise pigs in Oñate? Though now farms are highly technologized . . . Hey, Morita, how do you think I'd be greeted in Spain? Can you picture it? A living legend . . . !" "A living legend isn't a legend, Aguirre, raw meat isn't cooked . . ." said the Moorish girl. "True, true . . ." Aguirre felt like a little boy. He had been on Earth for five hundred years, and had lost all sense of reality.

But she was a wonder, and here she was before him, more alluring than ever. As he filled his spoon with compote, Aguirre recalled a remark made by Cagliostro at dinner in the Palazzo Farnese: "Before death and during death all of man's desires are satisfied. No one dies with desire for anything. This is man's privilege, but also his limitation."

They spent the summer on Lake Titicaca. Ate fish, tasty *suches* fried on the grill, Santander-style, by Lope. In the evenings she played her yellow plastic ukelele with charm and skill.

2 6 7

Infinite, unforgettable nights. Now Aguirre knew how to be. He knew how to linger over love and not rush rashly toward orgasm like a rapist halberdier.

The Moorish girl! But a sweet Moorish girl, rid somehow of her usual irritating sadism. Though she yielded, yet she was infinite and unattainable. The Old Man felt a great stirring of gratitude for what was occurring: his rebirth in her body. At moments he supposed that it was a mistake, and that someone would come forward to protest, and to part them. And it all was enhanced by the old threat: that the Moorish girl would pull one of her predictable ploys and vanish, evanesce.

The long embrace never ceased (and why should it!). Together they rose and rose, crooning lustful sweet nothings in each other's ears, and then together they fell from the highest height possible for a human, a delicious plunge through plush and feathers.

From the Altiplano (the terrestrial location closest to Space) they voyaged among the erotic constellations, visible solely to the eyes of lovers: Octant (Octans). Painter's Easel (Pictor). Air Pump (Antlia Pneumatica). Stern (Puppis). Oven (Fornax). Sexagintanovem. Unicorn (Monoceros).

Traveling vastly on a vast path.

He felt that the Moorish girl's sleekness and heat and curves were sea, fire, Venice: never tiresome. The Old Man got plump and peace-loving and pantheistic.

Occasional mornings they rowed in a totora reed boat (made of Titicaca cattails) to the secluded Island of the Sun. The Moorish girl made him play hide-and-seek in the Temple of the Virgins. "Are you there?" "Yoo-hoo! Yoo-hoo?"

And the Old Man running on the golden sands and she like an arrow entraps him and together they roll entangled.

They reveled for the rest of the summer on one of those islands adrift on the Lake. Almost alone (on the other tip of the island lived an old Uro).

Aguirre unwisely took a long dip. That night his legs felt like boards: two lifeless stilts. As though one of Lorenzo de' Medici's cultivated courtiers had stilettoed him in the spine.

The Old Man had smelled his own death for some time (we all intuit the time of our deaths, especially the metaphysical one). Very pessimistically he lay down on his mat. Seeing him thus, Nicéforo rushed off howling in despair and rolled through the fields of cut cattails.

It was during this calamity that the Moorish girl revealed her remarkable talents. She doctored him vigorously: laid oven-warmed bricks on his kidneys; applied poultices of newly deceased dove; tried to draw out all the bad dampness with leeches.

Again her nature intrigued him: how it rose with firm poise to the challenge. Whence did she derive her power? He had seen her unnerve the toughest. Within a day or so, the meanest desperadoes—Sicilians and Maltese—were defending her like guard dogs, devotedly paying for her "favors." In the brothel at Córdoba, Lope had watched topflight intellectuals, like that famous priest Góngora y Argote, splutter at the Moorish girl's mocking gaze: words scrambled every which way like a flock of chickens when a regiment passes. Whence had she acquired this wisdom that permitted her to transform men into paper birds? Primeval earthly wisdom, long predating the clumsy, crutched wisdom of philosophers.

Seeing no improvement, he leaped from his cot, switched off the Balmaceda radio (though the chapter of the novel was still in progress), and went out to summon Nicéforo. "Stop whimpering and squealing like a kicked guinea pig and go get Gabriel, the Uro, at once. Tell him to bring his ointments. If he refuses, inform that damn fool Indian that he'll have to answer to me!" Nicéforo trotted off. The Moorish girl's face was tense; she looked like Manuela Sáenz rescuing Bolívar, or Evita on October 17th. In a short while the Uro turned up, smeared his concoction on Aguirre, and chanted litanies in his prehuman tongue.

"You were getting stiffer and stiffer!" Grateful and relieved, the Old Man nestled against the Moorish girl's breast and drifted off to sleep, feeling a dry fire seep through his back while she played "Solamente una vez," which Aguirre loved, on her ukelele.

In two days he was up and about. But he was troubled by forebodings. "That was the Madam, I saw her face . . . It's a portent, Morita. I couldn't avert my eyes . . . !" And the Moorish girl: "If that was the Madam, she saw you only in profile, which means nothing . . . I'm sure it was unintentional. You caught a chill."

But Aguirre did not improve. He felt that the portent had been quite clear and that he would not weather well in the storms of life. Summer was ending and soon they would find themselves like two lovers without libretti. The Moorish girl was growing restless; she knew it was time to speak.

What she told him shocked him as much as that time she fled Cartagena impersonating a Neapolitan waiter. It staggered belief. The Moorish girl had joined up with Diego de Torres's revolutionary group!

She confessed that she had come to Cuzco masquerading as a gypsy (and as a leper, to discourage police persecution) for a special mission: to recruit high school and university students and to make contact with arms dealers.

The Old Man flew into a jealous rage: "Diego de Torres! Sanctimonious bastard! Weakling who wants to be a martyr!" Nothing exasperated him like a lay saint. The Moorish girl let him let it all out. He tore into young people who chose to renounce life for the purpose of changing the world: salvationists and men of the cloth had always disgusted him.

But the Moorish girl calmly refuted his ideas. "We must fight, Lope! We have no choice: they're everywhere and we can't get in! Besides, love must be made in the Great Bed of the World! What can we do? Vanish like the Uros? The future is ours, Lope! Are we going to leave the world in the hands of the Priest and Carrión? Please! It would be better to blow it to bits!" Her wrath was irrepressible and dangerous. Apparently she thought revolution was the only possible future for love and life.

The Old Man spoke: "I can't bear all these people who instead of living spend their lives planning life, like that holier-than-thou Diego de Torres! They're nowhere near the present, they look only into the future . . ." "It's true, Aguirre, but they've stolen the present, we have no choice . . . ," said the Moorish girl.

Historical conditions, she explained, were optimal for phasing into action. Colonel Pécuchet and General Baltasar

Salazar were embroiled in an ugly struggle for power. They hovered like crows over Carrión's disaster, his downfall. What Aguirre did not know was that Carrión, who was so unbelievably clumsy with his hands, had castrated himself while shaving. All because he had shrieked uncontrollably at his stupid wife, la Perticari, for congratulating the German ambassador on the triumph at El Alamein.

"There will be a bitter struggle for power. This is the moment, Lope, make no mistake! Your experience will be indispensable, there's no better strategist than you. Your contacts are worth gold: you can convince Huamán to give us a share of the Treasure of the Inca! We'll buy Chinese weapons, surface-to-surface and surface-to-air rockets, neutron grenades! The future's ours, Lope! A new beginning: we'll summon Bolívar, storm the Bastille, burn the torture instruments, proclaim the rights of man! The future is ours! They had their chance and they made a mess of it! You're with us, aren't you?"

Next morning the Old Man emerged wearing undershirt and shorts. "Count me in. But first I need a good workout. After all that's happened, I must get back into shape."

Aguirre jogged around the floating island. Turned somersaults. Scaled homemade bamboo monkey bars. Again felt the urge for action and departure. "Expedition! Great Expedition, we're off!" He had made his decision: there was no other sphere for the necessary treachery than events themselves, than so-called History. He would have to traverse it to achieve his ends. He must now come forth and conspire, until such time as Diego de Torres, that sanctimonious killer, creator of the new required truth, fell among

the ruins of his life-negating Trotschristianity. Aguirre reveled in the thought of seeing him in chains. He would
reseize power! But he must not breathe a word of these
projects to the Moorish girl, who was so young and eager
and gullible, and still cutting her milk teeth in politics.

Perched on bundles of cattails, she clocked his laps and
cheered him on. She forbade him to rinse down with very
cold water. Within two weeks, the Old Man was circling the
island at 15:56, a speed that had at first seemed unachievable.

They returned to Cuzco because the Moorish girl had
to deliver a message to the arms dealers and to update a set
of secret codes. They were euphoric. Aguirre left his poncho
and espadrilles behind. From the Sears catalogue she bought
him a sport shirt with splashy red and yellow flowers reminiscent of Nolde and a North American sport coat in blue
and red stripes. A pair of white cruising loafers.

On their last night they stopped in the Tourist Hotel
to drink a few *pisco* sours. Poked fun, giddy and gay, at the
throngs of tourists touring the ruins. Chose not to dine in
this stuffy milieu, and went over to the Roma, which they
had so enjoyed the last time.

They went on drinking. Requested a well-chilled bottle
of white *ocucaje*. With hilarity and happiness they were bidding farewell to this municipal civilization, to its little men
like timid, tyrannized shadows.

"What'll Torres say when he sees me, that prig! I'll put
him in his place on the spot . . ." The Old Man obviously
lacked the least notion of revolutionary discipline and rank.

The waiter brought the duck they had ordered. A curiously elongated bird, with a neck almost like that of a swan. "Must be the Phoenix," Aguirre murmured. The waiter squirmed, as though they had accused him of serving cat in lieu of rabbit.

They drained their drinks to the last drop. The Old Man felt grateful toward the Moorish girl, splendidly seductive in her jeans and sheer blouse. "All I had left was wisdom, a lot of damn fool wisdom, and then you . . ." He failed to finish the sentence. The Moorish girl wished to say something about love, something solemn; she looked serious but found no words. Aguirre came to her rescue with a quatrain by Nalé Roxlo, which made her laugh:

> *Love is so pure*
> *that money don't count:*
> *I know a cobbler*
> *that married a count.*

Then the incident occurred. Aguirre was looking for the wishbone and the Moorish girl was telling her third off-color joke. The Old Man said, "Here it is, the wishbone, let's see who . . ." and began eagerly toothing it clean. She was coming to the end of her joke: "So the elephant carried the ant over the puddle and when the ant said thank you to the elephant, the elephant was furious: 'What do you mean, thank you? Come over here and pull down those little knickers.' "

Laughter broke over him in waves, and before he knew what had happened, he had swallowed the bone. The Moorish girl thumped him hard on the back. Some French tourists rummaged for a wire with which to rake his throat. The Old

Man turned blue. The Galician cook whacked a chair hard over his shoulder blades, but it was no use.

By the time they reached the Emergency Room, just beyond the Plaza de Armas, he appeared to be dead. The young doctor was not all that adept at certifying deaths. And besides, the Old Man had learned to require very little air for life.

The Moorish girl wept in the bus all the way to Puno. She then proceeded into the jungle to join the group, serendipitously skirting Carrión's spies and patrol squads. She had naturally been fertilized by Aguirre's fierce daimon and would soon infect Diego de Torres ("that bastard who likes sacrifice better than pleasure," in the hard-bitten words of Aguirre).

Nicéforo Méndez spent a month crying and trying to land a job with the police. (Secretly he doubted the Old Man's death. He was sure he would turn a corner and stumble into him: "How're things, *negro*? Feel like traveling?")

But nothing did happen and when they informed him that his application to the Police Department had been categorically rejected, he went off toward Puno, from which point he would join the group.

That must be Nicéforo Méndez standing beside Tania's corpse on the bank of the stream in the photo distributed by the Associated Press.

The translator wishes to express her gratitude to Walter Arndt, David Campbell, Tomás Eloy Martínez, Silvio Martínez Palau, and Alan Ryan for their assistance.

This translation was funded in part by a fellowship from the National Endowment for the Arts.